Pretty Boy

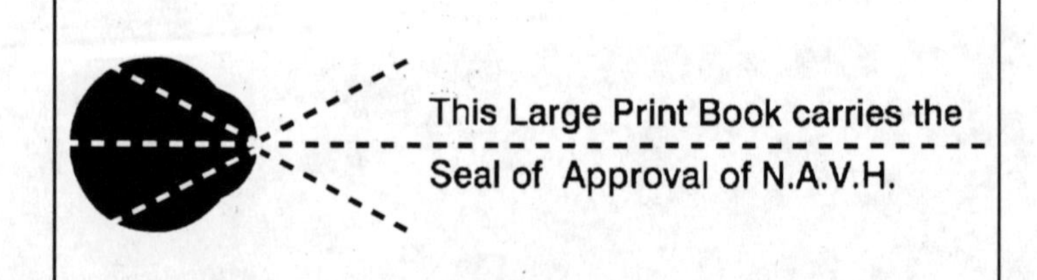
This Large Print Book carries the
Seal of Approval of N.A.V.H.

Pretty Boy

THE EPIC LIFE OF PRETTY BOY FLOYD

Bill Brooks

THORNDIKE PRESS
A part of Gale, Cengage Learning

Farmington Hills, Mich • San Francisco • New York • Waterville, Maine
Meriden, Conn • Mason, Ohio • Chicago

This is a work of fiction. All of the characters and events portrayed in this novel are either fictitious or are used fictitiously.

Thorndike Press® Large Print Western.
The text of this Large Print edition is unabridged.
Other aspects of the book may vary from the original edition.
Set in 16 pt. Plantin.

LIBRARY OF CONGRESS CATALOGING-IN-PUBLICATION DATA

Brooks, Bill, 1943–
Pretty boy : the epic life of pretty boy floyd / by Bill Brooks. — Large print edition.
pages cm. — (Thorndike Press large print western)
ISBN 978-1-4104-8008-8 (hardcover) — ISBN 1-4104-8008-9 (hardcover)
1. Floyd, Pretty Boy, 1904-1934—Fiction. 2. Fugitives from justice—Fiction. 3. Large type books. I. Title.
PS3552.R65863P74 2015
813'.54—dc23 2015006729

Published in 2015 by arrangement with William Brooks

Printed in Mexico
1 2 3 4 5 6 7 19 18 17 16 15

To my sister, Patricia, who knows the old histories and roads once traveled

ACKNOWLEDGMENTS

To my friend, Peggy Jackson, who took time from her own writing to edit and offer suggestions on ways to improve *Pretty Boy*'s looks. To my agent, Carol McCleary, for her unflagging support. To the historians who do all the hard work of digging up the bones.

1

Pretty Boy Floyd

As I lay dying, I see Daddy Walter sitting on the porch, reading a Bible sold to him by a man wearing spats. A fancy dude under a straw boater, who drove up in the yard in a red roadster, his pink face sweating. I see that red roadster parked in the yard, the sun fracturing off its chrome, the smell of leather and success rising in the heat. I see the way the Bible salesman wipes his face with a silk handkerchief, saying, "No home is complete without a good Bible" and "Since I'm real anxious to get home to my wife and children, I can offer you a special price on the last one I got left" and "Good gracious but ain't you got a handsome young feller there." His porcine eyes falling on me like sin.

As I lay dying, I hear grasshoppers snapping in the dry grasses, see waves of heat rising off the tarry road, hear the screech of the screen door, the hard pistol shot sound when it slaps shut.

As I lay dying, Daddy Walter says, "These are hard times, Charles Arthur." He sips from a fruit jar some illegal shine he has left over from his last run to Ft. Smith under the hard blackness of night. "Folks like us never stood much of a chance to amount to anything but moonshiners and dirt farmers. 'Bout the only thing raised in these hills is misery and outlaws, hell and high hopes."

As I lay dying, the sun bleeds red into my eyes and a calm settles over me.

Daddy Walter repeats stories about Belle Starr and Henry Starr and the Daltons and Cherokee Bill — all from the same hills we Floyds are from. Daddy Walter tells me again about meeting Henry Starr:

"Dark-eyed little fellow liked to wear checked suits. Spoke out the side of his mouth a lot. He got killed robbing a bank over in Arkansas. Died slow of his wounds, bled out like a pig. Let that be a lesson to you Charley. Crime don't pay."

As I lay dying, I hear the whispers of the men circled round me standing my death-watch. The same sort of men I knew all my life growing up in those Oklahoma Hills — dirt-scratch simple men with simple desires.

A circle of faces closing in above me, spelling my doom.

As I lay dying, I see Daddy Walter hand Mother a fold of green dollar bills she puts away in a sugar bowl top of the cupboard calling it their "rainy day money." She is lovely in his eyes, and he in hers — they pull the harness together through the rocky ground of life and my love for them both overcomes me and fills me with great sadness.

As I lay dying, men cough and spit and hold their guns close to their chests and some avert their eyes from mine and some do not. I am a thing they have hunted, an early autumn kill like a deer or rabbit or fox. Blood bubbles in my chest turning my heart into a faulty engine. Time shifts under me, the sun shifts above me, the world is turning me loose and I feel no wings sprouting from me to fly away.

As I lay dying, I taste the widow's kiss dry as paper on my mouth. Her name is Ruby and she was my wife until now, until a moment from now when the sun will burn me up forever. Ruby, Ruby, my heart cries out, but no words come forth and blood warm and thick spills from my lips red as a ruby.

As I lay dying, I see Daddy Walter in his small grocery store giving out credit to busted farmers and their dried-up wives, their sad-faced children. They shuffle in and out all day long, every day, except on Sunday when the "Closed" sign hangs in the door and voices rise out of the little white Baptist church, Daddy Walter's basso holding up the very walls of everything sacred.

As I lay dying, I feel the handle of hoe and scythe burning the palms of my hands into watery blisters, the razor-sharp cotton bole refusing to give up the small fluff, the taste of dust. I see too the oil fields with their grimy-faced wildcatters, big-knuckled men with flash-fire tempers who know nothing of love and fancy cars and easy money. These men who cannot even dream of such things, whose lives extend no further than the next paycheck, stare at me in perfect repose. They are drinkers and brawlers but never dreamers. They are alive while I lay dying.

I was the dreamer, the runner after all things beyond my reach, the dandy, the dancer, the lover of countless women, the bank robber, the husband, the father, the son, the brother. I was the most wanted man in America.

Look at me now.

As I lay dying, I am again swaying to the

soft seductive song of cocaine pills and high-priced liquor, and beautiful women. I am lying in hotel rooms under the blue-black color of night atop chenille bedspreads naked and faceless with naked and faceless others. From the streets below, a crescendo of traffic rises out of the madness of a world unable to satisfy itself. I hear footsteps in the hallway, unknown voices, a telephone ringing somewhere in the distance.

As I lay dying, I see Fred the Sheik with two listless but pretty girls named Dot and Ida — dope fiends. I hear their laughter as Fred the Sheik prances around the room with a lampshade on his head, his dick swinging like a small rope. I smell sex and alcohol and stale cigarettes. Dot shows me her blue breasts and her glowing blue cunt, blue because of the light of a movie marquee seeping into the room.

As I lay dying I taste Dot's salty blue cunt.

As I lay dying, a shadow falls over me; it is the shadow of a tall, well-dressed man smoking a cigar.

"Welcome to the end of the line, Pretty Boy." His words crackle like the static on a radio. It is autumn and I am soon dead. The winter will come and wrap me in blankets of snow and eternally I will keep vigil over the seasons and all time will pass away as quickly as the blinking of an eye. A hundred, a thousand, a million years from now, I will still be keeping vigil.

As I lay dying, a fine young woman full of Indian blood bends to kiss my lips. She is tall, with cascading auburn hair and unflinching truth in her almond eyes. She says, "No man has ever been inside me" and I say, "That's about to change." She says, "Your words are like rain in a dry season" and I say, "There's more to me than words, I'm a man full of dreams." "Yes, yes," she says. "Yes, yes," I say.

We are parked at the edge of a cornfield under a lopsided smile of a moon. She lets me fondle her breasts and kiss her red, red lips. "You are like fruit in my mouth," I say. "You are like a fire burning up the night," she says. We burn each other up as something flies silent and swift through the night, its wings thrumming like a lost heart. Her heart pulsates under my hand, the firm roundness of her breasts heavy and soft and electric.

As I lay dying, the face of my son hovers near, his sweet small eyes dance on my skin. "Daddy, daddy, what have they done to you?" I reach out and he turns to air and a man kicks at my hand, a mean hateful act and says, "Sumbitch is hallucinating."

As I lay dying, my heart flutters like a bird in the cage of my chest, wounded, trying to right itself, to fly away, its wings horribly and forever broken.

"Let's get married," I say. "Run off, you mean?" "Why not?" "Yes, why not."

Ruby's skin is like the silk of China, the world spins us round and round until our laughter rakes the night, until the katydids stop buzzing, until stars fall from the sky. She dissolves into me as her smoky mouth breathes my passion. My ache is long and deep and it feels as though her sex has split me in two, has sliced a chasm across my soul.

"I'm a hothead, impatient as a man can be," I say. "You will break my heart someday," she says. "No, never, I promise you." She sighs and leans back and lets me nibble at the buttons of her dress, lets me kiss the curve of her breasts.

As I lay dying, an airplane drones overhead.

"Goddamn Pretty Boy, they even got cops in the air lookin' for you," a man's voice says. His laughter is phlegmy. The circle of faces comes closer, fades back, comes closer again blotting out the sky. Into their strange eyes I look but find no solace, no comfort, no refuge. A kid about the age of my Jackie leans in so close his freckled nose nearly touches mine. " 'At really him, Pa?" "Yes son, that's Ol' Pretty Boy Floyd in the flesh." *Har, har, har!*

As I lay dying, Ruby straddles me, lifts her dress and lowers herself onto my hardness, her bare brown legs aglow in the little light of moon seeping through the windshield of Daddy Walter's old sedan. I am plunged into the warm wet folds of her sex. She moves and it is like electricity shot through me.

"Angels blow your horns." "What?" she whispers throatily. "I didn't say anything." "Yes, yes, you said, 'Angels blow your horns.' " I am there with her and I am somewhere else, in another place. I hold tight to her for fear I will become lost.

Our rhythm is intense, like gunfire at times.

"Oh Jesus, Charley, oh, Jesus."

"Yes, yes!"

She is undone, out of control, grasping and clawing, lurching, biting, a dervish of auburn hair and exposed throat and dark hard breasts. I feast on her. I drive into her like a storm tearing up everything in its path. I try and rip her to pieces, to let her know my passion is a reckless thing. Our eyes glitter in that small safe light of a night where the dark is not quite dark enough to hide everything.

"Oh, Jesus, Charley."

I like the way she says it. I like the way it sounds almost like a plea for help.

"Don't hold anything back, Ruby. Give me everything you've got, I want it all, I want to own every inch of you."

She chokes on her pleasure. I do everything I can to savage her.

Wind rakes over the corn standing in ragged thin lines like weary soldiers.

As I lay dying, I hear a justice of the peace, his hair combed over the bald rock of his head, saying, "Do you take this . . ." "Yes, yes." "And do you take this . . ." "Yes, yes, oh God, yes." "Then I pronounce you . . ." "You may kiss the . . ."

Daddy Walter hunkers on his heels, his gaze adrift, then cuts his eyes suddenly in my direction.

"I've come to take you home, son."

"I'm not ready."

"Your time has come. Let's get away from these fellers."

Someone has brought the men sandwiches and bottles of Co-cola and they eat and drink contentedly as though they've come on a picnic. They throw their waxed paper wrappers aside and the wind tumbles them along to snag on branches and food falls from their mouths as they chew and talk and sip their Co-colas.

"Move him out of the sun," the man with the cigar says. "Put him up under that pear tree where there is still a bit of shade."

The air is cooler under the pear tree, but touching me, lifting me with their rough hands is like a fire through me. I bite the inside of my mouth so hard I taste blood.

I'd rather drink my own blood than give them the satisfaction of hearing me scream. Daddy Walter is there under the tree waiting.

"How did you plan on supporting a wife, Charley? You with no job and no prospects but the harvests and the oil fields, you who never liked to get your hands dirty and always talking about fancy cars and fancy clothes and lots of money."

"I'd sell all my dreams just to be with her."

"No you never did. You said you would, but a month or two after the shine wore off the marriage bed, those dreams came back on you like the plague and you wanted them worse than you wanted her and did anything you had to get them."

"Never, never!"

His mouth is full of words that sting like stones.

As I lay dying, someone puts a jug to my mouth and spills water over my lips and down across my cheek and it comes to rest in the cup of my ear like tears I've wept.

"He about done," a voice says. "Shit, I'd say so, the light's going out of his eyes." "Well, his kind deserves what they get." "Damn straight." "Somebody should call a preacher." "You think it would make any difference?" "It seems only decent."

As I lay dying, Ruby is ripe, as they say, with child, her belly full and round and hard as a ball. I lay my head gently upon her rounded flesh and listen to the mingling sounds of life inside life, feel the little kicking thumps against her swollen tummy and understand the need to escape. Even a velvet jail is still a jail.

As I lay dying, I strangle on my own regret.

As I lay dying, I see Ruby sitting, big-bellied, at the table of my people: my mother and sisters, Rossie Ruth, Ruby Mae, Emma Lucille and Mary Delta. A table of women, of givers of life. The last supper of women, I think.

"A wife's an awful big responsibility, son," Daddy Walter says.

"Yes sir, I know it."

"They ain't like a dog you get yourself. They expect certain things."

"Yes sir, yes sir, do we need to keep talking about this?"

And in the luscious nights I plant my seed in her over and over and over again, as if she is a field I need to raise straight and true, as though I cannot rely on sun or rain or circumstance to see my seed grow and come to something, and bear something for the time of harvest.

As I lay dying, I hear the little sharp yelp of our son from the back bedroom of the little house we live in and Mother comes out with blood and mucus covering her hands, says, "A boy for you, Charley" and I know my labor has paid off.

"Yes, I can tell by the sound of him. He's just like me, doesn't like to be caged in."

"He looks just like you too, Charley. A real little tough guy."

Just like me. Ruby, eyes brimming with tears, says, "Kiss me sweetly, for we have a son, you and I — a beautiful son sprung from the seed of your harvest and the field of my love." I kiss her sweetly and smell life all around her and gaze into the staring blue eyes of my son.

As I lay dying, I remember these things and say to you who do not know me, to you who have hunted me like a wild thing and killed me with lust and fear and awe in your hearts, that I was the same as any of you — just a man, a child who grew to become a man, who was born with the restless spirit in me just as the wind is born restless and the water is born restless and all things are born restless. And you cannot kill the wind or the water or the spirit of a man. So try if you will, but you cannot.

Fractured sunlight falls through the tree limbs, and lies upon the ground and across my face and my "grievous wounds" and I am fractured too.

"He's near gone," I hear a fading voice say. "Yes, sir, yes sir."

"Lift my head up."

It's my only request, the only time I'll plead with them. "Lift my head up" and someone does, his hand strong under my neck.

"What's he looking at?" "Don't know?" "I don't see nothing what he's looking at, do you?" "No."

As I lay dying, upon the far hill I see the figure of a man who stops momentarily to look back. The figure is surrounded by sunlight. It takes me a minute to realize that the figure is me. Then I watch myself go slowly over the hill and know I am following Daddy Walter.

And in the book of life, my name is writ.

2

Pretty Boy Floyd

When I see farming isn't in the cards for me, I trade a neighbor man a few gallons of shine for a pistol.

"I hope you rob banks with it," he says. "Goddamn bankers ain't nothing but robbers with neckties their damn selves."

The pistol is hot and heavy in my hand and I don't know what is in store for me, but I know that gun fits my hand better than a hoe.

Then by providence, you could say, I meet Fred the Sheik working the harvests.

"They call me the Sheik," he says, "because women say I remind them of Valentino."

He's just a kid from St. Louis, but even I have to admit, he's as good looking as the real Valentino. We became pals fast.

One day we are picking cotton and the

pistol falls out my pant leg. Fred the Sheik says, "That's a good way to blow off your pecker, carrying a gun in your pants loose like that."

"What would you know about it?" I ask him, brushing dirt out of the chambers, wiping off the bullets one by one on my shirttail.

"I'm from St. Louis."

"So what?"

Then Fred the Sheik tells me how he robbed some electric company back in St. Louis and got away with almost two thousand dollars and how he's a "two-gun" man himself.

"Shoulder holsters," he says. "That's the only way to pack heaters."

"That's why you're working as a harvest hand?" I say. "Because you're so terrific as a robber?"

"Laying low right now till things cool off, boyo."

We keep picking that cotton, the sharp boles nicking our fingers. I feel the weight of my pistol in my waistband, the butt pressed up hard under my ribs, my fingers sore and bleeding, the sun scorching my back, sweat dripping in my eyes. I see the field boss riding the water can, jawing with men who drag their long sacks up to empty them in the wagons. I see how fat he is. Smart men don't work like mules and I wonder why I'm not smarter than that fat man.

"Listen," Fred the Sheik says. "I know how we can make a lot easier dough than doing this."

"You know so much, how come you're not out doing it? How come you're here same as the rest of us damn dumb bastards?"

"The action I'm talking about needs two guys."

"I'm listening."

"I know where there's some Kroger stores we can rob if you're interested."

Kroger stores?

I thought of Daddy Walter, that little grocery store he had started and how hard he had to work to make an honest dollar, the credit he gave those poor people who came through his door. I wasn't going to rob any damn grocery store and I told Fred so.

"I'm not into robbing grocery stores. My old man's a grocer."

"No, it's not the same thing at all, boyo. Kroger's is a big chain. They're like the banks. They're all owned by rich men with fat wives and fat kids and big black Packards."

I had my doubts until Fred the Sheik said, "Look around you, tell me what you see."

"See lost men, no future."

"That's right."

"See dust and cotton and a fat field boss hogging the water can."

"Go on."

"See another year of my life gone with nothing to show for it."

"That's what I see, too, boyo. I'm about fed up with working like a nigger, ain't you?"

I had a twelve-foot-long sack slung out behind me, dragging it along like the gray shadow of a dead man. A fellow could pick all day and not fill such a sack if he didn't go at it hard, didn't take no more than ten minutes to eat lunch. And if he did fill it, he got two dollars. Walking those rows all day under that sun for two damn lousy dollars.

I thought of Ruby and our boy Jackie, and that little shotgun shack we lived in and how none of us were going anywhere fast. I thought of Daddy Walter and all the other men around those parts and how it seemed everyone was living just to be waiting to die. I thought of the rich bankers and their big fancy houses and the tax collectors and the prohibition agents the government sent to bust the whiskey stills. I thought about a red roadster and what it would feel like to have a nice suit of clothes and cash in my pockets. I thought about a lot of things as I humped up and down those rows of cotton.

But most of all, I thought about that easy money Fred the Sheik talked about.

"What's the use of carrying that pistola if you don't intend to use it?" Fred the Sheik says.

It was a good question, one I had no answer for.

Ruby Floyd

Charley stole my heart the first time he spoke to me. We met at a pie supper in Bixby and he took up all my dance time. Other boys asked me, but I only said yes to Charley. I guess it was the way he danced with me. Close, so our bodies never stopped touching. He was smooth and hard all at the same time, a dream lover, his hair blond from the sun. I could feel his desire pressing through my dress. I wasn't wild or anything, but Charley just brought the wild in me out. He courted me for several weeks. My daddy wasn't crazy about him, but I was.

"That boy's got trouble written all over him," my daddy said. "You be careful Ruby."

"A girl's reputation means everything to her," my mother said.

"There's no food for extra mouths," my daddy said. "I don't want you coming home someday knocked up."

But it was already too late for such warnings. That first night Charley and me made love I knew I was already knocked up. I could feel his seed deep in me glowing like a match head. Charley and me were a wildfire right from the start. A flame that never got blown out.

The world seemed filled with lonesome smiles.

&

Charley Floyd was my first and only true love.

&

I his.

Fred the Sheik Hilderbrand

I'm a two-gun man and I took down the Kitlark Electric Company in St. Louis, Missouri for almost two grand — that figures out to a grand for each gun. I use my guns as I need them. I've clubbed guys over the head with them and I've shot guys with them and I wear them in shoulder holsters under my coat wherever I go.

I've been shot at and I know what trouble is and I know what the risks are when you take up the gun. But I ain't dead yet and don't ever plan to be. But if I were dead, I'd be the best looking corpse in St. Louis.

I met Charley Floyd in the harvests fields. We had one thing in common: we both hated working like niggers under a hot sun all day, our backs near broke from the work. One, two dollars a day was the best a man could make, just enough to blow every night at the roadhouses on booze and women, which we did regular. That goddamn Charley was a dancing fool and so was I. The girls went crazy over good-looking guys who could dance.

Once when we were picking cotton a pistol dropped out of Charley's pants — a Police model Smith & Wesson with rubber grips and most of the blue wore off the barrel. I told him a guy could lose his pecker carrying a gun inside his pants like that. He laughed, said it would take a bigger gun than it to do the job. I laughed. We got along good and at night hit the pool halls and gin joints in whatever town we happened to be near. I could shoot pool like nobody's business — Charley couldn't shoot worth a shit. I made us a little extra dough shooting pool with farmboys who thought they were a whole lot better than they were. You get inside a man's pride, there's no telling what you can do. Hell, they never seen anything like me around those parts until later when Charley got to be famous and would come back wearing his flashy clothes and driving his fancy cars — wanted by every lawman in the country.

Charley was as much hell on girls as I was. We were both crazy about girls and fast cars. I told him about the electric company heist. He didn't believe me at first. Then I told him about how easy it would be to rob the Kroger stores — St. Louis was loaded with them. He didn't want to, he said his old man owned a grocery store. I said what kind and he said, a little one where he gave credit to dirt farmers. I said, it wasn't the same thing. We argued back and forth over it, our backs sore, our hands raw from picking that damn cotton.

"I'll have to think on it," he said.

"You do that, boyo."

"Just because I got a gun doesn't mean I'm willing to shoot anybody."

"Who says you got to shoot anybody?"

"Chances are good you go to stealing people's money, you're going to have to shoot somebody sooner or later."

I lied, told him I'd done a lot of robbing and never had to shoot anybody.

Two, three nights later we were sleeping under the stars and Charley said, "You sure about that money being easy and lots of it?"

"Sure as I am me and you are going to starve to death picking cotton."

Two nights later we just stole a car and drove to St. Louis.

We took down five Kroger stores in one week and made almost six hundred dollars. We stole some cigarettes and candy too. I don't think we worked more than an hour total for the lot of it. Charley said he knew then why Henry Starr had taken to robbing banks — it beat hell out of being poor-assed in Oklahoma.

We had us a couple of girls we'd picked up in a speakeasy and they were on the bed and we covered them with that money and that's all they were wearing until we took it off them.

Pretty Boy Floyd

Daddy Walter stands on the porch looking at the roadster Fred the Sheik and me stole in St. Louis after our last robbery and rode back to Sallisaw.

"Picking cotton must pay a lot more than it did when I was doing it," Daddy Walter says. I think he knew we didn't earn enough for a roadster picking cotton.

We stayed close to the Hills for a time, shooting pool, dancing with pretty girls, me trying to smooth things over with Ruby, which was nearly impossible to do because of her Indian temper.

"You go away and come back whenever you want and I never know from one minute to the next what you're up to," Ruby says. I hold Jackie up to my face and can see me in him and it makes me feel bad I can't easily patch things with Ruby.

I think she knew that the Sheik and me were up to no good. I feel sorry for that part of my life, for what I put Ruby through. She didn't deserve my wildness. I was young and crazy about the fast life. It didn't take me long to go through that easy money and find myself needing more of it.

Still, I was able to get Ruby over her mad and we played like children, went for drives in the country, had picnics, fished, went out dancing, made love in the late night and early mornings when the land was still asleep. In between, I read the newspaper and paced. It doesn't take long doing the same things over and over again, no matter how good they are, before I start to grow restless.

"You got itchy feet, boy," Daddy Walter says when I tell him I'm thinking about taking off again for a while and would he and mother mind keeping an eye on Ruby and Jackie.

"I know I got itchy feet, Daddy."

"You hear that highway calling you like it called me once."

"That's where I get it from."

"I was a hellion before I met your mother."

"I'm as poor a hand at marriage as I am at being a farmer," I say.

"Hell, it don't take a genius to figure that out."

I go see Fred the Sheik. He's staying at the hotel in Sallisaw.

"Man, I don't know how you people do it," Fred the Sheik says.

"Do what?"

"Stay around this one-horse town and not go nuts."

"Most folks like it just the way it is. Nice and peaceful."

"St. Louis is starting to look good to me again, ain't it you?" Fred the Sheik says.

My pockets are as empty as government promises.

"All a fellow needs is one good score," Fred laments, "and he'd be on easy street the rest of his life."

By then I was feeling untouchable. Robbing was so damn easy it was scary.

"Kroger's got their headquarters in St.

Louis, you know that, Charley?"

"So what?"

"That's where they do the payroll for all the Kroger stores in Missouri."

"How much you figure?"

"Got to be at least twenty grand."

"Twenty grand."

Fred whistles, says, "Shit, what do you think?"

I drove back to Aikens and kissed Ruby good-bye in the middle of the night.

As I lay dying, I still see that look in Ruby's eyes when I tell her we are going.

"Don't count on us being here when you come back," she warns.

Her words were like fire on my skin. I tried to make it up by getting in the bed, but she won't let me.

"It's me or the road Charley Floyd, you choose."

Too late, too late.

My fate was planned by a hand greater than my own.

Daddy, I'm wearing a silk suit, spats, two-tone shoes that cost forty dollars a pair. Got women, guns, and money like you wouldn't believe. Got a friend named Dillinger. A real cool customer.

I swallow the night wind.

And the night wind swallows me.

3

Pretty Boy Floyd

St. Louis rises out of the fog, a jagged line of gray bleak buildings. Already I miss my wife and son. We pull up in front of a boardinghouse with trash cans out front, a scruffy butterscotch cat pauses atop one of the cans to look at us with amber eyes. Fred and me get out of the car stiff from the long drive and climb the stairs of the house to the second floor, go down a hallway to the end where Fred knocks on a door. A guy in an undershirt opens it partways, looks at Fred the Sheik, then me, then Fred again and steps back allowing us in.

There's an old brown sofa and a threadbare carpet and a canary flittering around in a cage with crap-covered newspaper on the bottom. There are smells: fried grease, cheap aftershave, an unflushed toilet. There's a side table with *True Detective* magazines stacked on it.

"This is my pal Joe," Fred the Sheik says, introducing me to this guy I never met before. "Joe's going to throw in with us on the Kroger job."

Joe doesn't offer to shake hands, says, "I was just in the toilet, excuse me while I finish my business.

I ask Fred the Sheik why we need another guy once Joe goes to finish his business.

He laughs, says, "Kid, you got a lot to learn about robbing. Joe's the best wheelman in St. Louis."

"Wheelman?"

"Oh, Christ!" he laughs, then tells me a wheelman is an expert at driving getaway cars.

"Hell, anybody can drive a car," I say. "I can do the driving, why we need him?"

"Let me ask you something. You know your way around St. Louis, do you?"

I shake my head.

"Joe knows his way around St. Louis, that's why we need him as our wheelman."

I'm thinking of how the payoff split three ways will be a lot less than split two ways. But I don't say anything more about it because I know I got a lot to learn about the robbing business and maybe it's better I keep my mouth shut for now. You know how you get certain feelings about some guys? Well I got a certain feeling about Joe the Wheelman. It wasn't good.

We drive around St. Louis in no particular hurry in Joe the Wheelman's Ford, which I can hear is not hitting on all eight cylinders. I wonder what sort of wheelman Joe is to drive around in a car with the timing bad. It's early morning yet and the streets are wet and empty from an all-night rain and the sun hasn't come up and everything looks gray and dead. Joe the Wheelman's got a sawed-off shotgun next to him on the seat, and me and Fred the Sheik have pistols. I'm hoping I don't have to shoot anybody.

Joe the Wheelman pulls up behind a parked Cadillac with a chauffer behind the wheel, an old black man wearing a cap and driving jacket and drinking coffee, sitting out front of a nice building like he's waiting for someone. Joe walks up and sticks his sawed-off in the window and tells the guy to get out.

"Start walking there, Dad, and don't look back," Joe tells the chauffeur.

"Yes suh," the chauffeur says and marches off down the street.

"What do we need another car for?" I say.

Joe the Wheelman and Fred the Sheik look

at me and shake their heads.

Joe the Wheelman drives the Cadillac and Fred the Sheik drives the Ford with me riding passenger. We drive for a while then park the Ford in an alley and get in the Cadillac and drive two more blocks to Kroger headquarters.

"You ready for a big score?" Fred the Sheik says to me.

By now it's too late to turn back. I wouldn't anyway; I've been spending all that dough ever since we left Oklahoma talking about what we were going to do once we got rich.

In we go, up the stairs to the second floor, guns out, burst into the room where they're counting the payroll — four employees: one woman, three men.

"First one screams, you're all dead," Fred the Sheik yells. "We just want the cabbage."

"Yeah, ain't this a grocery store?" Joe the Wheelman says. "We just come for the cabbage," then laughs waving that sawed-off at them. I grab up the bags of money.

Next thing I know we're running down the stairs, jumping into the Cadillac, only it's not Joe who's the wheelman, it's me.

"Drive you damn Okie!" Fred the Sheik yells.

"Yeah, kid, drop me off at my Ford," Joe

the Wheelman shouts.

I pull up to the Ford and Joe jumps out, but he's no sooner behind the wheel and away from the curb than a cop car screeches around the corner and gets on his tail.

"Get up close," Fred the Sheik yells.

I get up so close we're almost touching bumpers with the cop car ahead of us, and Fred leans out the window and opens fire shattering the back window. Then I hear lead bouncing off the hood of the Cadillac and realize the cops are shooting back.

"Go, go, kid!" Fred the Sheik is yelling. He's got a look on his face like he's happy and drunk as he empties his pistol at the cop car then grabs mine and empties it too.

I'm half sick praying nobody gets killed, least of all me.

Fred the Sheik

Next day we read in the papers about the heist. One of the clerks said, "The one guy was just a boy, a pretty boy with apple cheeks." That's how Charley got his name, Pretty Boy. They called the heist the most sensational payroll robbery in St. Louis history.

"Hey Pretty Boy," I say to Charley. "You're a real outlaw now — like your hero, Jesse James."

"Don't call me that," he says. But I can tell he sort of likes the moniker.

We split the loot three ways, counting it out on the bed in Joe's apartment: three stacks of tens and twenties, all of it green like cabbage. We spread it out on a cream-colored chenille bedspread. Close to twelve grand total.

"You guys gotta blow town," Joe tells us after we celebrate and split up the dough. "This place is going to be hot for a while."

I can tell Charley is not a big fan of Joe Hlavatry's.

"Next time we do a job," Charley tells me later, "I'll be my own wheelman, okay?"

"Sure, Pretty Boy, anything you say."

"You keep calling me that, I'm going to have to teach you a lesson," he says.

All the guys I know, Charley Floyd is the most dangerous. He's like deep water with a strong undertow — looks okay on the surface, but underneath there lurks danger. He doesn't want me to call him Pretty Boy, I won't. I got a feeling, Charley Floyd is going to be the biggest name in the crime business one of these days.

Pretty Boy Floyd

Fred the Sheik and me buy new suits, silk underwear, two-tone shoes, nice dove-gray snap-brims, and a new Studebaker, fully loaded.

"We're going kind of whole hog, ain't we Charley?" Fred says, when I peel off the money and hand it to the salesman.

"I didn't get into this business just so I could act poor," I say.

"You got style, Pretty Boy."

"Keep calling me that and I'll hit you in the mouth."

He throws up his hands and I throw up mine and we dance around like we're boxing. Then he says, "I was just kidding with you, Charley." So I let it go, his calling me that.

We hightail it out of St. Louis and stop that night in Springfield where we find a speakeasy with some hot jazz music and plenty of booze and girls. You'd have thought we were a couple of movie stars when we walked in, every eye was on us and we didn't mind. We slipped the doorman a five spot for a table up front and it wasn't long before we had company in the form of two dolls said their names were Annabelle and Josie. I liked the looks of Josie and gave Fred the Sheik Annabelle. We danced the foxtrot and Josie wanted me to dance the black bottom with her and I did, but mostly just watched her shake her stuff. We drank bourbon like it was good for us and ended up at a fancy hotel downtown.

"What is it you and your friend do?" Josie says as I am taking off my trousers and hanging them over the back of a chair so they wouldn't get wrinkled.

"Do?" She's as pretty as a picture, platinum hair and talks sort of smart. So I figure to impress her, I'll talk pretty smart too.

"We're in the financial business."

"Oh, that must be very interesting."

"Yes, it is. You'd be surprised at how much money is out there to be made."

She sips her bourbon and watches me, then when I'm down to just my underwear she says, "Those silk?"

"Yeah, you want to feel?"

"No, I want to wear them," she says, and reaches out for me.

There is something sweet about her that I like. I always liked the sweetness in women.

Making love to somebody for the first time is always exciting. Every woman's different and it's like going down a new road you never been down before. Josie giggles when she comes. Seems like I was making her giggle all night long.

Next morning Fred the Sheik and me head back to Sallisaw, the sun rising behind us red as a bloodshot eye.

Ruby Floyd

Charley has been gone several weeks and he never said where he was going or when he'd be back and I am mad at him. And when at last he does comes back, driving that new car I'm even madder because I know he didn't make enough working harvest to earn that kind of money. And even if he did, I felt he was spending it on the wrong things.

He brings presents for me and Jackie and smells like another woman's perfume and I can see there's some lipstick on his shirt collar.

"Don't ask," he says, when he sees me staring at it.

"I'm your wife, Charley. I've got a right to ask what you been up to."

"No, you don't," he says. "Ask me no questions and I'll tell you no lies."

"Is that how we're going to live our lives from now on?"

"Take it or leave it, Ruby. I'm doing what I have to do to make things better for all of us. You might want to live like some poor Indian, but I don't."

I slap him. It makes me mad, him calling me a poor Indian.

He rubs his cheek, says, "Fine, that's the way you want it," and drops the presents on the couch and walks out. I don't see him again for three days until Daddy Walter comes and gets me and takes me down to the police station where they've got Charley booked on armed robbery charges.

"They think Charley and his friend robbed a payroll in St. Louis," Daddy Walter says. I can see his eyes are full of hurt over what they say Charley did. Daddy Walter has a good reputation around Aikens and Sallisaw.

Charley looks a lot less sure of himself when we visit him at the jail.

"I didn't do anything," he tells Daddy Walter and me. "It's all a frame-up, they got me mixed up with somebody else."

My heart aches for him, and it aches for me and little Jackie too.

I want to curse him and hit him and make him understand what it is he's doing to us. But he looks so pitiful locked up I just can't be anything but sorry for him. He promises me that once things get cleared up, he'll change.

I want to believe him. The heart is a foolish thing, and love only leads to regret in the end. I kiss his mouth between the bars.

Pretty Boy Floyd

I can't explain how it felt to have my family see me locked up like that, Daddy Walter's eyes full of shame. But mostly having Ruby on the other side of the bars, the deep disappointment in her eyes. I'd have given anything to walk out of that jail and go right home with her and pick up my son and stay with them forever. Even if I'd had to farm again or work the harvests or oil fields, I think I would have done it and given up the life of crime.

But the police cracked Fred the Sheik easy as an egg and he gave up Joe the Wheelman Hlavatry and Hlavatry gave them me. I never liked that son of a bitch from the first moment I met him. I don't think he was much of a wheelman either.

When all was said and done, they gave me five years in Jeff City — the Missouri state pen. They stuck me in just seven days before Christmas. A hell of a note. I stood and watched the snow falling into the black waters of the Missouri River from my cell. It felt like it was snowing inside me.

Ruby Floyd

I get my first letter from Charley just two days before Christmas. In it he says:

Dearest Ruby,

I know I haven't been as good a husband to you as I promised. I miss you and

Jackie something terrible. This is no place for a human being to be in and certainly not at Christmas when I should be home with you and my baby boy and Daddy Walter and my mother and sisters and all the rest celebrating. I just hope you can find it in your heart to forgive me and know that I'll do right by you once I get out. I've learned the error of my ways. No more robbing grocery stores for me. Daddy Walter told me a long time ago about crime not paying, he was right. It don't. Guess what? They made me a waiter. Imagine your Charley, a waiter. All my love and give Jackie a kiss for me and tell him I love him. Your Loving & Faithful husband, Charley.

The thin sheets of paper were stained, some of the ink smeared, like maybe Charley's tears had fallen across the words then dried again. I felt sorry for him. But I felt sorry for our son and me too. It was a hard life and the times were hard and not much work for anybody. I resented Charley for what he did to Jackie and me, how he left us in favor of a fast life. He had broken my heart just like I told him he would that first time we made love. I should have known better, but when you're crazy for someone, everything you do is crazy too.

Daddy Walter

I can't tell you how it hurt me to see them take my boy off to Jeff City. Cage him like a dog for five long years. Charley was a good boy. He fell in with the wrong people and that cost him, but it don't stop the shame we all feel. I pray every night that the good Lord will see fit to take hold of him and turn him around before it's too late — before he goes so far wrong somebody shoots him down. God, I don't think I could stand to live to see my boy shot down.

I don't know what sins I committed in my life to have them visited on my child, but surely God must be angry with us Floyds to shatter us like He has. I just pray that we can find the right path to walk on before it is too late.

Pretty Boy Floyd

With less than three months to go on my sentence, papers arrive from Ruby's lawyer asking me for a divorce. *Neglect* is the stated cause. I guess maybe so. I don't argue with what they say, I just sign my name: *Chas. Floyd,* and send them back to the lawyer. What else can I do? It hurts to think that maybe Ruby will end up going off with another man, my boy under another man's roof, taking orders from another man. I feel black inside. Black and empty. I almost wish one of those policemen's bullets had found me that day we were shooting it out. All that fast easy money doesn't mean a thing if you've got no way to spend it. I got empty pockets and a hole in my heart, and the snow is still falling.

The last five years have seemed like one long winter. I promise myself to change when I get out. I dream of those Oklahoma hills and me in them.

I try and pray for redemption but how do you pray to a god who would curse you?

4

Pretty Boy Floyd

Red says Kansas City is where the real action is.

"I don't know," I say. "I've seen about all the action I can stand. Look where it's gotten me."

Red's an okay guy and my cellmate here at Jeff City. Quiet, not loud and boastful like Fred the Sheik or Joe the Wheelman.

"I used to be a baker," he says. "All kinds of breads, rolls. But man, I hated getting up early. I got insomnia and don't ever sleep good at night. It makes it rough, you have to get up at four in the morning to bake bread."

Sometimes I hear him thinking up in his bunk.

"How was it you went from being a baker to a robber?" I say, after we'd gotten to know each other well enough. In the pen, you've got to know who you can trust. Red is the only guy I really trust in here.

"I just got tired of getting up so early with no sleep. I'm by nature a night owl. So after awhile I start looking for alternatives. Then I meet a guy who has all the answers — you know the type, don't you, Charley?"

"Yeah, I know the type."

"So this guy tells me he's a stickup artist. Stickup artist! Like it's something beautiful what he does — like he's Rembrandt, only with a gun. But I listen and he says it's easy money, and best of all, you can set your own hours — no more getting up at four in the morning." Then he says, 'Unless you want to rob a bakery.' "

"You sorry you did it now?"

"No. I mean, I'm sorry I got caught and all that. But to tell the truth, once you get a taste of that lifestyle, that easy money, it's hard to think about going back to a regular job."

I knew what he meant. When he got his walking papers he told me to look him up in Kansas City — gave me the phone number and address of his sister, said she'd know where I could find him. I wrote it down on a piece of paper. But I didn't have any intention of going wrong again.

Alfred "Red" Lovett

I had me a flop on the second floor of the Dixon Hotel in K.C. when Charley showed up. I was a little surprised in a way that he did, after all that talk in Jeff City of how he was going to go straight once he got out of the pen. "Straight to what?" I said. His wife had divorced him while he was pulling his time. A thing like that can ruin a man and whatever good intentions he might've had.

There he stood when I opened the door, a cardboard suitcase in his hand and wearing his prison suit, those cheap shoes they give you. He probably had ten bucks gate money in his pockets, maybe not even that. I remember in Jeff City him telling me how he liked to dress nice. But standing there he looked like what he was — an ex-con just got out of the joint.

It was March and still cold outside and Charley had the collar of his suit jacket pulled up and no overcoat and was shivering like a wet dog.

"Don't just stand there," I say.

He comes in, looks around.

"It's nothing much," I explain. "I'm still setting up some scores."

"Jesus, Red, it's a lot like the room we had at Jeff City."

"Only no bars, in case you ain't noticed."

We have a beer and talk this and that. Then Charley says, "Were you serious about this town being a good place for a man to get some real action?"

"Why you think I'm here?"

We have another beer.

"Thing you got to worry about more than anything in K.C.," I tell Charley, "isn't the police — they're all on the take."

"If not the cops, then who?"

"Guys like Blind Harry Brewer and Johnny Lazia."

"Who are they?"

Charley's real innocent. Even though he's done time, he don't know squat about how things work in a place like Kansas City. Charley's from Oklahoma — somewhere in the sticks. I said to him the first time he told me where he was from, "I thought all they had in Oklahoma was cowboys and Indians." He laughed, said, "Red, get real." Tells me there were a lot of pretty tough customers come out of Oklahoma. I say, yeah, like who? And he says, the Dalton brothers and Cherokee Bill and a guy named Henry Starr and I say I never heard of them. Then he shakes his head like I'm the one who don't know nothing.

"Blind Harry runs a big gambling setup," I say. "And Johnny Lazia is connected to the Democratic machine and runs all the bootlegging. You want to wet your whistle, you drink Johnny's hooch. You want to buy you a woman, you buy one of Leroy Maxey's girls. Anything else you want, you go see Benny Portman or Solly Weissman. See, Charley, in this town, you don't get away with or do nothing illegal that ain't connected to one of those guys. Cops are the least of your worries."

"Then let's go see who we've got to see," he says.

"It ain't that simple."

"Why isn't it?"

I can tell Charley's got a whole lot to learn, but looking into those serious eyes of his, I got no doubt he's going to learn fast and be a contender.

Pretty Boy Floyd

The cops pick me up two days after I move in with Red. Red tells me it's just a warning because I'm new in town and they want to check me out, make sure I know the score and who's in charge. They let me go that same day. Then two days after they cut me loose, I get arrested again on a charge of vagrancy. I'm having a cup of coffee in a diner figuring out what my next move is when two detectives in plain clothes come in and take me out again in cuffs.

"You best go back to the sticks where you come from," one of the dicks says.

"You mean some of the local boys don't want any competition," I say smartly. For this I get backhanded by the dick hard enough to split my lip.

"Keep talking wise guy and somebody will find your body dumped in the river."

When I tell Red the cops want me to hit the road, he tells me they're watching his place and maybe it's better I find a new place to hole up in. I move my things to a rooming house on Holmes Street run by a woman named Sadie Ash who Red says has a fondness for ex-cons: "It's like they're stray dogs to her, or something."

"No funny stuff while you're staying here, Mr. Floyd," Mrs. Ash tells me in a stern voice. She's small with a pinched face and red hands, like they've been scalded from being in too much hot water. It's not exactly the picture Red painted for me of this kindly old lady. I find out later that her two boys Willy and Wallace are pimps and petty crooks. I also learn they are dope addicts and police informers. Real beauts.

The good news is, if you could call it that, Willy and Wallace are married to a couple of good-looking sisters named Beulah and

Rose and I get to look at them every night across the dinner table. I say good news because soon as I take one look at Beulah and she takes a look at me, we both know it's all over. I'm maybe at the house a week and the next thing I know, Beulah and me are doing it in the bathroom while the boys are eating Sunday dinner with their ma.

"Oh, god, Charley!" Beulah keeps saying. I got her up against the door with her skirt hiked up over her hips and I can hear Willy and Wallace saying, "Pass the mash potatoes, Ma" and "How's about some more of that bread, Ma" the whole time I'm shoving into Beulah. "Oh, god, Charley!" she says with her hot breath on my face.

"Pass them peas," the boys are saying.

"Oh god, Charley, I'm coming."

"How about some of that coffee."

"Hurry, baby, hurry."

"Go ahead, cut loose," I tell Beulah.

"I am," she says and I have to kiss her hard on the mouth so the boys and Ma don't hear her when she cuts loose.

Grunt, grunt, bang, bang. And it's like we're parachuting to earth, Beulah and me, there in that small bathroom, those boys feeding their faces.

The whole world is crazy and I'm just as crazy but I don't care anymore. Five years in the pen leaves a guy hungry for a lot of things and I'm starved to death for a woman.

A few days later, Beulah and me move in together in some walkup across town and she files for divorce from Wallace. I should have known this would ultimately bring me more trouble. Women always were for me the bearers of bad tidings.

Beulah Baird

I just knew the first time I laid eyes on Charley I had to have him. He spoke to me with his eyes and I knew everything he was saying. My husband Wallace sitting right across from us stuffing his face with Ma's potatoes and pork chops while Charley's hand slid up my leg under the table all the way to the top of my nylons. His hand was strong and gentle all at the same time and I wanted it there on my thigh. I thought I was going to cry out when his fingers moved higher. I had to bite the inside of my cheek. Pretty soon I excused myself from the table and next thing I know me and Charley are in the bathroom and he's got me up against the door and no way I can resist him. Charley whispers sweet things to me as he lifts my skirt . . . it's been forever since anybody's whispered sweet things to me. A woman needs to hear sweet things whispered to her and Charley knew how and what to say.

"You're as beautiful as the rain," he whispers.

He is all hardness, a force of muscle and bone.

"I can't stand looking at you and not touching you," he says softly, his mouth pressed against my ear. "I knew I had to get you alone, and now I got you alone and I'm not ever going to let you go."

"Touch me," I say. "Let me burn you up, Charley."

"Yeah, burn me up baby."

His hands discover all the lost places of me, his words reach into the secrets of my heart and take them out one by one and fondle them and never put them back.

And when he enters me it is like salvation itself and I cling to him, hold on tight.

Ann Chambers

Charley came around my establishment lots of times. I kept a house of girls down near Cherry and Thirteenth and he'd show up there dressed to the nines, right down to silk underwear.

"What's a pretty boy like you having to buy a date for?" I said to him once.

"Don't call me that," he said soberly. He was two sheets to the wind on gin and there was this scary thing about him. He said he hated the name, Pretty Boy, that the newspapers gave him that name. I said, "It fits."

He sulked a bit then told me to take my clothes off, but leave the lights on.

"I like to watch a woman undress," he said. I didn't see anything unusual in his request, lots of men are like that. But what was different was the way Charley watched, the way his eyes seemed to look into your thoughts. Made me shiver a little.

"Charley, lots of girls would give it to you for free," I said, taking off my kimono — I had great tits and liked to show them off and I could tell when Charley saw them he thought they were great too.

"Lots of girls give it to me for free," he said, lying on the bed in his silk shorts. "But those kind of girls aren't always around when you need them, and besides there is a wonderful difference between *those* kind of girls and girls like yourself."

"Oh really?"

"That's right, kiddo. With girls like you, it's always about business, straight to the point, no miscommunication. I always know what I'm getting, what I have to pay for it."

"Should I take that as a compliment or an

insult?" I said, climbing into bed with him.

"Take it any way you want, I didn't come here to talk."

The man loved to screw. I think he screwed every girl in my establishment, sometimes two at a time. "I just love women," he said. "Women have always been my one great weakness. I wouldn't be surprised they'll be the downfall of me."

He told me later, after we'd gotten to be something of friends, he had a wife and a girlfriend. I said, gee, ain't that enough women for you, and he said, a guy like him could never get enough of a good thing, that he was the sort of man who appreciated the pleasures life had to offer and that his time on earth might be short and he was going to enjoy every minute of it

"Live till you die, right."

"Yeah, exactly."

After awhile I stopped charging him for it because I got to like him a lot.

Pretty Boy Floyd

Even when I'm with other women I still miss Ruby. I think about her and little Jackie all the time. Sometimes I think about her even more when I'm with another woman. Every time I see the snow falling or watch it rain, I get lonely for them. There's something lonely about the snow falling or rain hitting the empty streets late at night. It's like I'm the last guy on earth and it's always going to be that way. I go out with other women because I hate being alone, I hate thinking about Ruby and my son being alone and a long ways away. I think I'll go see if I can find them. I'm getting tired of getting rousted by the cops and I'm getting tired of Kansas City. I never did anything wrong, and if I did, it was because they wouldn't leave me alone. All I ever wanted was a decent life for me and my own. What's wrong with that?

I leave K.C. on a bus, same way I arrived. I don't see any future for me in K.C. and I'm not sure I see a future for me anywhere. Nights without a woman, somebody to keep me company are like little deaths. I die every night.

Daddy Walter

Charley didn't come home this time in a fancy new car. He came on a bus and walked the last three miles up to the farm. I was reading Leviticus; it's a hard book about hard rules for living a good and righteous life. I don't think Charley ever read the Bible.

"Daddy," Charley says. "I sure miss this

old place."

We sit and talk while the women make him a big supper — his mother and sisters. His brothers look at Charley like he's some sort of hero — like he's Jesse James come back from the grave. I need to talk to my boys before they get it in their heads to follow Charley. Having one go down that road is bad enough, I don't know what I'd do if the other two went as well.

After supper I tell Charley I need to speak to him alone and we take a walk out into the fields where we can see the evening star standing alone in the blue-black sky.

"Charley, I need you to talk to Bradley and E.W.; I need you to tell them not to get any ideas about joining up with you. Those boys get envious when they see you. You're like the prodigal son in their eyes."

"I'll do it, Daddy," he says. "I sure would hate to see either of them spend as much as a single day behind bars — it's not a fit place for even a dog to be."

"Lord, son, I wish you'd find it in you to turn your life around."

"Tell the truth, I've come back to find Ruby and little Jackie," he says. "I want my family back and to start over."

It made me want to cry. He seemed so lonely, my own flesh and blood, like the apple that fell too far from the tree. Charley was always different than the rest of us Floyds. It was like he heard and saw things none of the rest of us did and it got him to dreaming about things none of the rest of us had it in us to dream about. I can't say why. We are all of the same blood, the same bone.

But not Charley.

Pretty Boy Floyd

It was hard hearing Daddy Walter asking me to steer my brothers straight, knowing I'd brought disgrace to the Floyd name. I was more determined than ever to do the right thing — even if it meant digging my hands into the dirt, picking cotton, working the oil fields. If I could just get Ruby and Jackie back, I promised myself I'd stay straight. It was my sister, Mary Delta, who finally told me the sorry news.

"Ruby met another man and she and Jackie moved away with him."

It was like hearing Ruby had suddenly died. I thought maybe if I could find some honest work, put a little stake together, I could find her, talk her into coming back to me. So I went to work in the oil fields, but I didn't stick with it any longer than I had the other times. Red was right about how once you got a taste of easy money it made it impossible to do anything else. Pretty soon, I was back in Kansas City, no Ruby and no Jackie.

I was back at doing what I knew how to do best.

I was half hoping for God to tell me I was doing wrong. But God never told me anything, or if he did, I must have been asleep.

Beulah Baird

Charley was restless as a cat when he came back to K.C.

"Where'd you go off to?" I asked him.

"Don't ever ask me about my personal business, Beulah." He made me take my clothes off and get in the bed with him. He was cold and shaking like a child in my arms.

If Charley would say jump, I'd ask how high. That's how crazy I was about him.

We went to Pueblo, Colorado because Charley thought the change of scenery would do us all some good and he said he wanted to see some real mountains before he died. I said, you think you're going to die, Charley, and he said, sooner or later.

But the cops rousted us in Pueblo too, and Charley said if I'm going to get rousted, it's not going to be in some one-horse town like this. Two weeks later we were back in K.C., Charley still restless. The police kept picking him up on one charge and another. I'm not saying Charley never did anything to draw suspicion to himself, but he sure didn't do what the crooked police claimed he did.

We got some real bad news not long after Thanksgiving: Daddy Walter had been killed in a fight. Me and Rose and Charley went to Sallisaw for the funeral. I guess nobody in Sallisaw ever saw anything like the three of us. I can only imagine what everybody was thinking. But I didn't care what they thought of me. I was Charley Floyd's girlfriend and that's all I cared about. Let them look, let them talk.

Pretty Boy Floyd

Daddy Walter's own neighbor, Jim Mills, killed him. I used to play doctor with Jim's girl Shirley when we were kids. According to the testimony at the trial, Daddy threatened him with a knife after they got into an argument over some shingles. Shingles! Who the hell ever killed anybody over some damn shingles? Jim tells the jury he shot Daddy Walter in self-defense when he come at him with a knife. Tell me how it's self-defense when it's a shotgun against a knife? They let

Jim go scot-free. He disappeared right after the trial and nobody ever heard of him again. I know a lot of folks think I took revenge on him. I've gotten accused of lots of things, so one more accusation doesn't bother me. If something bad did happen to Jim Mills, maybe he deserved it.

I saw Shirley at the trial — she was pregnant, sitting with a farmboy in overalls who wore a slouch hat, his jaw fat with a chaw of plug tobacco. I wondered when she saw me did she think about those days in the corncrib when we played doctor with each other, or if all she thought about now was how her daddy had killed mine.

I remember the sun coming through the slats of the corncrib, the way her skin was pink and warm to my touch, the slight sour smell of her mouth, the rough hard cobs of corn shifting underneath us.

I remember the innocence, the sweet, sweet innocence of us there on the brink of the rest of our lives and wondered if it had led to this day, this place, this sad occasion where death overtook us and overtook the memory of that day.

Oh sweet girl, let me kiss thy innocent mouth.

& brush this death away and stroke thy hair
and bring forth a new god.

Beulah Baird

Charley and Rose and me drive back to Kansas City in a snowstorm. We stop at a little grocery store to get some cheese and crackers and liquor for the trip (Charley said he knew the man ran a still and sold shine under the counter) and I say, "Charley, ain't you coming in?" He says, "No, I hate goddamn grocery stores."

Christmas is an unhappy time — Charley is so blue even making love doesn't cheer him up.

"Come on, hon — don't you want to unwrap your present?" I say. I'm wearing nothing but a big red ribbon. Charley just looks at me then looks out at the snow.

"Every time I see snow falling," he says glumly, "it reminds me of Jeff City and every bad time I ever had."

I do my best to get him out of the blues, but nothing works.

Rose and me go to the movies. Charley stays home.

Charley is a mystery always to me.

Ruby Floyd

I got word that Charley had come back to Sallisaw for Daddy Walter's funeral and the trial that followed. I would have liked to have gone to visit Daddy Walter and paid my respects, but I'm with another man now and I know if Charley were to see us together he'd go crazy, maybe do something that would get him in more trouble with the law. Seems like trouble just dogs Charley.

A hundred times I started to write him a letter and a hundred times I threw it away. I've got a good man now, a baker, and he works hard and he takes good care of me and Jackie and loves us to pieces — so much so, sometimes it's smothering. I go for walks alone in the park and sit on a bench and try not to think of Charley as I watch kids flying kites in blue skies. I love the way the paper kites sound when they snap in the wind. Mostly when I think about Charley, I think of the way things used to be between us before he went off and got in trouble. It's easier remembering the good times than the bad.

I read what they say about him. I hear talk. But nobody knows Charley like I do. If they did, they'd know he's a good man with a lot of weaknesses.

A flight of geese in a long dark V wing

their way south. Their honking is an alarm to the heart and I look up and watch them disappear beyond a line of bare trees and realize that it feels like winter inside me and that love flies away no matter how much I try and hold onto it.

I will Charley to fly away from my heart as I watch the geese and listen to the kites snapping in the wind, then walk back to my small apartment above the bakery and to a man who loves me desperately and leaves me feeling starved.

Pretty Boy Floyd

I can hardly stand the thought of Ruby with another man. Her daddy tells me she married a baker down in Coffeyville, Kansas. It's like she's living in another world than me, and it feels too strange to contemplate. A baker! I wonder if he dances with her and makes her feel the way I did.

I wonder if she has given him her heart along with everything else.

I wonder does my boy call him "Daddy."

I wonder all the time, my head too full of things not my own.

I wonder if she is with him right this moment as I am thinking about her.

Lying with this new man in a bed, her

arms wrapped round him.
Christ, I hope not.

5

Pretty Boy Floyd

I decided an alias might keep the cops off my back. I told Beulah and some of the boys from now on they should call me Joe Scott. But somebody must have had a loose lip and spread it around because the cops still rousted me every chance they got. I even got rousted for the robbery at the Sears-Roebuck plant. There was a heist anywhere in Kansas City, the first person they mentioned was me. I knew how Jesse James must have felt when they said he robbed every bank in three states all on the same day.

Then I get approached by some guys, who I won't name, to take down a dick that's been giving the whole K.C. underworld a hard time: a dick by the name of Burt Haycock. A crack detective the papers call him.

All I know is this: one morning the dick is on his way into work when a car pulled alongside him at a traffic light and some guys opened up on him with machine guns. How the hell he didn't get killed is anybody's guess. Of course the shooting makes all the headlines and outrages the cops to no end and my name gets mentioned around as one of the gunsels. So what's new, I say to myself when I hear. But I figure I better clear out of K.C. quick. I've got no real friends but Beulah and Rose. I'm not even sure I can trust them. It gets so after awhile you don't trust anyone.

It reminds me a little of a dame I used to go see in a cathouse in Ft. Smith. She said to me, "I used to be a good Catholic girl, went to church and confession regularly. I prayed and did penance even though I never committed any real sins. Then I went out with the wrong boy in high school and he spread it around I was a tramp. And after that, all the boys treated me like I was a tramp, and after a time, I figured if I was going to keep getting accused of something, I might as well do what they're accusing me of, so I did, and that's how I ended up a tramp."

That's how I was beginning to think, too. As long as they were going to accuse me of being an outlaw, I might just as well be a real one.

Beulah Baird

Charley is in a panic.

"They got my name down as one of the shooters of that dick," he says, throwing clothes into a suitcase.

"But Charley, you didn't do it, right?"

He takes the glass of hooch sitting on the dresser and tosses it back then packs some socks and underwear to go along with the clean shirts and shave kit.

"You didn't do it, right, Charley?"

"I told you don't ever ask me my business, Beulah. Didn't I tell you that?"

"Sure, sure, you told me."

"Then why you asking me?"

"Where're you going?" I say. "You planning on taking me with you?"

"Not this time, kiddo. I've got to travel fast and light. Besides, I don't want you mixed up in nothing as serious as trying to kill a dick. You know what they do to cop killers, even if they just think you tried to kill one."

His skin is flushed. Maybe it's all the heat in the room coming from the radiator, or maybe he's concerned the cops will bust in any minute and roust him. Or maybe the reason he's flushed is I'm standing there with my kimono hanging open. I push up close to him and say, "Take me with you, Charley. I'll go anywhere with you, you know that, don't you?"

"Sure, I know it, kiddo. But . . ."

Then I take his hand and slip it inside my kimono and it's warm and strong against my breast. A girl knows the power of her own body.

"Jesus, you got nice ones, kiddo, but this ain't the time or place."

"Don't I know it, Charley, but take me with you, huh?"

I kiss him long and hard and I think maybe he's going to change his mind because while I'm kissing him I reach for him down where he likes it best. But just as I do, we hear a car door slam outside and next thing I know Charley is running down the hallway toward the back stairs, his suitcase in one hand, his gun in the other.

I figure as long as I'm in love with Charley Floyd, I better get used to seeing him disappearing. Charley always said he was born to run.

The cops come in and ask where Charley is. I tell them he ran away. "Which way?" "Your guess is as good as mine." "Dames like you," one of the cops says. "Yeah, dames like me."

Run Charley, run.

Bert Walker

I knew Pretty Boy in Jeff City. He once helped me whip a couple of spades wanted my smokes and I appreciated his help and told him he ever needed for anything to look me up once he got out of the joint.

"I thought you were pulling a hard thirty," he said.

"I am, but you think this place can hold a guy like me?"

I don't think he believed me until I went over the wall. Charley had already gotten out by the time I made my escape and I know there are those who say he helped plan it. Maybe he did. Maybe he didn't. I'd never rat any guy out, especially a guy like Charley Floyd.

Things got hot for us in K.C. because of too many crooked cops, and too many bad gangsters if you know what I mean. Loyalty don't mean nothing to some guys. I introduced Charley to my old partner Nate King. Nate at that point was doing time with Nellie Maxwell, someone who I also have a bit of history with and who also happened to be one of the best boosters in town. Nellie said she'd cook and clean for us while we pulled jobs. Charley liked the idea we'd have somebody to cook and clean for us.

"Sort of like the rich guys do," he said.

Yeah, I told him, but I didn't tell him the rest of it.

"How you feel about Akron, Ohio?" Nate said, while we were all sitting around contemplating our futures in K.C.

"Ohio?" Charley says. "Gee, ain't that a long ways from K.C.?"

"Yeah," I said. "But I cased some banks there — they look easy. You boys ever see how easy those farmer banks look? Some of them are in towns don't even have a stop sign. Christ, I think you could open most of 'em with a spoon."

We look at each other and say, "What the hell."

I don't think Charley had ever been farther east than Kansas City. He said, "Man, they grow a lot of corn here" when we drove through Illinois and Indiana.

Corn, farmers, banks. Charley sniffs the air. He's wearing a pinky ring, dressed like a swell. I think to myself, wait till these farmers get a load of him.

Nate's right. Lots and lots of farmers in Ohio, which means there are lots of little farmer banks just sitting around. I guess we're a gang now: me, Bert Walker, Nate King and Nellie Maxwell. But we don't have any name like the Ma Barker Gang or anything like that, and we don't want any. I tell the others the key is not to draw any attention to ourselves.

We rent a small yellow house near downtown Akron.

"We don't rob any of the local banks," I tell the others once we get settled in.

This I tell them one morning while we're eating some of Nellie's flapjacks the morning after we arrive. The air outside is so cold you could break it with a hammer. I'm still trying to figure out the deal between Bert and Nate and Nellie. The two of them have eyes for Nellie and she seems to have eyes for both of them. The weird thing is their sleeping arrangements. Some mornings I see both Bert and Nate coming out of Nellie's room. And sometimes when I'm in my own room at night, I can hear them all in the next room together. But I don't want anything to do with that kind of action. I don't share, for one thing. But hearing them in there like that, laughing, making noises makes me miss the hell out of Beulah and Ruby. I wonder if I'm not in somebody else's dream, for it's like I'm outside myself watching this guy with my face living like this, doing these things. I wear myself out pacing the floor, watching the moon slip beyond the trees. Can't sleep.

"What banks do we rob if not the local ones?" Bert says, the syrup dripping off his chin as he stuffs his mouth with a big brown flapjack.

"I hear they got some big banks up in Toledo," I say.

"Toledo? That's what, four, five hours by car from here?"

"All the better. We drive in, do our business, and drive out again."

"Like dogs who don't shit where they sleep, right?" Nate says.

"Yeah, something like that."

I can see they like the plan.

"Bank robbers, huh," Nate says, twirling a revolver on his finger.

"Like Jesse James," I say. "We rob banks like Jesse and Frank did."

"Yeah, I remember you got a thing for Jesse, always talking about him while we were up at Jeff City."

"He invented bank robbing," I say.

Nate looks up, still chomping on those

flapjacks and says, "Didn't somebody shoot him in the head?"

"His cousin," I say. "He was just thirty-nine. Live fast, die young."

Nate swallows down his pancake. He looks at me, then Bert, then Nellie. I can see in his eyes he's trying to gauge what a bullet in the brain feels like. He gets this look on his face like he's not going to like it if it happens to him, forks himself another flapjack. I'm young but I feel old.

Bert Walker

I got pals I owe. I figure we're going to start hitting banks we need to go in loaded for bear. I tell this to Charley and Nate. Charley's sitting at the table in his undershirt, his hair combed straight back, shiny with Brylcream. I'm not sure I trust him any more than I trust Nate where some things are concerned. I see the way Nel looks at Charley sometimes. I know he's a real ladies' man. I figure it's enough I got to share her with Nate. But Nel's wild and more than one guy can handle. Nate calls her a nymphomaniac. Was up to her, she'd probably say, sure, invite Charley to our party too. Hell with that. I got a feeling I might be in love with her.

"This extra guy you're talking about,"

Charley says, when I tell him I think we need some more firepower. "He ever do heists before?"

"This is a solid guy," I say. "Solid as you and Nate."

A cigarette is dangling from Charley's lips and when he speaks he don't bother to remove it, talks around it, the smoke curling up into his eyes so he has to squint.

"Solid, huh?"

"Yeah, real solid guy."

Charley nods, sips his coffee. I never seen such a cool customer for having such a hick background. He says he's married to an Indian. Has a kid by her. He's like a Chinese puzzle, hard to figure out. I know this much, I wouldn't want to go up against him in a fight. Some guys just have that way about them, guys you don't want to fool with when push comes to shove. Charley's one of those guys.

Bill Gannon

I get a call from Nate asking how I'd feel about pulling some jobs. I got a wife that's pregnant and three kids running around biting my ankles and most the factories shut down. There are soup lines all over the place: good, honest, hard-working guys standing in line to eat like they're a bunch of bums or something. Guys a lot smarter than me. I did it myself a time or two — stood in those soup lines, and I hated feeling like a fucking beggar. So when Nate asks me how I feel about pulling some heists, I say, how you think I'd feel about it? I'm in.

Nate says he called a couple of other pals of his — Lefty Salazar and Joe Horvath, but that Lefty's in a wheelchair from getting his foot amputated by a railroad car he was stealing coal off of, and Joe's in the Ohio state pen — again. Guys like us never come to a good end. The good life wasn't meant for guys like us, it was meant for other guys.

My wife wants to know where I'm going when she sees me putting on my overcoat and slipping my .45 in a special inside pocket.

"Get these kids and you some food, get some rent money, that's where I'm going," I say.

"Oh Jaysus, Willy, tell me yar not going to do what I think ye are."

She's straight off the boat from County Cork, still got that mick accent.

"Don't worry, Colleen." I kiss her pretty red hair.

"Shar, shar, don't wary," she says. "Like I ain't got a right to wary about me future, about me kids' future, about you, me own husband, Willy."

It's snowing the day I drive off toward Akron. Perfect, I think. Even the weather is against guys like me.

Pretty Boy Floyd

Bill Gannon seems like a solid enough guy. Quiet, the way I like them. Bert tells me Bill's married, got three kids and another on the way. I wonder what his family will do if he gets caught or shot. But I guess that's on his plate not mine, I've got my own worries.

We knock over three banks — all around Toledo, and one across the line in Michigan — this little farmer bank with a cornfield across the street. It's all easy work, but the payoff's not that great. Nobody's all that happy with the take, the risks we take. Bill says he knows of "a sweet little number just outside Toledo." He says, "I thought about knocking it over by myself once — it looked that easy."

"Why didn't you if it was so easy?" I ask him.

"I was working in the factory, had a good job until recently when all the factories closed down. I didn't need to rob no banks. But ever since Black Friday there's no work. I haven't had a decent job in months. Now,

I'd rob a church if I had to."

I look at Bert and Nate. They shake their heads.

"We're in," they say.

"I'm tired of hitting nickel and dime jobs," I say.

Bill says this one is different.

"How is it different?" I say.

"They got rich farmers up that way."

Bert and Nate laugh.

"Who ever heard of a rich farmer?" I say.

"You'd be surprised at what some of those old farmers got in banks."

"I hear they keep their money in tin cans buried in their back yards," Bert says.

"I hear they keep it sewn in their mattresses," Nel says.

I think of Daddy Walter, think there were probably guys like us running around thinking the same thing about him, how he must have had money to have a grocery store. Rich farmers! Shit, I doubt it very much, but the others seem sold on the idea.

I've got no choice but to go along with the rest of them. When I think about it hard enough, I don't believe any of us have any real choice in how life plays out for us.

Nellie Maxwell

I know there have been lots of things said about me, some true, some not so true. Sure, I made a living shoplifting and I was good at it. And if I got busted, I'd just cry me a river and usually the cops let me go. Sometimes I had to do more than just cry a river — some of those cops take advantage of a girl they get the chance. Cops are just like every other guy I ever met — they all want the same thing when it comes right down to it. But before you label me a tramp, remember in those days there wasn't any work to be had and everybody was doing what they had to do to survive. I admit, I enjoyed the work and I enjoyed the people I met and I enjoyed Bert Walker and Nate King and Charley Floyd too. Of course you could say I enjoyed Bert and Nate a lot more than I did Charley. But that's because Charley never gave me a chance to enjoy him. I don't think Charley ever approved of me. But it wasn't like he had any room to point fingers at others, if you know what I mean. Charley wasn't exactly a saint. Still, he was a damn good-looking guy and if he had asked me, I'd have done it with him. I mean I like men, what can I say. But still, there were mornings when I'd awake before the sun came up and I'd be in bed with Bert and Nate and wonder what the hell was I doing with my life. I'd feel blue and low-down and even thought about killing myself a couple of times. But then the sun would come up and break against the snow and sparkle so prettily I'd want to cry with happiness. For I had men who loved me and took care of me and that's a lot more than some women could say.

Pretty Boy Floyd

The bank job in Toledo went wrong right from the start. I learned my lesson that day about listening to other guys telling me how easy a job was.

We go in guns drawn and line everybody up, only Nate's got them lined up right in front of the window while me and Bert are making for the safe. Bill is outside in the getaway car with the engine running.

Next thing I know Bert is conking the bank manager over the head with his pistol, screaming at the guy, "Open the fucking vault! Open the fucking vault!"

The guy's curled up on the floor holding his bleeding head saying, "It's on a time lock, oh Lord, it's on a time lock! Please don't hit me no more."

Bert is giving the guy the toe of his shoe.

"Stop it," I tell him. "Let's just get the

money and get out of here."

"We can't get the money, it's all in the damn vault!" Bert is yelling at me now, his face red as a beet. "This prick's got it all locked up in a damn time-locked vault!"

Then I see that Nate has got the customers lined up in front of the window, their arms up in the air and I'm about to say to him, "Are you nuts?" when we hear this siren go off so loud nobody can think.

"What the fuck is that?" Bert says to the bank manager, who is trying to wipe the blood out of his eyes.

"Alarm," he says. "They got you bastards now."

"Cocksucker!" Bert kicks the guy again and his eyes roll up in his head.

I hate this sort of action. I just want to rob banks; I don't want to hurt anybody.

I start grabbing what I can from the teller drawers and order Bert to stop kicking the guy and grab what he can and in less than a minute we're running out and jumping in the car.

"What the hell went wrong in there?" Bill says.

"Everything. Drive and ask questions later!"

I'm not even sure I know where we're going, but Bill says he knows Toledo like the back of his hand, that he grew up around here. It's the only reason I agreed to let him be wheelman.

"We got a tail," Bill says, looking at the rearview mirror.

Bert turns and looks out the back window.

"It's a fucking fire truck," he says. "Jesus, these farmers. I'm surprised they aren't chasing us with a tractor."

"Yeah, a goddamn John Deere with a plow on the back!" Nate says.

"Lose them," I say.

It's all so ridiculous I don't know whether to laugh or cry.

Nellie Maxwell

The boys come in all breathless, drop two bank bags on the kitchen table. Charley's mad, you can tell by the way he's quieter than the others, the way he paces the floor like a tiger. We count out the money: less than two grand. Two grand split five ways is a lot less money than any of us were counting on.

That night I ask Bert and Nate what went wrong.

"Don't ask," says Bert.

"Everything," says Nate.

"You hadn't lined those folks up in the front window so's everybody could see what we we're up to we would have gotten out of there clean," says Bert.

"You said line 'em up, I lined 'em up."

I'm thinking I wish I were spending this night with Charley instead of the two dummies. But Charley has gone out for the evening by himself and I'm stuck with Bert and Nate and nobody's having any fun. They stop arguing long enough to paw at me and I feel like we're just a bunch of animals off in the woods somewhere without any feelings, just going on instinct and animal lust. It makes me sick to feel like that. I get up off the bed and say, "You two want to screw somebody, screw each other."

I go out into the empty living room and drink what's left of a bottle of gin and taste Charley's mouth on the lip of the bottle. The night is just outside the window and I hate looking at it and I hate everything about my life just then. But I know in a day or two, I'll be okay again — until the next time. But I wonder if the day will come when I won't feel okay again, when I'll never feel okay again.

God, it seems I'm always waiting for the next good time to come along, the next bad time to pass.

I'm getting a bad feeling with this group. Bert's got a mean streak in him a mile long and Nate's a dummy. Bill's just in it for a quick score then back to his wife and kids which means he's not a pro, and in this business you've got to be a pro or you're headed straight to the slam or a waiting bullet. Nellie is just Nellie, a woman with empty eyes. I miss Ruby and Jackie. I miss Beulah too. I miss Daddy Walter and how it was before I realized how damn poor we all were. I write my brother Bradley a letter:

> Dear Brother,
> I sure do miss everyone. Tell E.W. and Rossie Ruth and Ruby Mae and Emma and Mary Delta I miss them all. Tell Mother I miss her too. I wish I could be there with you now. Things are fine with me. Don't believe everything you might read in the newspapers about me. They have me robbing every bank from OK to NY. Hell, I never even been to NY. Ha. Ha. I don't suppose you ever hear from Ruby? I sure miss my son and her. I've got lots of things to tell you when I see you again. If I see you again. Boy, I don't know why I said that. Don't worry. Nothing's going to happen to me. I'm

even looking for honest work, thinking I'll change my life around like Daddy Walter wanted me to. He was right, crime don't pay. Make sure you and E.W. stay on the straight and narrow. Take care. Your loving brother, Charley.

I carry the letter around in my pocket for three days before I mail it. It has the weight of lies. And when I drop it into the mailbox, I can still feel the weight of its lies in my pocket.

Somewhere I hear church bells
&
It sounds like a toll of those dead
&
those yet to die
&
Mine is tolling among the names.

6

Pretty Boy Floyd

A month goes by, we play cards, drink beer, and stay close to the house. We read in the papers about the bank heist — small article, but we all agree to cool our heels for a time. I hear Nellie in there with Bert and Nate every night, going at it. They're either fighting or doing the other thing, almost always drunk. Sometimes I wonder how long it's going to be before Nate kills Bert over her, or the other way around. I don't know how people can live like that.

One night Bert says he's taking Nellie out on the town, and does Nate want to come along or stay and play gin rummy with me.

"Sure, I want to go," Nate says. "What do you think?" They ask me if I want to go, too. No.

I've had enough of the bunch of them to last me a lifetime. I'd just as soon be alone.

I'm thinking about heading back to Sallisaw, see if I can locate Ruby's whereabouts. I got three hundred dollars left of my share of the last job — the one where the farmers chased us in a fire truck.

Yeah, I think I'm going to go look for Ruby.

Bert Walker

We were all drinking that night. Never drink and drive, ain't that what they tell you? Me and Nate are up front, Nel is in the back with this tart we'd picked up at a local club, the two of them making out like schoolgirls. The tart says it's her birthday and she wants to celebrate. I see in the rearview mirror Nel has got her hand up the tart's skirt and they're kissing. I'm about to clue Nate in to check it out when suddenly a cop car flashes its red lights. A spotlight hits the rear window and lights us all up. Jesus, what's this? I get blinded by the spotlight and end up crashing into a parked car.

"What the fuck!" Nate's yelling. Nel's got a cut on her forehead. Just a little one. The blood looks like red rain dropping over her eyelid. The tart's not saying anything; I can see she's too drunk to be scared.

"Get outta the fucking car!" Voices outside the windows shouting at us.

I look, see two big mugs pressed up against the glass. Cop mugs. Akron's finest. Nate's door gets jerked open and one of the cops has him by the lapels dragging him out. The cop on my side is trying to do the same thing — to pull me out, but I got a surprise for him. I don't pull easy. And when he sees my gun, it's too late. There's a bang like the sound of a door slamming shut and the cop folds, sits down on the walk. He has this look on his face like they all get when you shoot 'em.

I'm yelling at Nate to get back in the car when I feel something hot go through my arm. I don't have to look to know I'm shot. There are bullets flying everywhere. I can see I got just one chance — that's to run like hell. Only I don't get half a block when I get shot in the other arm. I'm like a goddamn chicken with two busted wings. But I keep running.

Nellie Maxwell

It all happened so quick. We were having a good time, me and Bert and Nate. We'd made a new friend at one of the clubs and she and I were in the backseat talking nice when all of a sudden Bert crashes the car and there are cops everywhere and Bert's shooting and the cops are shooting. The whole world seems lit up by spotlights and red flashing lights and it's madness. Beverly, the other girl, didn't say a word the whole time. Me, I'm going crazy because I think, this is it, we're finally caught and they're going to kill us.

Then there is this loud bang and I see Bert standing there with his gun in his hand, smoke curling out the barrel and this cop is sitting on the sidewalk holding himself, saying, "Oh Jesus, oh Jesus I been shot." A bullet shatters the windshield and whizzes past my ear. I got glass in my hair. Something sharp cuts into my brow then there are these little drops of blood. Beverly says, "Hey, you're bleeding" and tries to kiss the blood off my face. Her breath is warm and sweet and smells of gin.

Next thing I know there are more cops everywhere, everybody running around, shooting and shouting like crazy. Bert is running down the street, the cops shooting at him, even the one on the ground bleeding through his fingers is trying to shoot him, but Bert doesn't even slow down. While all this commotion is going on, I say to the girl, "Maybe we ought to take a powder while we can."

"Right," she says, and in the confusion, we escape down an alley.

Nate's not so lucky.

Pretty Boy Floyd

I hear people coming into the house, have my gun ready just in case. But it's only Bert and Nellie and some woman I've never seen before. Bert's bleeding from both arms and Nellie's got some dried blood on her face.

"What happened?"

"The cops shot the hell out of us, Charley," Nellie says, leading Bert to the bed in their room. She tells me the cops have Nate. My bad feeling is getting worse.

"You know what you did, don't you?" I say.

Bert is moaning about his arms hurting him.

"You led them straight here," I say.

The girl with them takes off her coat and gloves and Nellie brings some hot water and bandages. A couple inches either way and Bert would have been a dead man. I might have minded that a lot less than them leading the cops back to the house. I start packing my things.

Footsteps. Lots of them. Voices. Fists pounding on the door.

I got no place to hide but under the bed.

Jesus, whoever said it was a glamorous life being a gangster?

Nellie Maxwell

The cops show Bert no mercy. They show Charley even less when they drag him from under the bed. Two cops hold him and one beats on him with his big fists. Charley doesn't say a word as they beat his face to a bloody pulp saying, "So, you like shooting cops, eh?" I get sick and want to puke. The cops make me and Bev watch them do their work. I can't help but think that just a few hours earlier we were all having such a good time. That's the true ugliness of life, how fast things can go from being good to bad. I should have slit my wrists the other night, just let myself sit in a warm tub of water and ended it all. Too late now, too late.

Pretty Boy Floyd

I don't tell the cops my real name, no matter how much they beat me. And they beat me pretty good. I tell them my name is Frankie Mitchell. That I'm only nineteen and that I've never been in trouble before, that I never shot anybody. But by the next day, the newspapers have me as the ringleader, report that we're a gang out of New York and Chicago, that we're responsible for all sorts of crimes. I am surprised they haven't blamed us for the Lindbergh kidnapping. Reporters show up and want to take pictures of me and the cops together. The cops let me hold a tommy gun while the flashbulbs go off in my eyes. No bullets in the tommy gun of course.

The bad thing is, the cop Bert shot died. The good thing is, the cop fingered Bert for the shooting and not me before he died. I knew someday Bert's quick temper and mean streak would catch up to him. Now it has. Daddy Walter used to always say, be kind to everybody, treat every man with respect. I guess Bert never learned that lesson.

They take us to Toledo and a few days later they bring down some of the employees from that bank, that sweet easy bank Bill Gannon was so high on where the farmers ended up chasing us in a fire truck. They finger Bert, but not me. One of the farmers looks at Bert and says, "That's him, I know by that twitch in his neck."

Not long after, the cops have it all figured out who we really are: James Bradley (Bert's real name), me, and Nate.

They've got us cold.

The judge gives Bert the chair for killing the policeman. I get twelve to fifteen, hard time. Same thing for Nate.

Toledo looks like hell in the winter as I stare through the bars waiting for the train to come and take me to the big house in Columbus. I still have the note Bert sent me before they strapped him in the electric chair.

Dear Charley,

This is it. I'm gone. It's going to be a shocking night for your old pal. Ordered steak, fried potatoes, shrimp and strawberry shortcake for my last meal. I asked for a bottle of Irish whiskey to wash it down. Guess what? They said no. I should have never done it — shot that cop. I would be a free man, or at least not a dead one. Now I got to go to my grave knowing I never accomplished anything in life. Nel's probably already got herself a new fellow — but at least it ain't Nate. True love never did run smooth. Take care pal. James Bradley.

The note is written in pencil.

Bert Walker (Alias James Bradley)

I got a few hours to go. It's snowing outside the guard tells me. I can't see nothing but gray walls. Me and the grim reaper have come to terms. You want me, I tell him, you can have me. I hear the hum of the dynamos as they shoot the juice to my cellmate. They took him down a half hour ago. Christ, it must give a guy a real headache, shooting all that electricity through his brain. He says to me as they are taking him away: "I'm scared, Bert."

"Buck up, kid. It can't last more than a minute or two. How bad can it be?"

He starts crying and the guards have to hold him up, drag him like he's already dead. He's just a young guy, no wonder he's scared.

I hear him bawling all the way down the catwalk. Then nothing until I hear the dynamos humming and know they're giving him the juice. Then nothing. Just silence and waiting on my last meal.

I think about Nellie, how the last time I seen her she had her hand up this tart's skirt in the backseat. How we were all drunk, getting ready to have us a hell of a good time. I never minded that Nel liked the ladies as much as she did men. Some women are like that. Who can blame 'em? Hell, it even lent a little excitement to our love life. Nel loved everybody, maybe a little too much. At least Nate's not going to get her for himself. He and Charley have landed a suite in the big house. Nate's pecker will rot off before he ever sees the light of day again. I'll think about those boys when I'm in hell. I'll probably see them soon enough.

They bring my last meal.

I can't believe I'm hungry, but I am and eat everything on my plate.

The guard says, "You want anything else, Bert?"

"Yeah, a swell piece of ass."

He says, "You ought not to talk that way, Bert. You're about to meet your maker."

He has peaceful gray eyes, like the walls in this place. He tells me he's a Christian. I say, "How can a Christian keep a man caged up like an animal, shoot him the juice? Tell me that?"

"It's just a job to me," he says. "Like digging ditches. I see it as a duty."

"Some duty," I say.

He looks at his watch, says, "You still got an hour, you want we could pray together." Hell with that, I tell him. "You want to play some checkers, then?"

I listen down the hall at the silence where the chair is. I wonder will the afterlife be just this great big silence or will it be like they say: streets paved with gold? I sure could use an easy time of it.

Pretty Boy Floyd

I tell myself I'm never going to prison again. I tell myself that a thousand times. I'd just as soon be dead as to be locked up again. Bert was the lucky one — he got juiced. His troubles are over. Mine have just begun.

Nate and me are given haircuts in the jail barbershop before we go up for sentencing. I see my chance and take it by slipping out the side door. Christ, I can't believe the guards aren't paying better attention. Lucky for me, they're not. I taste the outside air. The sky over Toledo is sooty, but it could just as well be blue. Freedom looks like blue sky. I start to run.

I hear the alarms going off behind me back at the jail. I keep running.

Deputy Packo

Charley was like a goddamn rabbit. One minute he's there getting a haircut, the next he's bolting down Michigan Street, running between cars, like a goddamn rabbit. I'm running like hell chasing after him. He doesn't get far. Charley's no track star. I snatch him up. The judge throws the book at him. These crooks are all the same, think they can beat the system, think they're never going to get caught. They all get caught sooner or later or end up eating a lead sandwich, or in the electric chair. Me, I'm just a guy who likes to see them get what they deserve.

I took my chance and lost, but for a few minutes, I was a free man. I was like an Indian back in Oklahoma, running free and wild. I was a horse untamed. I was the wind. I saw Ruby behind my eyelids standing at the finish line. I saw my boy, Jackie. I saw heaven.

They catch me, throw me back in jail, but they still got to get me from Toledo to Columbus and that's not going to be so easy.

I made a vow that I'll never go to jail again. And I won't.

I jump off the train an hour out of Toledo. It's half an hour before the cops even know I'm gone. So long suckers.

Running through weeds and swamps.

Running through backyards and ditches.

Running through the long darkness of night.

Running ahead of my shadow.

Charley Floyd is a running son of a bitch!

7

Pretty Boy Floyd

Kansas City looks better to me this time than it did the last time. I thought I'd never come back here, but beats hell out of a seven-by-nine room in the big house. I look up my old flame, Beulah. She's living in a boardinghouse, maybe with her old man Wallace for all I know. I toss pebbles up at her window until her light comes on and I see her face. She opens the window and says, "Hey, that you Charley?"

"Who do you think? You got company?"

"Ah, jeez, Charley, what sort of girl you take me for?"

I sneak up the backstairs.

Her room is warm.

"Get in the bed with me Charley," she says.

"Let's have a drink first."

We do. Bourbon neat. We kiss. Touching

her under the blankets makes me feel terrific.

"You're on the lam?" she says.

"No, they let me off for good behavior."

She laughs. She sits on my lap. Jesus, that's all it takes.

We make love with the lights on. I insist. I want to see her eyes, her mouth, the curves of her body, everything. I want to see what I've been missing. That's the worst part of being in jail — not having a woman to keep you company, nothing soft and warm except your thoughts. Sure, there are guys in the slam who are into doing anything for the substitution of a woman, but I'm not one of them. Never was, never will be.

Beulah's soft flesh is warm like a lake in the summer and I sink into her.

Later we lay in bed and smoke in the dark and Beulah makes little circles of orange light with the tip of her cigarette. She giggles and sips bourbon and tries to tickle me, but I'm not the ticklish type. She's like a playful child. I love that about her. Ruby is the more serious type. Maybe because she has to be, being my wife and the mother of my son and all I put her through. Jesus, I miss Ruby and my boy.

"Look it, Charley," Beulah says, drawing the orange circles in the black air.

"Just tell me one thing," I say.

"What, baby?"

"How many other men have you had since I been away?"

"None!" she swears. I don't believe her, not even for a minute. A woman like Beulah isn't happy without a man. These are hard times and loneliness is a bullet that can kill you. I try not to think about the other men she's been with.

"What about your old man, he ever come around looking you up, wanting something from you, wanting you to go back with him?"

"No." "Nothing, huh, not even a jingle?" "No, Charley, I've been faithful to you." "Faithful, huh?" "Yeah, sure." "Sure you have, kiddo."

I pour bourbon between her breasts and lick it up. We make love again, in the dark this time. I pretend it's Ruby I'm making love with, that I'm back home in Sallisaw, and me and Ruby are together and happy again. It's not all that hard to pretend when you're in the dark. A woman still feels like a woman no matter what her name is.

I slip into dreams somewhere between Beulah's last gasps of pleasure and my own and I dream of crazy things: that I'm locked in a cell with the devil, drowning in black water, being kissed by a corpse.

I wake up with the sun in my eyes.

Beulah's making breakfast on a hot plate — scrambled eggs.

"How's Rose?" I ask, after I get dressed and sit down at the little table. The window looks out onto the alley. There's a stray cat poking in the garbage. Fragments of the dreams still skitter around in my head.

"She's got herself a new guy," Beulah says.

"Who?"

"Billy Miller."

"He a solid guy?"

"Yeah, Charley, he's a solid guy."

"He do jobs?"

"Yeah, he does jobs, just like you Charley."

I'm thinking, among other things, I could use a new partner. We eat our eggs then do it again and fall asleep and I have those dreams again, about kissing a corpse.

Billy the Killer Miller

The girls introduce me to Charley. Rose and her sister Beulah. He's a quiet guy. I like quiet guys. Loud guys make me nervous, always spouting off what they're going to do, but they never do anything but talk. I hate loud guys.

"Beulah tells me you do jobs," Charley says.

"You don't beat around the bush do you?" I say.

"What's the point? I do jobs and I need a partner. Beulah says you're a solid guy."

"Solid as the rock of Gibraltar," I say. "Solid as they come."

"You want to do a job?"

"Sure, you?"

"That's what I do," Charley says. "I do jobs."

"Same here."

Charley sees the gun in my waistband because I haven't bothered to button my shirt all the way because I wasn't expecting company. Me and Rose were just sitting around drinking coffee. Before that we were on the bed. I still got the taste of her in my mouth when Charley and Beulah knocked on the door. I was reading about John Dillinger in *Startling Detective.* I like to read when I have my coffee.

"You ever shoot anybody with that gun?" Charley says.

"With this gun?" I say, rubbing the handgrips. "No, not with this gun. This gun I just got from a pawnshop. I ain't shot nobody with it yet, but I might if I get the chance."

"I don't like to have to use a gun if I don't need to," Charley says. "I never shot anybody and I don't ever intend to. But if you listen to the cops and the newspapers, I've killed all sorts of guys."

"Some guys are like that," I say. "They don't like guns. Me, I'm not like that."

"So you shot some guys?"

"Yeah, my brother for one."

Charley looks at me like he thinks I'm joking, a sloppy grin on his puss.

"What you shoot him over?"

"A dame, what else."

"You ever shoot a dame?"

"No, not a dame, just some guys."

He grins like he doesn't believe me. But it's the truth.

"I think me and you can do some business," he says. "I like a guy with a sense of humor."

Pretty Boy Floyd

Me and Billy Miller are out having a drink a few nights after we first meet. The girls are at home. We're talking about doing a job together — a bank.

"You want to know what I hear?" Billy says.

"What do you hear?" I say.

"That those Ash brothers are ratting to the cops."

"You think they'll rat on us?"

"Yeah, I'm thinking maybe they will because of us being shacked up with their wives."

"If they were going to rat us out, why wouldn't they have done it before now?"

Billy is drinking sloe gin fizzes. He likes sucking the lime slices. He bunches his shoulders.

"Who knows why dope fiends do what they do? Any guy who would stick a needle in his arm, who knows about a guy like that?"

"Maybe you're right. Maybe those guys will rat us out. What do you suggest we do about it?"

"There's only one thing you can do with rat pricks," he says. I see him rub the pocket where he's got his gun. "Shoot them in the fucking head. Guys shot in the head don't do a lot of talking."

"I don't want to kill anybody if I don't have to," I tell him. "I'm not a killer. I'm a bank robber. That's what I do: rob banks. I don't kill people."

"You know what they call me?" he says.

"What?"

"Billy the Killer Miller."

"You like that name?"

"Probably a lot more than you like being called Pretty Boy," he says.

"Yeah, the newspapers all got names for guys like you and me," I say.

"Fucking dope fiends," Billy says. "You can't trust 'em."

We don't talk about what to do about the Ash brothers because I already know what Billy wants to do about them. It's something I've got to think about long and hard. We drink until the bar closes and drive home in the rain.

"I don't see killing some guy over a woman," I say as we pull up in front of the rooming house. I can see Rose and Beulah up in the second floor window dancing.

"You don't, huh?" Billy says.

"No."

"What's the diff why you kill a guy, dead is dead."

Rose Ash

I'm gone on Billy. Completely gone. I'm probably even more crazy about Billy than Beulah is about Charley. Beulah never stayed all that faithful to Charley after they sent him to jail in Ohio. I mean she tried. I'm not passing judgment on my own sister, mind you. But Beulah likes good-looking guys with dough and there are plenty of good-looking guys with dough in K.C. who were more than happy to take an interest in my sister.

She saw a few guys while Charley was gone. She even saw her ex, Wallace, once or twice rather than be lonely even for a night. Of course when Charley came back, Beulah told him she'd been faithful. But Charley's a smart guy and I'm sure he figured out what's what with her. Like Charley's always saying, ask me no questions and I'll tell you no lies. I think that's the way they both looked at it when he came back.

Billy and Charley are a lot alike in some ways: fancy dressers, good-looking guys who aren't afraid of anyone. A girl can feel safe with guys like Billy and Charley.

The only thing about Billy I'm not so crazy about is when we make love he likes to finish with me face down on the bed. I like to look into his eyes, to see how happy I'm making him. But for some reason that's the way he prefers it, me face down. I asked Beulah about it, making her swear never to say anything to Charley because I don't want it to get back to Billy I'm telling anyone about our love life. Beulah says maybe it's because Billy was in jail.

"So what does that have to do with anything?" I say.

"Jeez Louise, you're a real babe in the woods, Rose," she says. "Don't you know nothing?"

"What is it I'm supposed to know?"

Rose looks at me, snapping her gum as she's ironing a dress for that evening because we're all fixing to go out together. She's standing in just her slip and hose.

"There's no women in the joint," she says. "Sometimes guys have to . . . you know, do it with other guys."

"Oh jeez, Rose, that's so sick," I say.

"Maybe Billy got used to doing it that way, is all."

I don't even want to think about such things. But every time Billy makes love to me and finishes up that way I can't help but thinking about what Beulah told me.

To try and keep from thinking about it, the next time Billy and I are doing it, I ask if we can please do it so I can look at his face.

"Why you want to see my face?" he asks.

"I just do, you're such a good-looking guy and I feel so lucky."

"Okay," he says and finishes up with him on top and me looking into his face, but I could tell he didn't enjoy it as much. Whatever Billy wants, whatever way he wants it is fine by me. I'd do anything for him.

Billy wants to rub out the Ash brothers. He says it's the only way to deal with a rat. I tell him I'm not interested in doing any killing, that I'm a bank robber, plain and simple, that they'll never give you the chair for stealing somebody's money but they will for stealing a life. I think about Bert, that note he sent me while he was on death row. I still got it in my wallet. I don't want to end up like Bert, waiting for them to strap me into the chair knowing I'm going to get juiced and can't do anything about it. Anybody can shoot someone, but it takes a real artist to rob a bank and get away with it without hurting somebody.

I could care less about the Ash brothers, I tell Billy.

Then two days later, I get rousted by the cops in a speakeasy while I'm entertaining a young woman: Gloria, the hatcheck girl. Three dicks in gray suits burst into the private room I've rented.

"Stand up," one of the dicks orders. I just got my coat and hat off.

I stand and he pats me down.

"Let's go," he says.

"Where?"

"Where do you think?"

"You mind I get my hat at least?"

"Go ahead."

My hat is in the closet on a shelf next to my two .45s. The dicks are real surprised when I start shooting. I don't want to shoot anybody, but it's me or them at this point. I shoot out the lights. The hatcheck girl is screaming her head off.

Then I'm out the door running into the black Kansas City night with bullets whizzing past my skull. One bullet snatches my hat off and sends it flying. Another rips through my coat sleeve. I keep running until the bullets aren't chasing me anymore. I keep running until there is just the sound of me running.

And when I stop to catch my breath with the sweet scent of garbage there in the alley behind a Chinese restaurant all I can think about is just one thing: Those Ash brothers set me up.

Billy the Killer Miller

Charley calls from a payphone, says he almost got nabbed, says he had to shoot it out with the cops. I ask how, where, when. He says he thinks it was the Ash brothers who set him up.

"We better blow Kansas City," he says. "Those dope fiends are going to be the death of us."

"Sure, sure," I tell him. "We'll blow this place, give me until tomorrow night to tie up some loose ends."

"Loose ends?" he says. "You know what will happen if you do what I think you're going to do and they catch you."

"You stick to what you do best and I'll stick to what I do best," I tell him.

I arrange to meet him at a bar on Holmes Avenue the following night and tell him to lay low in the meantime.

"You bring Rose and Beulah," I tell him. "I'll meet you there just after midnight."

"Okay," he says, then adds: "Whatever it is, these loose ends you got to tie up, I don't want to know about."

"Don't worry, Pretty Boy, there's only going to be three guys who know about it and two of them won't be doing any more ratting after tonight."

Rose asks me where I'm going when I put on my jacket after talking to Charley on the phone.

"Meet with your ex old man."

"What for?"

"Me and him has got some business to discuss."

"Jesus, Billy, you're just asking for trouble."

"Nah, everything's aces between us. I just

want to talk to him is all."

"Billeeeee," she says.

Sometimes Rose acts like a kid, but you can't beat her in the looks department.

Rose Ash

Billy tells me to call up my ex.

"What for? I hate the guy."

"Just do what I tell you," he says.

He tells me to tell William that I'm at a joint outside of town, that Billy and me have gotten into a fight and he's abandoned me and that if William really loves me, he should come and get me right away. "Make it sound real," Billy says.

So that's what I do: I cry and everything over the phone and my ex says, "Stay put, I'll be right there."

"Tell him he should bring his brother, too," Billy whispers in my ear. "Tell him in case I change my mind and come back there might be trouble and he'll want to make sure he's got some backup."

So I tell my ex that and he says, "Damn straight, Rose! I'm bringing Wallace and if that dirty prick Miller shows his face, I mash it in for him."

I'm scared after I hang up the phone.

"What you going to do, Billy?"

"Nothing, just talk to them is all, a business deal. Pack your bags, and tell Beulah to pack hers. We're going to blow town — the four of us, you and Beulah and Charley and me."

I got a bad feeling, but I love Billy so much I'll do anything he wants and I won't worry about anything else. I don't care. Billy sticks his gun in his pocket — he calls it his heater.

J. A. Reid

I get up because I have to take a pee. Since I hit fifty, I pee a lot. I guess it's after midnight sometime and as I'm going to the bathroom I hear a couple of gunshots off in the distance. Then a couple more. Who the hell hunts at midnight, I'm asking myself. It sounds like the gunshots are coming from out by the road. I go to the window and look out. Nothing. I go in and pee and come out again and look out the window again and I see a fire. A fire! I call the fire department, then get dressed and walk out to where the fire is.

Here's what I see when I get out to the road: A car on fire and two guys lying half in the ditch, their feet sticking up toward the road. One of the guys has got a hole in the bottom of his shoe. I shine my lantern to get a closer look at them. Off in the distance I can hear the sirens. Too late, too late. Those boys were stone dead, both of 'em with their brains blown out. The cops arrive and say it looks like a gangland murder. Lord almighty, you think this stuff only happens in the city, not way out here in farmland.

Pretty Boy Floyd

I'm with the girls at the speakeasy Billy and me arranged to meet at. Half hour after midnight he pulls up in a nice sedan: a Hudson Hornet.

"Get in," he says, without getting out.

We pile in and thirty minutes later we cross the state line.

Billy's sweating even though it's a cool night. He's wearing his overcoat and a snappy fedora and he's sweating and grinning and driving fast.

I want to ask him what he's done, where he's been, but I think I already know.

We stop at an all-night diner around three in the morning.

"I'm hungry as a goddamn wolf," Billy says, and orders two burgers and a cup of black coffee for himself and something for the girls while they visit the powder room. I just have coffee. Every now and then a truck goes down the highway, its headlights like yellow eyes peering into the long dark. The whole world right about then has the feel of a lot of loneliness to it.

"I'm not going to ask you what you did before you showed up tonight," I say to Billy. I sip my coffee and smoke a cigarette and stare out into that deep darkness where a hidden world is.

"I did what needed doing. You want to hear?"

"No."

He lights a cigarette, knuckles his fedora back away from over his eyes.

"You got to know something about me, Charley," he says.

I wait for him to tell me.

"A guy does me wrong, I don't give him a chance to do me wrong a second time. That's the way I am. I hate a rat. I hate a rat worse than anything. You want to know the only thing I hate worse than a fucking rat?"

He leans across the table, his face in close to mine.

"What?" I say.

"Two fucking rats!"

The corners of his soft boyish lips curl up like a piece of paper thrown in a fire.

Beulah and Rose make their reappearance, their noses freshly powdered.

"What are you two talking about?" Beulah says cheerfully.

"Rats," Billy Miller says.

"Oooh!" Rose says. "I hate rats."

"Me too," Billy says.

"Oh kiss me," Rose says.

& Billy the Killer Miller winks
his conspiracy and seals her red mouth
with
his
&
another truck rumbles along into the night
leaving behind the silence of death,
scattering
tattered dreams in its wake of wind and my
heart & eyes are stone.

8

Pretty Boy Floyd

We drive all night and half the next day with the girls asleep in the backseat, Billy and me taking turns at the wheel.

"Where we going?" I say.

"Toledo."

"The hell with that, I'm still a wanted man in Toledo."

"Okay, so not Toledo," Billy says out of the side of his mouth.

The black endless night eventually turns gray. I can see the shadows of trees off in the distance, fields still asleep under the early dawn. Then the sun rises above the trees and it looks like an egg cracked open in the bottom of a beer. By the time we stop for gas again it is close to noon and I see a sign that says: TOLEDO, 25 MILES.

"Listen," I say. "I'm not showing my face in Toledo."

By now the girls have been awake and have begun complaining about how cramped it is in the backseat, how tired they are of driving, how hungry they are.

"Shut up!" Billy tells them, "or I'll leave you along the side of the road."

"Jesus, Billy," Rose says. "You don't have to be so mean."

He looks at her in the rearview mirror, doesn't say anything, just gives her a look.

The car smells of perfume and stale cigarettes and unwashed bodies.

Next thing I know, Billy is turning off the highway on to a little two-lane road.

"Now where?"

"You don't want to go to Toledo, we won't go to Toledo."

I see a sign: BOWLING GREEN 2 MILES.

The name makes it sound like a nice place.

Billy the Killer Miller

By the time we hit Ohio, everybody's getting on my nerves — the girls especially. They want to stop, they want to get something to eat, they want to know when we're going to get there. Get where? I don't know myself, except I know a little about Toledo, know my way around because I knocked down a couple of banks around there. Never got caught so I figure what the hell — it must be a good place for me, Toledo. But when Charley asks where we're headed and I tell him, he about has a fit. "I ain't going, I ain't going," he says over and over again. Then Rose and Beulah are barking at me and I'm already tired from driving all night and what I did to those Ash brothers. I keep seeing those two rats, how they looked just before I shot them.

Rose's ex, kneeling and sobbing like a damn baby, snot running out of his nose. His goofball brother, Wallace, doped up as hell so he don't even understand the consequences of what is about to happen to him for ratting Charley out.

"You fucking rat dopers," I say to them, because I'm mad and I know I'm going to kill them both and it doesn't matter what I say or don't say by this time. It's always easier when you're mad at a guy before you shoot him.

"You fucking dope fiend rats!" And I point the gun at them.

"Oh shit, don't kill me!" Rose's old man is sniveling. "Oh don't kill me. You can have that fucking cunt for all I care. Who gives a fuck about her!"

"I do," I say, and I pull the trigger and it's just this loud bang of a sound because I'm using my .45 with the grips wrapped in electrician's tape so they can't lift my prints. I could have used a smaller gun, a .22 or a .38, but a .45, you don't have to worry about nothing. *Bang! Bang!*

"I care about her," I tell him as I pump another round into him. The night seems big and empty with nothing in it but me and those dope fiends and maybe a couple of farmhouses. And when I shoot Rose's ex, the sound soon gets swallowed up, until I shoot the other one and that sound gets swallowed up too.

Bang! Bang! Then it's real quiet again.

The other one, Wallace, looks at his kid brother as he flops over and says to me, "Hey you just shot my fucking brother!" His eyes are rolling around in his head because he's doped up. He doesn't know if he's in Kansas City or Timbuktu.

"Yeah, I shot him," I say, "and now I'm going to shoot you, you rat prick."

He giggles.

Fucking dope fiends.

I don't think he knew what hit him. Two in the head.

I toss the heater into the ditch, down into that muddy water and get in my car and drive away because what's done is done and I don't look back. But now, with everybody getting on my nerves, I'm thinking it would be just as easy to get rid of everybody just to get them off my nerves — Rose, Beulah, Charley — as it was those two rats.

Beulah Ash

Rose tells me she thinks Billy did something to our exes — that that is why we left K.C. in such a hurry and in the middle of the night.

I'm not sure how I feel about this at first, to think Billy may have killed my ex-husband. But the thing is, I'm with Charley now and I can't be overly concerned about Wallace. He had plenty of chances with me, but he chose morphine and his brother over me. I asked him one night when I caught him sticking a needle in his arm why he did it. I could never do anything like sticking a needle in my arm.

He looked at me and said, "Jesus, Beulah, it's better than fucking sex!"

"Better than sex with me?"

He just smiled that stupid dope smile of his, said, "Better'n sex with anybody."

Maybe if Billy did do something terrible to William and Wallace, maybe it was God's will. Maybe if he hadn't done something to them, somebody else would have. I tell this to Rose. I ask her, "Does it trouble you that Billy might have done something to them?"

"No," she says. "I don't care. I mean, yeah, I'd be a little sorry to know William's dead, but I love Billy more than anything. You think that makes me a bad person, because I don't really care or want to know what Billy might have done to them?"

"No, I don't think it does, Rose. Love is a two-way street. Problem was, Willy and Wallace were traveling one way and we were traveling another. They loved their dope more than us."

She smiles, we're both dead tired.

I try not to think anymore about Wallace or Willy.

Pretty Boy Floyd

It's Sunday and nothing is open in town. Bowling Green looks like a sleepy little place where nothing bad ever happened. Maybe nothing good ever happened here, either. We drive past the same bank three times. The only bank in town any of us sees.

"They're not open," I tell Billy, after the third time he drives past the bank.

He looks at me the same way he looked at Rose earlier when he told her to shut up. Maybe he thinks he can scare me the same way he does her, but he can't. His gun doesn't scare me, and neither does he.

"Ah screw it," he says, after the third time

past the bank. "Wrong time, wrong town. Let's go find us a place by the lake."

"What lake, Billy?" Rose says, sweeter now, trying to get back on his good side. It seems to work, for his mood changes; he laughs, says to Rose she ought to wise up and that there's more to the world than just "Kansas fucking City."

Rose pouts. Then Billy the Killer Miller explains to her which lake he's talking about:

"Lake Erie," he says. "I love being by the water."

We drive across the state line into Michigan — through a little town called Monroe. We see a sign telling us that Monroe is the home of General George Custer.

"Hey, that's that Custer's last stand guy," Billy says. Rose and Beulah look at each other. I don't think they're big on history.

We drive until we find Lake Erie. We drive right up to the water's edge so that our front tires are practically in the water. The lake is flat and smooth. It looks like sheet metal under the early afternoon sun.

There are some cottages for rent and we rent two of them and then find a grocery store not far up the road. One of those old stores that reminds me of the one Daddy Walter had before he was killed: old screen door with rusty hinges, a metal Dr. Pepper sign, fly tapes hanging from the ceiling with about a million flies stuck to them.

"Should we rob it?" Billy says, as we walk in. But he's laughing when he says it. We buy cold cuts, bread, beer, potato salad, cigarettes, some cold Dr Peppers, licorice sticks for Beulah and Rose because they beg us for them. The guy sells us some bottles of homemade beer.

Back at the lake, Billy and me sit on the stoop of one of the cottages while Rose and Beulah fix lunch: bologna sandwiches to go with the potato salad and bottles of beer.

"Why are we here?" I ask him.

"Figured a little vacation might do us all some good," he says.

We see some guys out on the lake in a small boat, fishing. And later that evening, we watch the sun sink into the lake way out beyond a buoy while bats or starlings or something dart across the darkening sky.

Out in the reeds along the shoreline, frogs begin to croak in an uneven rhythm. Other than the sound of the frogs, and the moths flapping against the screen door, it's all very peaceful. Billy doesn't say anything, and neither do I. Then we hear the sound of a radio playing a torch song from one of the far cabins. It seems to fit the mood: sweet and lowdown. The yellow lights inside the cottages fall through the windows and lie in small squares in the sandy, stump grass yards. The shoreline of the lake curves gently and waves come in and caress the land then retreat again. I think of Ruby, wishing she were here with me, just the two of us on vacation here in this place, watching the sunset together, sipping a beer and doing nothing.

The girls come out and we sit in silence and watch the moon rise out of the water just to the right of where the sun sank into it. We drink and listen to the music coming from the radio and Rose says, "It's really dreamy here."

Something splashes in the lake.

"We should go fishing in the morning," Billy says.

"What with, our guns?" I say.

We all laugh.

Rose is right, it is dreamy here. I just wish it was Ruby here instead of Beulah.

Billy the Killer Miller

For a couple of days we laze around and do nothing. We rent a boat and row it out into the lake but the wind comes up and makes the water choppy and our feet get wet in the bottom of the boat.

“Ooh, ooh,” the girls say, so we row back to shore.

Charley and me take a long walk down the shoreline until there ain’t no more cabins and I take out my .45 and shoot some rounds into the water.

“What are you doing?” Charley says.

“Fishing,” I say.

He shakes his head.

“What, you don’t think I can get any fish this way?”

“No, maybe you can,” he says. “But how you going to reel them in?”

We take turns shooting a piece of driftwood and watch it bob whenever we hit it.

“I’m about ready to blow this place,” I say when we run out of bullets.

“Yeah, me too.”

“You ready to pull a job?”

“Yeah, you?”

I look at him.

“That’s what I do, I pull jobs,” I say.

“Hey, that’s my story.”

“Then let’s go pull us a job.”

“Let’s go.”

We walk back toward the cabins, our guns empty, but happy.

That night I hear Billy and Rose going at it. It's a warm night and the windows are open and I can hear them laughing and going at it. Beulah says she's not feeling well, that it's her time of the month, so I get up and go sit on the stoop and watch the stars and think how far away from Aikens I am.

"Oh Jesus, Billy!" I hear Rose say, her voice full of heat.

I try not to listen, but it's hard not to. I think of all the things I could have become if I'd only set my mind to it: a lawyer, maybe an actor out in Hollywood, something, anything but what I became. I look up at those stars and wonder why I became what I did and why I didn't become something else.

I wonder why I wasn't born to rich folks or born in Africa or something. I wonder what the hell is life about but chances. We all take our chances, we're all born to chance. Everything is just a matter of chance — like why I met Beulah instead of Rose first.

I got a heart full of questions but no answers.

That night I dream they kill me: faceless men in gray suits with guns.

9

Pretty Boy Floyd

The way we work doing the job is we steal a car: a pearl Hupmobile from a parking lot. Big sedan. We tell the girls to take our own car and meet us at a diner we know a few miles outside of town. Then Billy and me drive to this small bank that's got plate glass windows with gold lettering: FIRST CITIZENS OF WHITEHOUSE, the sun glaring off it.

"That's the one," Billy says.

"Looks small."

"All the better," Billy says. "Who worries about a small bank in bum fuck Ohio getting robbed? You see any armed guards inside? Small banks don't hire armed guards. You know why?" Before I can answer, he tells me: "Because they're too cheap and they figure, like most folks, nothing bad is ever going to happen to them.

Cheap and stupid is a bad combination, but good for us."

"You want me to go in and you wait behind the wheel?"

Billy shakes his head; he's already got his .45 in his hand.

"Nah, piece of cake," he says. "I'll be right back."

I drum my fingers on the steering wheel as I keep an eye open for any police cruisers that might be coming down the street or cops who might be walking a beat. Though I doubt a town this size they even have police. I look around. It's not much of a town. I wonder why they call it Whitehouse. I don't see anything that looks like *the* Whitehouse if that's what they named it after. I see chestnut trees and old homes. I see a hardware store and a jeweler's. I see a gas station and I see the bank Billy's just gone into. I see a lovely little town where nothing ever happens.

Billy the Killer Miller is back out in less than five minutes and we drive off.

Billy's grinning as he's counting the dough.

"That's the easiest eighteen hundred dollars you're ever going to make Pretty Boy," he says. "And all you had to do was sit in the car and watch the birdies."

"I didn't see any birdies," I say.

He gives me a screwy look.

We meet with the girls and ditch the stolen car.

"What now?" I say to Billy.

"Oh, man," he says. "These are some easy pickings — these Ohio banks, Charley. We're going to do real well for ourselves around here."

I'm thinking maybe he's right. Things have gone pretty good for me since I joined up with Billy. Maybe he's my good luck charm. Later when we're back with the girls and sitting around watching the same two guys out fishing in their boat I say, "Hey, let's go to a speakeasy in Toledo tonight."

"Now that's the spirit," Billy says. "And if we have to, we'll shoot our way out of the joint."

The girls giggle, kiss our faces and hug our necks.

Beulah Baird

I like it that we're all so happy. I've never been so happy. Charley and Billy are in good moods and Rose is draped all over Billy like she's something he's wearing. The boys suggest we go to a speakeasy in Toledo and of course Rose and I both say we have to have something nice to wear. "You mean like new dresses?" Billy says, and hands us a hundred dollars. Rose's kisses leave little red lipstick bows on Billy's dark cheeks.

That night we dance and drink gin at a club where you have to knock and whisper your intentions through a small slot in the door. Billy slipped a ten spot through the slot and they let us in.

"Oh jeez Louise," Rose says when we get inside and hear the music and see what a good time everybody is having. "Ain't this the greatest!" Charley orders us a round of drinks — gin and bourbon. He and Billy look nice the way they're all dressed up in new suits, new hats, white-on-white shirts with blue silk ties. Billy looks a little like James Cagney and Charley a little like George Raft. I feel like Rose and me are out with two movie stars. The cigarette girl comes around and Charley buys a couple of packs of Chesterfields from her and gives her a five dollar bill and tells her to keep the change and you never seen such a big smile.

I'm feeling very loving toward Charley. I tell him I want to dance with him.

"Sure," he says. "I'm a hell of a dancer." And he is.

"Oh dance with me, Billy," Rose says.

"I don't dance," he says.

Rose looks disappointed.

"Well, maybe I should find me a guy who likes to dance," she says.

"Go ahead, and make sure he takes you home too and buys you new dresses."

"Oh, Billy, I was just teasing."

"I wasn't."

Sometimes Billy can be a real stick in the mud. Charley and I dance until our skin is warm and damp the way it is after we make love and I can tell looking into his eyes he wants to take me home and make love to me for real. And I want him to.

Except for Billy's refusal to dance with Rose, we have a great time and don't drive home until three in the morning. Home is a set of hotel rooms Charley and Billy rent us in Bowling Green. Billy says there's a nice bank there he wants to take down and the hotel is closer than the cottage at the lake. Charley says about the bank: "The same one we drove past three times the Sunday it was closed?"

"Yeah, I got a feeling about certain banks, and I'm telling you this particular bank will be even easier than the last one. And I'm betting it's got a lot more money than the last one, too."

Charley's in a really good mood, and says, "Sure, Billy the Killer Miller, whatever you say." Billy grins like a fox showing his teeth. We go up to our rooms and I was right about when we were dancing, for we barely get in the door and Charley's all over me, kissing me and pulling me in close to him and I say, "I like it Charley, the way you handle me."

And he says, "I like it too, kiddo. I'm a real lady killer."

We kiss, and oh my god I just can't stand it.

"You want to turn out the lights or just do it?" I ask him.

"Just do it," he says.

So we do.

Pretty Boy Floyd

Beulah gives me anything I want and all of it I want, but it still isn't the same as it was with me and Ruby. Ruby isn't as sexy as Beulah, and she never tried as hard as Beulah tries when we're in bed together. But there is just something about Ruby I can't describe, the way I feel about her deep down in my bones. I think a man can only know that kind of love once in his life. All the other women that come along can't touch me the way that Ruby does. I know she's probably right now somewhere lying in bed with another man and I hate the thought of it, but I still love her.

It's maybe an hour before daylight and I still can't sleep. I'm thinking about Ruby and Jackie, and I'm thinking about the bank me and Billy are going to take down in a few hours. I'm thinking about my kinfolks, about them nesting in the sand hills of Oklahoma all safe and warm in their beds, how they must worry about me at times, reading about all the mean things I'm supposed to have done. Daddy Walter is resting in his grave and maybe the man who killed him, too. I think about how innocent I used to be and how I'd like to be back there now with them, safe and warm in my bed too without the cops looking for me. But I know that's never going to happen.

Billy told me something disturbing while we were at the club and the girls were powdering their noses.

"You remember asking me when we first met if I'd shot anybody?" he says. We were watching people dancing, listening to the music. We already had a load on from all the booze.

I say, "Sure."

"And I told you I'd shot my brother."

"Yeah, that's what I liked about you," I say. "Your sense of humor."

"It wasn't a joke," he says. "I did shoot him."

I look straight into his eyes and I can see he's dead serious.

"Why'd you shoot him?"

"Over a woman, like I told you," he says. "I shot him over a fucking broad we both wanted."

Something cold runs down the back of my neck because of the way he says this, the way he looks at me and grins.

"You're pulling my leg again, right?"

"You think?"

But I know he isn't pulling my leg.

I can see the streetlights glowing in the predawn darkness; they are like watchful eyes watching out for Billy and me. I'm tired but I can't ever sleep more than a couple of hours at a time. Beulah is dead to the world and from the little light that filters into the room, I can see her sprawled on the bed, the covers twisted between her legs, one fleshy hip exposed as though offering it to whoever wants it. I think of how it is a man can be so jealous of a woman that he would shoot his own brother over her. I tell myself that I must be careful of Billy Miller, for he takes offense as easily as some women take compliments.

I should write a letter to the folks back

home and in it ask them if they've heard anything of the whereabouts of Ruby and Jackie. I smoke and watch the darkness give way to the dawn. I feel like I've lived a lifetime already.

Rose Ash

Billy takes me face down after we get back from the club and later I dream of William. The dream makes me feel pitiful. I awake and Billy is asleep, on his side, his head resting on his arm. He seems quite innocent this way. I see his gun hanging in a shoulder holster draped over the back of a chair when I get up and turn on the bathroom light and it falls out into the room over Billy and the bed and his hanging gun. I see myself in the mirror above the sink and ask this woman I see what she is doing here with a man who kills people and robs banks. But she doesn't answer and I don't ask any more questions and turn out the light and sit on the floor with my head in my hands. I think if I listen hard enough, I can hear the gunshot that killed William.

Pretty Boy Floyd

We have a nice breakfast in the hotel dinning room. The tables are covered with white linen and the silverware is polished and the coffee served in small porcelain cups with red roses painted on them. The girls have big glasses of orange juice. They both look exhausted, but happy. I look at Beulah and I look at Rose and wonder what it is they see in Billy and me. Why would a woman want to run with outlaws? Billy is reading the *Toledo Blade,* looks up and says, "Hey, the Mud Hens are playing a game tonight, wanna go watch?"

"Who are the Mud Hens?" Rose asks, bits of orange pulp on her upper lip.

"They're a baseball team, minor leaguers," Billy says, looking at her like she's from outer space.

Rose looks at Beulah and rolls her eyes, as if to say, oh, how boring.

"Sure," I tell Billy. "Maybe it would be fun to go watch a baseball game. I used to play — shortstop."

"Yeah, I used to play too, only I was a pitcher. You think you could hit one off me, boyo?"

"You as fast with a baseball as you are with that heater?" I say, ribbing him a little.

"Faster."

"Maybe we'll have to give it a try next chance we get," I say. The waiter brings our breakfast eggs over easy, buttered toast, bacon, sausage, hash. We order just about everything on the menu because we're flush with dough and what else are you supposed to do with money but spend it?

Rose eats like a bird, Beulah like a horse. Billy eats without closing his mouth. Look at them. It's like we're all in a gangster movie.

The sun is shining outside and Beulah says it looks like it's going to be a great day.

The girls want to go shopping. Again. Billy and me decide to get haircuts and a shave because it's little things like that make a guy feel ready to take on the world. But all we really have in mind is to take on one little bank. We agree to meet up with the girls in front of the barbershop.

Billy looks at me with those dark menacing eyes. But what I don't know and what he doesn't know is that in less than an hour, they'll be a dead man's eyes.

Uncertainty is everywhere.

I feel like loose change in a poor man's pocket.

10

Pretty Boy Floyd

The barbers wrap our faces in warm towels. I feel just like a rich man. I think back when Daddy Walter used to cut my hair sitting on a bucket, his shears going *snip, snip, snip.* "Don't cut my ears off, Daddy."

"I might," he'd say. *Snip, snip, snip,* my hair falling in light brown clumps, itching my bare skin, the sun warm on my back, E.W. and Bradley waiting their turns, snickering and poking each other in the ribs.

Now look at me, getting four-bit haircuts and two-bit shaves like I was J. P. Morgan. Smoking fifty-cent cigars and tossing ten-spots around like confetti.

Billy says from beneath his face towel, "Ain't this the life?"

The razor glides smooth over my cheeks.

In my head I write Ruby a letter:

Darling wife,

I miss you and little Jackie terribly. I don't blame you for divorcing me; after all, there was no reason for you to think I'd ever be different than what I am. No woman wants to always be worrying about her husband and have to end up staying alone so much, never knowing where her man is at. But I think of you with another man now and it breaks my heart. I tried to do right by you, I tried that damn farming and working in those damn oil fields and I just couldn't do it, no matter how much I loved you and our son. I guess you lost your love for me because I couldn't go straight. I don't blame you. I miss the warmth of you lying next to me in bed at night, the tender way you were with me. I miss what it feels like being inside of you and hearing those little love sounds you make. When I think of you making those little love sounds with another man inside you it drives me crazy. And when I think of another man's hand disciplining Jackie, saying harsh and angry words at him, I want to kill that man, whoever he is. Ruby, I'm sorry for all the grief I brought down on our house. I never meant to hurt you. All my love, your

Charley forever.

The barber pats bay rum on my cheeks causing them to sting; the fragrance fills my senses, my letter to Ruby momentarily finished. He unclips the sheet from around me and snaps it in the air then folds it over his arm and smiles.

I look in the mirror as he turns my chair about.

He smiles proudly. I think how boring it must be for a man to stand and cut other men's hair all day, how it must make him feel knowing that's all he will ever do in life — cut other men's hair. I give him a dollar tip and he brushes the shoulders of my suit jacket. In my pocket is a gun. I look over at Billy. The barber is just finishing him up. Billy's wearing a new pair of two-tone shoes: white with black trim. His dark cheeks glisten with the aftershave lotion.

We stand on the street waiting for the girls.

"We smell like whores," Billy says, sniffing the air.

"You maybe." He gives me a look.

Beulah Baird

Rose and me shop for some new clothes. We don't find much. The stores here in Bowling Green don't have the selection they do in Kansas City. I tell Rose we should ask the boys to take us to Toledo, that we'll find a better selection of clothing.

She is standing in front of a mirror holding up a green dress, turning this way and that. It doesn't suit her.

"What if something happens?" she says.

"What do you mean?"

She looks at me in the mirror as she examines the way the dress hangs, its row of ivory buttons, the wide white belt around the waist.

"I mean," and she turns slightly to see that there aren't any clerks close by, "what if things go bad one of these days. What would we do, Beulah, without Billy and Charley?"

I tell her to shut up with that kind of talk.

"We've had nothing but bad luck when it comes to men until Charley and Billy came along. Nothing bad is going to happen to them, or us. We're on easy street, Rose. Easy street."

Now she turns, holding the dress in one hand and looks at me like I'm a simpleton.

"Jeez Louise, Beulah. They rob banks. It could happen that something might go wrong one of these days."

I tell her to hush her mouth in case somebody hears.

"I'm just saying," she says in a rushed

whisper, "we can't expect that nothing is ever going to go wrong . . . it's not like they're factory workers, or something. They carry guns."

"Let's go," I say, taking her by the arm and hustling her out of the store. We see the boys up the street standing in front of the barbershop.

"Listen, Rose, I don't want to hear that kind of talk, okay. Nothing's going to go wrong. Nothing is ever, ever going to go wrong."

"All right," she says. "All right, nothing is ever going to go wrong."

I'm hoping she hasn't jinxed us with her crazy talk.

Shorty Galliher

We get word there are some suspicious characters in the area. Bowling Green's just a small town where everybody knows everybody and we all look out for one another. It's my town and I'm proud to be the chief of police and I don't mind we got hardly no crime to speak of. I like it quiet. Except for the college kids some Saturday nights, it's real quiet. We don't need no Johnny Dillingers or Al Capones coming around causing trouble. We're good people. We've got lots of churches we go to. We're farm people. We go to church and treat each other right and work hard for what we got. So when we get word that there are some suspicious types hanging around, driving up and down in front of the bank and spending money around town like it's water, I call up my patrolman, Ralph Castner. I tell him to come pick me up in the squad car so we can go have a look at these birds.

"You think it could be some real trouble?" Ralph says, as we're driving down Main Street.

"Could be," I say. "But let's hope it's nothing. We don't need trouble."

"I hear that."

"But just in case," I say, "make sure you got all your chambers loaded." I can see he's got a worried look on his face. Neither of us has ever had to shoot anybody in all our lives and I'm praying we don't have to today. But being police officers, we both know that the day could come when you're one minute dunking doughnuts in your coffee and the very next you could be ducking bullets.

We spot two couples out front of the barbershop. The guys are nattily dressed and the women are real lookers. You can tell just by looking at them they're not from around here. The one guy is wearing black-and-white shoes. I get a bad feeling about these birds.

"Pull over," I tell Ralph. He cuts the car sharply to the curb.

I get out one side and Ralph gets out the other and I say to the strangers: "Hold it right there!"

That's when all hell breaks loose.

Pretty Boy Floyd

The patrol car comes up fast, stops hard, the brakes screeching and I know we've got trouble. I see the cops with guns in their hands. I yell for everyone to duck.

Bang! Bang! Bang!

Suddenly, everybody's shooting everybody.

Billy says, "Cocksuckers!" Draws his .45.

Bang! Bang! Bang!

Billy doubles over like somebody's hit him in the gut with a sucker punch.

"Ooof," he says. A flower of blood flows out in a bright-red pool from underneath him as he lies on the sidewalk. He's gasping like a fish out of water.

Bang! Bang! Bang!

Beulah bends over Billy to help him or reach for his gun. I can't be sure, because I'm also busy shooting. Then Rose screams and I think she's been shot, but instead she's standing over Beulah who is lying across Billy. Beulah's hair is sticky with blood. Christ, it's all madness. I've never shot anybody before, but I think I shot one of the cops because he goes down in a heap. But maybe his own guy shot him. I don't know with all that lead flying around anything is possible.

"Oh, goddamn! Oh, goddamn!" Rose is shouting. Bullets shatter glass, clang off the car fenders, chip chunks out of the curb. I can hear them ricocheting. I'm too scared to be scared. Sirens coming, I hear more sirens.

"Oh, goddamn! Oh, goddamn!" Rose wails as I'm running for my life, as the bullets zip past me slamming into the brick buildings. I hear sirens off in the distance. I run the other way, down alleys, across back yards. I hear a dog barking. I run and I run because I'm never going back to prison. I hear a radio playing in some open window. I want to see Oklahoma and Ruby and my son, and my kin who are all waiting for me. I want to see them one last time and I run straight into their arms where it is safe and warm. I feel the sun on my neck like I felt it in the harvest fields. My heart beats against my chest so hard I think it is going to burst any second. I want to dance with Ruby in the kitchen of my mother's home.

I run and run.

Rose Ash

I had this funny feeling all morning long, even before we got dressed and went down to breakfast, even while we were eating breakfast and later when Beulah and me were in the store trying on dresses. I don't know why I had the feeling, I just did. I thought something bad would happen to us but I couldn't tell you where or when, just that it was going to. I've had such feelings all my life, even as a child and something bad always did happen.

We had it so good for so long, maybe that was part of it — you can't ever have anything good for too long.

I told Beulah about my feeling in the store and she told me to shut up, said I would jinx us all with such talk. I could tell she was as scared as I was to think we might end up dead or in prison. We always had bad luck when it came to men. I look at Beulah's pretty hair wet thick with blood. She is laying across Billy whose mouth and eyes are open, but I can tell that he is dead, dead, dead.

Oh, God, the insides of me cry out. Oh,

God! I can hear someone cussing, I think it is me.

Then somebody grabs me, one of the police and gives me over to another police and his hands are rough and he says to me, "Shut the fuck up with that screaming, lady!"

I see Charley running fast as a deer, the police shooting at him, blood everywhere, on the sidewalk, Billy lying in a puddle of blood, the blood in Beulah's hair glistening with sunlight.

Oh, God!

Shorty Galliher

Ralph took a bullet to the neck. It bled him out. I think I shot the woman, and Ralph may have shot Billy Miller. Hard to tell who shot who. Bullets everywhere. You don't think about nothing except killing the other guy. I shoot and shoot until my gun is empty and watch the one guy run. He doesn't stop. I shoot at the air, at the emptiness, at the places where he was, my hand shaking like a goddamn leaf until I'm all out of bullets. Help comes, too late, too late.

We find a pocket full of cash in Billy Miller's trousers pocket when we search him at the funeral home.

"Some big-shot life, these gangsters, eh?"

Parkinson, the funeral director says, taking out the bloody money and dropping it in a metal basin. "You and me don't make that much in six months, Shorty."

"Yeah, some life. But look what good that money's doing him now," I say.

"Help pay for his burying," Parkinson says.

In death, Billy the Killer Miller doesn't look so vicious. He looks like every other stiff I've ever seen, just another guy who's run out of time.

At the hospital they say the woman will live. For this, I'm grateful. I never wanted to kill anyone, especially a woman.

I question the other one who says she's the shot woman's sister. But that's about all she'll tell me.

"Look," I say. "It'll go a lot easier on you and your poor sister if you tell us the truth."

"The truth?" she says. "Ha, that's a good one. All you police want to do is kill us. The truth is something you can buy anywhere for a dime, or ain't you heard?"

She's pretty and pretty tough, but when I tell her that her boyfriend is dead, she breaks down and cries. Some gals just never learn.

I drive west, toward the setting sun, my gun empty. I take the back roads. I take them nice and easy so I don't arouse any suspicion. Billy had half our money in his pocket. I can still see Beulah lying across Billy like they were two lovers who fell exhausted in a heap of dead passion. Billy and Beulah, I think. I wonder if he was one of the men she had when I was in the big house. It doesn't matter. I guess everything has a way of working out for the best. I was getting the sense we were all going to die one way or the other as long as we were keeping company with Billy. You could look into Billy's eyes and see he was drawing death near to him.

I take my time, stop at a small café and get a hamburger and a chocolate malted. Gunfights make you hungry I guess. I smoke a cigarette and half-flirt with the waitress. She has ginger colored hair and tired green eyes.

"You want anything else?" she asks after I'm finished with my lunch.

"Yeah," I say.

She looks at me with that tired look. I tip her two bucks.

I ditch the car somewhere across the Ohio state line, a little burg called Angola, Indiana. I go into a movie theater and watch a double feature and when I come out, it's dark. I steal a car — a nice maroon DeSoto — and head for home. I want to see my kin again, to see Ruby and Jackie again. I want to see them one more time because I'm thinking of Billy the Killer Miller's dead eyes and how they're never going to see anything ever again and how I don't want to end up that way.

I want to see my wife and son.

I want to see the way it used to be.

I want to rest in the arms of love.

I want to be just a regular guy.

The sun balances itself at the end of the road and when I reach it, I'll be home.

I try not to think about what happened as I drive toward the waiting sun.

There is just me and the waiting sun and love at the end of it.

I am swept along by time and fortune.

11

Pretty Boy Floyd

My future seems always just beyond the grill of my car. I drive for two days and nights, the solitary land is like a sleeping giant under a black blanket. Gunshots still ring in my ears. I may have killed my first man.

"What you doing, son?" Daddy Walter says. It is midnight and he is sitting next to me on the passenger seat, his face aglow from a cigarette.

"I know you're dead, Daddy Walter. I know you're not real."

"Yes, but I came to warn you, Charles Arthur, before it's too late, son."

"What's it like being dead?"

"It's a lot like not being dead. They's some good to it and some bad."

"I might have killed a policeman."

"Then your sins increase."

Rain falls gently and I switch on the wipers. They slap the water back and forth and the oncoming headlights make it seem like diamonds are flung across the windshield.

"Did you come to warn me about it all?" I ask. "Or just the bad?"

"All, boy. It's all or nothing, this game you're in."

"Then take me soon if you're going to."

"I will darling boy, I will."

Then a truck passes, its high beams awash inside the car and I close my eyes for a moment and when I look again I am once more alone and there is just the quiet darkness. The rain falls steadily, gently. The highway ahead runs straight and true and the highway behind runs just as true. Angels and monsters watching from heaven and hell would see only the red glow of my taillights and the twin beams of my headlights snaking along in the dark strange country I cannot see.

I drive on through hours of time until I arrive at last at our old place. The farmhouse sits empty of life and seems to me like a tired thing. It needs a good painting, the windows washed. Weeds have grown up around the foundation. A note pinned on the screen door reads: *Gone to town, be back later.* It is written in my mother's hand.

I go inside to the kitchen. The linoleum is

yellowed and curled at the edges and the room smells of a thousand cooked meals. There are skeins of red dust on the sills and small quadrants of sunlight fall through the unwashed windows and lie on the floor. The room is warm and dry. Mother has let the place go. Who can blame her? Her children are all grown and gone and Daddy Walter lies in his grave. I leave fifty dollars on the kitchen table then drive to brother Bradley's place.

I see his children first: Glendon and Bayne, swinging on an old tire held by a rope tied around the thick branch of a gum tree. Their yellow hair is spun gold falling in their faces. Their laughter raises a racket. Chickens scratch and peck in the yard, an oily red rooster struts about. The children turn and stare at the big plum-colored DeSoto as I drive up. I park and pull the hand brake and step out.

"It's your uncle Floyd," I say. "Don't you youngsters recognize me?" They stare in frozen anticipation; they are too young to recognize anyone who has been gone from their lives for more than a week. Bradley's wife, Bessie, comes out on the porch, says, "Lord almighty!" and runs to me and throws her arms around my neck. She smells like yeast dough; flour coats her wrists.

"Careful Bess," I say. "Old Bradley's liable to think we're up to something."

She blushes.

"Go on with you, Charley. Such talk ain't Christian." She's a hardshell Baptist.

"Where's Bradley?"

"Down sick with a cold," she says. "I think it's gone into his chest."

Bradley's the best of us boys. He's got a heart of pure gold. He's a lot more like Daddy Walter than me and E.W. or any of the girls except for maybe Rossie Ruth.

I hand Bessie the keys to the DeSoto and tell her to take the young ones for a ride if she likes. She looks at the car and says, "Oh, I could never drive nothing that big and fancy."

"I don't see why not."

"Suppose I was to wreck it, Charley? Drive it smack into a tree or something."

"Why I'd just buy me another one," I say. "Go on, those kids are about ready to bust."

I go in the house and start up the stairs where I know Bradley's bedroom is. He's lying on the bed, his eyes closed. His breathing is ragged, like something's broken in him.

I pull up a chair and sit next to him. His

face is bloodless, his lips cracked as rain-starved earth. I can feel the fever coming off him without even touching him.

"Bradley," I say.

He doesn't open his eyes. I sit there a long time quiet.

I remember when we were just hard-running wildcats, how Bradley helped me whip some Choctaw kids who wanted to steal our bikes. What they didn't know was the bikes were already stolen. Bradley and me had taken them from behind the library in Aikens. We only intended on riding them down to a small lake we knew to go for a swim then take them back where we found them. I just never did like walking anyplace that I could ride if I could help it. Neither did Bradley.

We got down to the lake and that's where we ran into those Choctaw kids — the Dexter boys. Their daddy was a freighter and a drinker and was always getting arrested for disturbing the peace. Mostly he got arrested for fighting with the husbands of women he took up with, least that's the way I heard Mother tell it. Back then, I didn't know what a womanizer was, but I thought it must take a special sort of man to become one, for Mr. Dexter didn't seem to be afraid of anything or anyone.

One of the boys, Truck, I think his name was, weighed as much as me and Bradley put together. We were thin as sticks because we were always running and never sitting still long enough to eat much of anything; I guess that is where I got my running ways from. I was a lot faster than Bradley and a lot faster than just about any boy in the Cookson Hills. I won marbles, pennies, jackknifes, and one time a one-eared dog in foot races. Nobody could catch me. They still can't.

Anyway, this boy Truck said he was going to whip our white asses and take our bicycles and Bradley popped off and said, "Go ahead, redskin, give it a try." And the next I knew everybody was socking everybody in the nose, the eye, the mouth. By the time we were wore out and had run them off, Bradley and me looked like we'd been hit by a freight train. But those Choctaw kids didn't get our bikes.

"Why you think we fought so hard over stolen bikes?" Bradley said, as we washed the blood off our faces. He had gotten a back tooth knocked loose and was wiggling it between his finger and thumb. "Hell, we must be the biggest fools in Oklahoma. We should have just let them have the dang bikes and then called the law on them."

I wanted to laugh but my mouth hurt.

"It was your idea to go to fighting," I said.

"Yeah, I am a dang bigger fool than anybody. Look, I lost me a tooth."

He showed me the thing: small and bone-white with bloody pulp where it come out by the root.

"Bradley," I said again and he opened his eyes.

"Oh, hey, Charley, what you doing here?"

"Came to see how you were."

He blinked a couple of times and coughed and said, "I'm about all used up."

"I can see that."

Then he closed his eyes and I went back outside and stood in the yard and watched Bessie running those wild children up and down the road in the purple DeSoto. I felt like I was home again where I should be. I could smell the earth and it smelled like home.

Emma Floyd

I come home from town to see my son sitting at the kitchen table. I thought I'd seen a ghost the way he was sitting there in the afternoon sunlight all lit up like an angel. He didn't move or say anything at first and I thought for a moment it wasn't Charley but Walter and I nearly fainted.

"Hey, Mama," he said, and came and took the sack of groceries from my arms and kissed me on the cheek.

"Praise God," I said.

We sat and talked and he told me he was doing fine and I said we'd all been reading things about him in the newspaper and he said, "Don't believe everything you read in the newspaper — most of it is just a pack of dang lies."

"I know it," I said.

"Those papers are all run by yellow dog Republicans Mama and you know the Republicans has always been against the working man. That's all I am, just a working man."

"Lord, ain't it the truth."

But honestly, Charley didn't look like no working man I ever knew. He was dressed fancy. Even his shoes were two different colors and he wore a silk tie. He was pretty enough to be a movie star.

"I never saw a working man dressed like you, Charley."

He smiled, said, "There's work and then there's work" and slid some money that had been on the table over to me.

"What's all this?"

"Just a little something," he said. It was a whole lot of money.

"I don't need it, Charley."

"Go ahead, take it. That's all honest money there. Case you're wondering. I mean it's not stole money."

"Charley, you know the thing I worry about most, don't you?"

He smiled in the only way a boy can smile at his mother and it near broke my heart, for we both knew what I was talking about.

"They are never going to catch me Mama. And if they can't catch me, there is nothing bad can happen to me."

"Oh, son." I took hold of him and held him for a long time, for as long as it took to stop my tears from flowing. A mother knows things no other human can know, especially about her dark-star child.

Pretty Boy Floyd

The most interesting thing about life is you never know what is going to happen next. I went to Sallisaw that night because there was a roadhouse near there that had music and dancing and you could buy illegal whiskey from just about anybody there and I had a thirst for some because I'd not had any in a long time. And I had a hunger for some female company because I'd not had any since I left Ohio. I thought of poor Beulah. They say you don't know what you got until you miss it. I guess I will miss her in the same way I miss Ruby.

I wasn't in the place long before this tall drink of water under a cowboy hat with his feet shoved down in high-heeled boots came over to me and said, "You Choc Floyd, ain't you?"

I'd not heard anybody call me that since I first left the Cookson Hills.

"No, I'm Billy Miller," I say, because I don't know who the guy is.

"You mind I sit down for a minute, I've got a business proposal, you might say."

He sure didn't look like the law. He didn't have lawman's eyes.

"Go ahead." And so he sits.

"My name is Birdwell," he says. "George Birdwell."

"I've never heard of you George Birdwell."

"I sure have you."

"You got me confused with somebody else, George Birdwell."

"Maybe so. But I'm a man don't mind chasing a rainbow if there's a pot of gold at the other end of it, and what I heard about you is, you're a rainbow chaser."

"A rainbow chaser, huh?"

He nods.

"Say it straight what you're wanting from me, George Birdwell."

"I want to throw in with you, be partners."

"I look like I need a partner?"

"From what I read about what happened up there in Ohio, I'd say you do."

I asked him what he read and he told me Billy Miller was killed and so was a policeman and that the two women that were with us were taken into custody.

"One woman, you mean," I said. "The other was shot in the head."

He smiles, this George Birdwell.

"True enough, but they say she'll live."

"Let's go for a walk."

And that's how I hooked up with my next partner.

George Birdwell

I guess I knew the day I got shot in the leg by a jealous husband I wasn't ever going to be a real good preacher. It's mighty hard to concentrate on the Good Word when you got a woman under you and a man firing bullets at you and you don't know whether to get up and run or keep on doing what you'd been doing until he walked in. Sin is a powerful thing. Good as it was feeling, I got up and ran, and then I packed up my wife and children and headed to Oklahoma. I had some people down that way. I wasn't there long when I started hearing about

Choc Floyd. That's what they called him down that way; they said he got the nickname because he drank so much Choctaw Beer. His reputation was getting to be nearly as big as Henry Starr's or Jesse James's down that way. So I started reading everything I could on him in the papers: how he robbed dozens of banks and the law couldn't catch him and even when they did, they couldn't hold him.

I don't know why, but I got to thinking that if I couldn't make a living as a preacher, maybe I could as an outlaw, you know, from one extreme to the other. Because in those days, there wasn't anything in between the one or the other. About the only thing I knew about being an outlaw was that a gun is a powerful persuader (look how it persuaded me) and probably has converted more men to Jesus Christ than all the preachers in the world. So when I ran into Charley that night at the roadhouse, I took a chance he needed a new partner — his old one having been recently deceased up in Ohio.

As it turned out, he did.

Pretty Boy Floyd

I tell George Birdwell that before we go to taking down any banks, there is something I have to do first.

"Sure," he says. "Just don't keep me on a long rope too long is all. Man of my skills ain't likely to stay unemployed for very long."

"Well, I suppose you could always take up preaching again," I say. George told me about that period of his life. I laughed like hell when he told me about getting shot in the leg by a jealous husband.

"Were you trying to convert her?"

"Hell, I guess you could say I was trying my best."

"I'll get hold of you when I'm ready to roll," I told him.

"I'll be waiting, Choc."

He looked like he ought to have had a horse tied up outside.

"You believe in reincarnation, George?"

"Boy that's a hard one," he says. "I'm a man of God and don't hold much with pagan thoughts. Why you asking?"

"It could be that we're the James boys come back from the dead. Frank and Jesse."

"To rob again?"

"It's not out of the realm of possibility."

"Hell, you just might be on to something," he says.

I left him sitting there sipping his beer to contemplate the possibilities of the spirit world while I went out and drove under a sky flung with stars, some of which fell in among the hills and were forever lost.

I had it in my mind to find Ruby.

To redeem myself if I could.

12

Pretty Boy Floyd

I come and go like a shadow. I don't stray far from my people but I never stick around any one of them too long at a time in case the police are on the scout for me. I come and go in the evenings, sleep during the day. Summer is slow and hot as dog breath in Oklahoma. I read in the papers that Beulah and Rose got out of jail, pardoned for their sins. I wonder if Beulah's all right in the head. I send out feelers to some people I still know in Kansas City and get word back the girls have returned and are staying at the Sexton Hotel. I send money, a telegram:

Beulah, how's the head? STOP. Meet me in Aikens. STOP. You know the place. STOP. Mother's got the whole house to herself. STOP. You can heal here just as good as you can there. STOP. Charley.

Soon as I send it I wonder if I did the right

thing because I've got Ruby strong on my mind. I go see her kin and they tell me she's living in Coffeyville, Kansas with the fellow she married, her and my son Jackie. Coffeyville! The only thing I know about Coffeyville is the Daltons rode in fifty years earlier and got shot to pieces trying to rob two banks at the same time. Two banks at the same time! It's a hell of an idea that I might try myself sometime. I ask Bradley what he thinks of me going down and trying to get Ruby back.

"You sure you want to do that, Charley? She's a married gal now, that ought to tell you something about the way she feels."

"I know Ruby better than anybody. I know she loves me as much as I love her," I say. "Love like we had can't be broken."

"I think you'd just be asking for heartache."

"It wouldn't be the first time I've had my heart broke. Probably won't be the last either."

We sit and drink Choctaw Beer and it's cold because Bradley's kept it on a block of ice while I helped him do some weeding in his garden. It's close to supper and I can hear Bessie inside telling the kids where to place the knives and forks and to fill the glasses with water.

The sky is the color of a bullet and the sun is just beginning to melt beyond a ridge of trees that look smoky in the fading light. I can smell the river, a pungent smell of wet mud and decaying leaves. The river comes and goes free as anything. Sometimes I wish I were a river.

"I'm wanted in seven states," I tell Bradley.

"I know it," he says. "I read the same papers you do."

"E.W. keeps talking about wanting to join up with me."

"Don't let him, Charley."

"No way in hell. You neither, in case you were thinking 'long them lines."

"I wasn't thinking nothing."

Bradley's had his share of strife. He works hard but it barely seems enough to keep him and Bessie and their kids afloat. His hands are rough and scarred from work. I feel ashamed that I've spent as much as three dollars on a manicure and my hands show no labor.

"Listen, Bradley, you'd have to be crazy *not* to think about all that easy money. But let me tell you something, son, it ain't as easy as it seems. Yeah, the taking is easy; it's all the rest that can be hard on a fellow."

"Can I ask you something?" he says,

draining the last of the beer in his bottle.

"Sure."

"If it's so damn tough, why do you do it?"

"I'm good at it. Besides, I don't know what else I could do and have this damn much fun. It's just the running that's hard."

"You was always the wild one, Charley."

"Oh, hell," I say. "Let's go in and eat some of Bessie's chicken before you ask if you can shoot that machine gun I keep in the trunk of that fancy DeSoto."

"Can I?"

We go inside and sit around the table and Bessie say prayers, then we dig in.

A belly full of home-cooked food does wonders for the spirit.

Ruby Floyd Leonard

I met Leroy at a dance, just like I'd met Charley. He said I was the prettiest girl there and I liked it that he had clean hands and no dirt under his fingernails and was polite. We danced and I liked him well enough, but not nearly as much as I liked Charley the first time I danced with him. But then no man can live up to Charley in my book — even though Charley has brought as much grief into my life as he has pleasure.

Leroy came around regular and brought

me flowers and always brought Jackie a toy to play with and we'd go for rides in his motor car and go for picnics and he'd carry Jackie around on his shoulders. I liked Leroy's easy manner, but most of all I liked it that Leroy didn't have any big dreams of being something other than what he was.

"I'm just a baker," he told me when we began to get serious. "That's all I'll probably ever be, Ruby, just a baker."

"That's okay by me," I said. "A baker is a fine thing to be. Everybody needs bread."

Then he asked me to marry him and I agreed because Jackie needed a father even more than I needed a husband.

But when I dream, I dream of Charley Floyd. And sometimes I awake flushed and full of the need for Charley. And sometimes when Leroy is above me — his eyes full of desire — I pretend it is Charley. My husband tries hard to please me in every way including in the bedroom, but once you've been with Charley Floyd, no other man can satisfy you in the same way. For every woman there is a man who touches her in that special way and it can either mean the beginning or the end of heartbreak.

I read romance magazines and wait for Leroy to come home. I smoke out on the fire escape because he doesn't like me smoking in the apartment.

"I don't like the stink," he says. It's just a little thing we disagree on.

Leroy labors above me on moonless nights and I pretend he's pleasing me more than he is. It's the least I can do for him for all he's done for Jackie and me, to make him feel special, like he's the only man for me.

Sometimes afterward, he will lay beside me in the dark and say, "Dang, Ruby, I never loved any woman like I do you. I just can't seem to get enough of you. Was it good for you, hon?" And I tell him it was. Then he falls asleep and sometimes it is only nine o'clock in the evening because he has to get up so early in the morning to go to work, to bake his bread, to sell his bread, to be a baker. I wait until he's snoring then go out and sit on the fire escape and smoke and watch the stars and think Charley is out there somewhere probably looking up at the same stars. Charley always had a fondness for looking up at the stars. He thought his future was written in the stars. But I grow sad thinking of him. I try not to think of him with other women. But I can't always, and it hurts like hell to think he's with someone, giving her the same pleasure he gave me, leading her to a broken heart the same way he did me.

Love doesn't mean anything if it's the wrong person offering it to you.

Sometimes all that desire for something I can't have is like a fever that leaves me listless, as though I'm sick and near death. Charley has left me with a wound that won't heal.

Pretty Boy Floyd

It's raining hard the day I roll into Coffeyville with Ruby's address written on a piece of paper in my pocket. Her kin had come to respect me well enough once we were married. I always was good to them, always respectful. It was her daddy who gave me her address. He said, "You know what you're getting yourself into you go down there, don't you Charley?" I told him all I knew was I loved her and in my book, we were still husband and wife. He shook my hand.

Ruby will be surprised when I show up at her door. I stop at a store and buy Jackie a baseball mitt and Ruby some perfume. I buy a box of chocolate candy too.

The address leads me to a brick apartment building and I see over the mailboxes the name: Mr. & Mrs. Leroy Leonard #14A. I climb the stairs carrying the mitt and box of chocolates, the bottle of perfume in my pocket.

I can practically feel Ruby on the other side of the door when I knock. A man can sense his woman the way animals can sense their own. I feel like a lion looking for my mate. I want to roar and sink my teeth into her neck and hold her down and make her know I'm back and I'm still the only man for her.

Ruby Leonard

I open the door thinking it's another one of those door-to-door salesmen. I'm all ready to tell him I'm not interested. Then bigger than life there stands Charley, grinning like a raccoon, a ball mitt and a box of candy in his hands.

"I'd a brought you flowers," he says. "Except I couldn't find anyplace that had them."

Oh, Jesus, my heart almost jumped out of my chest.

"Well, you just going to stand there with your mouth open or are you going to invite me in, Ruby?"

"I'm married," I say. The words come out all strangled.

"So I heard." Charley looks up and down the hall, he tries to see into the apartment over my shoulder.

"He home, this husband of yours?"

"No."

"I sure would like to talk to you for a minute."

I feel the world unraveling around me.

"Charley, Leroy could come home any minute. If he were to find you here there'd be all sorts of hell to pay."

"Leroy, huh?" he says. "Come on, Ruby. Let me come in for a minute. I brought Jackie a ball glove, see. At least let me give it to him."

He holds out the gifts, the glove and box of chocolates and I don't know what made me reach for them except it had been a long time since anybody gave me a gift and I knew Jackie would be thrilled. Then Charley took a bottle of perfume out of his pocket and said, "Oh yeah, I got you this, too."

He came into the room and took off his hat and turned it round in his hands as he looked about.

"Awfully small," he says, after a moment or two. My heart is still kicking like crazy because partly I'm scared Leroy will come home and find him here and partly because I'm still crazy about Charley.

"Where's Jackie?" he says.

"He's playing with a friend, you want me to go get him?"

"Yeah, but in a minute, huh."

I keep thinking Leroy will come up the stairs, walk through the door and catch us even though we're not doing anything.

"You miss me, Ruby?"

"Look, Charley, I got me a husband now and it wouldn't matter if I missed you or not."

"Just tell me, do you?"

"Oh, Jesus, Charley."

The next thing I know we're kissing and it's like the very first time we kissed and my knees go weak.

"Charley, we can't do this."

"Sure we can, we're already doing it, Ruby. We're doing it right here and right now because in spite of everything, we still love each other and we still want each other. Tell me it ain't so."

I'm up against the wall and Charley is pressing against me and his mouth is warm and wet on mine and I can't do anything to resist him anymore because he's Charley Floyd, the man I loved, love still, and he knows it and I know it. I feel his hands on my thighs, working up under my dress. His hands are like a fever crawling up my legs, like a fire seeking a fire and I'm like a fire inside.

"I missed you like crazy, Ruby. I missed

everything about you."

I part my legs and his hand slips in between them and when they touch me there I about faint, but squeeze my legs together clamping his hand there because I don't want it to move, I don't ever want it to move.

"I missed hearing your voice and I missed waking up next to you and I missed this, too. I missed this more than anything," he whispers, his lips brushing against my ear.

I release my grip on him and his hand does things to me I can't explain. I reach for him too. I fumble with his belt, tug at the zipper on his trousers. I am no longer the wife of a baker but still the wife of Charley Floyd and it seems wrong to deny him what he wants and what I want.

Then I hear a car door outside.

"Charley," I whisper, barely able to get the words out of my mouth. His hand keeps working between my legs. "I think Leroy's home . . ."

But he doesn't stop.

"Charley . . ."

I hear footsteps coming down the hall. I hold my breath waiting for the door to open.

"Charley, promise me you won't do anything, you won't hurt anybody."

"Jesus, Ruby," he whispers in my ear. "I'm

not like that."

My heart is choked with terror and anticipation and I can hardly breathe. The footsteps go on down the hall. Charley eases himself inside me. I close my eyes and feel the release of my soul, of all things practical, of the scent of fresh bread and warm places and safe places and a quiet life lived from four o'clock in the morning until night has fallen over the little safe town we live in.

"Jesus, kid, I missed you like nobody's business," Charley says breathlessly, as he rocks gently back and forth taking what he knows is his, has always been his and is now reclaiming. I am impaled by passion and love and my heart is impaled as I cling to him, to Charley Floyd, Pretty Boy, they call him, impaled by the only man I ever truly loved.

"This is the way it should be," he says. "The way I've dreamed of it. Just me and you, like this, like this always."

I think of his cock as a key unlocking my soul.

Leroy Leonard

I come home from work and find them there, sitting on the couch together and I say to Ruby, "Who's this?"

But before she can answer, Charley says, "I'm Charley Floyd, Ruby's husband."

"You're mistaken," I say. "I'm her husband."

Ruby starts to say something but Charley says, "I'll handle this."

"You'll handle nothing," I say. "Get the fuck out of my house."

"Say," he says. "There's no need for that kind of talk."

I'm ready to hit him.

"Tell me what's going on here, Ruby."

"Leroy," she says, barely getting my name out of her mouth.

"I'm going to take her with me, Mr. Leonard," Floyd says.

"To hell you are. I'm going to call the police you don't get out of here."

"No, you won't," he says.

"I know all about you. You're a fucking thief!"

"Bank robber," he says. "I'm a bank robber, I'm not a thief."

He has this smug look and I'm wishing I had a gun or something because if I had a gun, I'd shoot him with it. The cops would probably give me a fat reward. But I don't have a gun and I know that he could kill me as easy as he could all those other guys I read about he killed and it eats up my guts knowing that I can't do nothing.

"Tell him you're not going, Ruby," I say to her. But I can tell she is going. I can tell by the look in her eyes when she looks from me to him.

"Wasn't I good to you? Didn't I treat Jackie like he was my own? What is this, Ruby? Tell me what the fuck this is?"

"Oh, Leroy. I'm sorry to have to hurt you like this. . . ."

I tell Charley again to get out of my house.

"I will, just as soon as Ruby packs her things. Go get Jackie," he tells her. "And pack your things."

She starts to leave, to go get Jackie. I want to kill her and Charley both.

"I'm just a baker," I say to her. "I told you that in the beginning. If you didn't want to be with me, you never should have married me."

She starts to cry.

"Look, Leonard," Charley says. "Ruby and me have something special between us, something a guy like you don't understand. Don't ever get in between a man and his wife, okay."

"If I had a gun I'd shoot you both," I say.

"No you wouldn't," Floyd says. "Go get Jackie, Ruby. Get him and pack your stuff, we're leaving."

The anger in me is hot and tastes like metal in my mouth, like a copper penny that's been laying out in the sun that I'm trying to eat. I want to gag as I watch them go — all three of them, down the stairs and out on the street. And from my window, I see them get in Charley Floyd's car and drive off. Charley Floyd stole as much from me that day as he ever did any bank.

Pretty Boy Floyd

Jackie is crazy to see me again, calls me "Daddy" over and over and hugs my neck. He sits between Ruby and me and we drive south again back into Oklahoma and I'm thinking this is better than robbing banks, better than anything, to have my family back again. I look at Ruby and she has this look of happiness but maybe a little sad too because of Leonard. I know I was a little rough on the guy, and I guess I can understand how he felt, losing something he probably loved so much. But Ruby's my wife not his and if he wants a wife, let him go find his own.

"It's always just going to be us," I say to her.

She looks over at me, looks at Jackie between us.

"I sure want to believe that, Charley."

"Believe it," I say.

"I really want to."

"I'm going to change now that I got you and Jackie back. I'm going to be responsible. I know you got a thousand questions, but let's wait until we get home and have time to talk."

"Okay, Charley," she says. "Okay."

I pull them both close to me and we drive home like that, just the three of us, like it should be. I really believe things are going to get better. They just have to.

13

Pretty Boy Floyd

I smell the two rivers — the Poteau and the Arkansas — and the smell is different at night than it is in the morning. I see fireflies bobbing in the dark. Ruby sleeps on our bed and Jackie in his in the next room. I haven't robbed anything in a month. I think about Ruby on nights like this with that baker inside her. It grinds me, I'll admit. I'm not sure I can trust her like I once did. How is a man supposed to trust a woman who gave everything of herself to another man? Like Billy Miller told me once about women: "You either own 'em or you don't. And if they give their cunt to another man, you don't own 'em." I think about that. Maybe I don't own Ruby like I once did.

Sometimes I drive across the bridge to Aikens and visit Beulah who is staying with Bradley while her head heals. She has to hold on to chairs and walls when she walks around or she'll fall down. The bullet did something to her balance.

I say, "You get dizzy when we make love too?"

"Sometimes, Charley."

Her left eye strays a bit.

"Can I ask you something?" I say, one time after we finished making love.

"Sure, Charley."

"What did it feel like when you got shot?"

"I don't remember nothing. I don't remember getting shot at all. One minute it's just you and me and Rose and Billy and the next I know I'm in a hospital."

"So it didn't hurt?"

"No. I mean I didn't feel anything. It hurt after I woke up, sure. It still hurts some and I've got the taste of metal in my mouth."

She looks at me, her one eye unsteady.

"Why you asking so much about getting shot, Charley?"

"I'm just hoping if they ever shoot me it doesn't hurt. I don't think it's the dying that's going to be so bad, but it's how you die. A bullet's got to hurt like hell."

We make love again but it's not the same as it was before Beulah got shot. I never know if she's going to get dizzy and pass out. I don't know what that bullet may have done to her thinking, either. Sometimes she says strange stuff. I can't trust her like I used to.

I don't go over very often to see Beulah. Part of me feels bad that I want to go at all.

Bradley says to me one day when I was getting ready to leave the house to come back to Ft. Smith, "Ain't you afraid Ruby and Beulah are going to find out about each other?"

"I've never been afraid of anything in my life."

"I know you ain't. But still, Ruby finds out about Beulah, she'll leave you again and take Jackie with her."

"I never could settle just for what I've already got," I say to Bradley. "That's always been my problem."

"That ain't no lie."

We watch a flock of geese flying north. They are a black V against a dingy gray sky and we can hear them honking. I wish I had wings. As I always did, I offered Bradley some money. He put up his usual show about not wanting to take it even dirt poor as he was and with all those kids and a wife to feed.

"It's for you and your family and for the upkeep on Beulah," I say.

"You know I can't take your money, Charley."

"Why the hell not? It's all free and there's plenty more where this came from."

"Charley, I hope you don't mind my saying I wished it wasn't money you stole from other people, maybe even people like ourselves who don't have all that much."

"I wished it weren't either, but those banks are insured and those bankers don't lose no sleep over it and you shouldn't either. I'm just robbing the rich to give to the poor you might say. Like Jesse James did." It's a lie I hate to tell my own kin, but Bradley's sometimes got too much pride for his own good.

"Still . . ." he says. I don't go out of my way to hurt his pride. I leave the money on the porch and put a rock on top of it so the wind doesn't blow it away.

The trips back and forth across the river always leave me feeling like I got no true home, no one I can trust except my family.

I hear water running and go down the hall to find Jackie standing at the sink with the faucets on.

"What are you doing, son?"

He doesn't say anything. I realize he's sleep walking again and carry him carefully back to bed. You wake a sleepwalker they'll die of fright. I kiss his forehead as I tuck the blankets up under his chin. He's just an angel and I sure hope he doesn't grow up wanting to rob banks.

Ruby Floyd Leonard

At first it is like Charley and me have never been separated. Charley buys me and Jackie all sorts of things and makes us feel swell. He takes us to the movies and we come out and the sun is bright in our eyes, or if it's an evening feature the stars are out and we stop along the way home to buy ice cream. Charley is really good to us, but underneath, as the days go by, I can feel his restlessness growing. About once a week he drives over the river into Oklahoma to go see Bradley and E.W. and some of his sisters. I ask to go along but he says it's too dangerous. He doesn't want Jackie or me to get caught in any gunfights in case the police pull him over. We're going under the name Douglas and we have this nice little apartment on Garrison Avenue in this quiet neighborhood.

Jackie's started school. We seem almost like everybody else. Sometimes I think about my legal husband, Leroy, how it must have hurt him to come home that day to find his wife getting ready to leave with another man. I know I've hurt some people that didn't deserve to be hurt and for that I'm sorry. Love makes everybody a little crazy.

Like the crazy way I love Charley even though I hate the life we have to live.

I was talking to a shoe salesman the other day where I took Jackie down to the store and Charley came in and he just looked at me and then he looked at the salesman and took me out of the store and said, "Listen, woman, I don't want you talking like that to other men."

"Talking like what? I was just asking him if he had any Buster Browns in Jackie's size."

"I don't believe that's all you were talking about," he says.

"Sure it was; what else would we be talking about?"

"I saw the way he was looking you over. Don't you know anything about how men are?"

"All I know about men, Charley, is what I learned from you, that's what I know about how men are."

And for the first time ever I saw what the bankers must have seen when Charley confronted them: a face like stone, cold pitiless eyes.

"I wasn't the one who left you sitting in

jail," he says. "Just remember that, Ruby."

It was our first blowup.

Later he tried making it up to me by buying me a pair of pearl earrings. That same night he whispered how much he loved me and couldn't do without me and Jackie. He made love to me gently saying all the while how sorry he was, and I cried.

The summer of our reunion was a good one and I was happy for the most part. I listened to the radio while Charley read the newspaper or wrestled with Jackie. I listened to all my favorite songs like "Love Letters in the Sand" and "Where the Blue of the Night Meets the Gold of the Day." Sometimes I get Charley to dance with me slow and we dance in the living room and he is like he was when we first met and we are like those young people fresh in love without a care in the world.

"I wish we could always dance to 'Love Letters in the Sand,' " I say.

"Me too," Charley says.

We go for days at a time like that, just happy and content and Charley is terrifically sweet and kind and makes me laugh with his pranks. But then he grows restless again, starts pacing the floor and looking out the windows. Some nights I awake to see him standing at the window smoking a cigarette, staring out into the darkness.

"Something out there?" I ask him, one time when I caught him like that.

"I was just wondering how far away the ocean is," he said. I didn't know what he meant by that.

George Birdwell

Me and Flora go to visit Charley and Ruby over in Ft. Smith. They've got a nice little apartment there on a tree-lined street. Ruby seems swell and is a good looker and I can see why Charley's crazy about her.

"You planning a job for us, Charley?" I ask him, every time we go there because it's been nearly the whole summer and we haven't robbed anything in some time.

"You know me, George, I'm always planning something."

"Good, because I'm about tapped out."

Charley slips me a deuce without saying anything.

"You like the straight life?" I ask him.

"Some of it," he says.

"Yeah, me too. I miss preaching."

"Never too late to repent," he says.

"The way I drink and chase skirts?"

"You wouldn't be the first sinner to turn it around you wanted to, George."

"Truth is, Charley, I'm not sure I want to."

Ruby makes us all a nice fried chicken dinner and I keep thinking what a terrific looker she is and how if I wasn't such a pal of Charley's I might make a play for her, even though I know thinking like that can get you in trouble.

Toward the end of the summer Charley tells me he's about ready to make a move.

"You still want to be an outlaw, George? It's dangerous work."

"You're talking to a man who got himself shot diddling another man's wife, Charley; things can't get much more dangerous than that."

"You do that a lot, diddle with another guy's wife?"

"I was pretty wild back in them days. I had God in one ear, the devil in the other."

"Just remember something, George."

"What's that?"

"I'm a damn good shot when I have to be."

I pretend like I don't understand what he's getting at, but you can't fool a guy like Charley Floyd, he aces on everything.

"Don't worry about me," I say. "I know better than to try something like what you're thinking."

"Good, keep it that way."

He tells me about the bank he's planning we hit. I'm starting to feel all revved up again, like how I used to get just before I preached, only better. That night I screw Flora's brains out and end up drunk on the bathroom floor I'm so goddamn excited me and Charley are getting back into the robbing business.

Pretty Boy Floyd

It's time to get back in the saddle. I don't need the money that much, we still got plenty, but it's not just the money. I don't want to leave Ruby and Jackie again, but I can only take so much lying around reading the newspaper, listening to the ballgames on radio, dancing with Ruby cheek to cheek. I can only play just so much catch with my son.

I tell George about a bank I'm planning to hit. His eyes light up. We both know the same thing: robbing banks is a kick in the head.

I go and see Beulah one more time.

This time she faints while we're making love.

She wakes while I'm getting dressed.

"Jesus, Charley, what happened?"

"You went out cold on me, kiddo."

"I'm sorry, hon. I guess it was what that bullet did to me made me go out on you."

"Nah, it was just that I'm such a terrific lover conked you out."

We both laugh.

"Yeah, Charley, I think it was that good."

"Yeah, maybe it was."

"You leaving so soon?" she says, seeing me put on my shoes.

"Time to go to work," I say.

"Let me go with you."

"No, I couldn't stand it if something happened to you again," I tell her. But that's not it. I just don't want to have her slow me down. I mean I care about her and I feel sorry for what happened to her, but I can't take the chance.

"You really love me that much, Charley?"

"Yeah, that much, kiddo."

I drive back to Ft. Smith. Tonight I'll tell Ruby we need the money and that's why I have to go back out on the road. I'll bring her and Jackie some presents and take them out to dinner, and afterward when we're lying in bed together and I've got her all calmed down, I'll tell her.

I promise myself that I'm not going to see Beulah again. I'll wait awhile and send her a good-bye letter with some cash in it and urge her to go back to Kansas City. I can't keep seeing her for lots of reasons.

I leave early. Ruby is still asleep. I kiss my sleeping boy. George and me drive through the foggy places along the River & drive until the sun pierces through & lights the Water with a thousand tiny candles & glows in us like unquenched desire, like unrequited love.

14

Pretty Boy Floyd

We hit the banks at Okmulgee, Maud, Earlsboro, Konawa. George says it's like plucking chickens. I'm not so sure. It was George's idea we should use machine guns.

"For a preacher," I say, the first time he mentions it, "you sure got some murderous notions."

"Never do anything halfway," he says. "I once preached for thirty-six straight hours in a tent during a thunderstorm. I ended up with eighty dollars in collection money and the affections of a sixteen-year-old farmer's daughter who thought I was the second coming. I might have married her but for two things."

"What two things?"

"I was already married, and her daddy came and stuck a shotgun in my face and said if I ever came to that town again it would be for my funeral."

So we buy Thompsons: three of them. George is right about a machine gun being a mean piece of work; you can see how in the eyes of the bankers when we point the tommy guns at them.

"If Jesse James would have had one of these he might still be alive," I say to George after we robbed the bank in Okmulgee.

"Yeah, but he'd be real old by now." We both have a good laugh.

We hit the bank at Castle same as we do all the others: I go in wearing a steel vest (my idea) and carrying a Thompson while George waits in the car, the motor running. I never stay inside more than three minutes.

We make so much money so fast we have a hard time spending it all. I send some home to Mother, always with a note telling her it's not stolen, and some to Bradley and some to E.W. and of course a bunch to Ruby. But still I got plenty. I still need to send the good-bye letter to Beulah along with enough cash to get her back to Kansas City and a fresh start. Will do that soon.

By now, I'm wanted in half the country.

I read in the *Daily Oklahoman* I've been charged with murder of the policeman in Ohio during the shootout that Billy Miller was gunned down in. Something inside me feels broken when I read that. I never meant to kill anybody. I guess had it been the other way around and the policeman had killed me, they'd be calling him a hero not a murderer. To me killing is killing, it doesn't matter who's doing it.

George says the day after we'd robbed the bank in Sallisaw, "The papers are calling you 'the Phantom of the Ozarks.' "

George carries a small Bible in his jacket pocket and reads it when he's not reading the newspapers. He hardly seems like a bank robber, spouting Psalms one minute, oiling his gun the next, dancing and drinking and chasing skirts every chance he gets. But when he's sober and reading the Bible, you can't touch him for righteousness.

"Also says here," George continues, his nose stuck way down between the pages of the paper, "that you're the King of the Bank Robbers, that you robbed more banks than Jesse James."

I'm shaving, trying not to cut myself because you can never strop another man's razor sharp enough to cut clean your face. It's Daddy Walter's old bone-handled razor that Mother gave me before George and me left the farm last time. She offered to give me his silver hairbrush but I told her Bradley deserved it more.

"What about this?" she said, showing me a small, pearl-handled pistol Daddy Walter kept in a cigar box along with some Indian-head pennies and a campaign button with President Harding's portrait.

"Too bad Daddy wasn't armed the day that fellow shot him," I said. "It could have made all the difference."

Mother looked sad sitting on the edge of the bed holding what was left of Daddy Walter in that little cigar box: just some memories, pennies, a button and a pistol.

"I'm worried about you, Charley," she said. "Worried you'll meet the same fate as your daddy."

"Nobody's going to shoot me," I told her. "Leastways not some fool over some damn roof shingles."

"Oh, son . . ." She wept and her tears caught in the folds of her face.

"I don't care what they call me," I tell George over my shoulder. The razor's blade is smooth and shiny like a narrow mirror I can see my face in. I take care around my Adam's apple. My luck I was to slip and cut anything, it would be my throat. I ask George why he thinks they call it an Adam's apple.

"It's because Adam took a bite out of the fruit from the Tree of Knowledge — which was an apple offered him by Eve — and it stuck in his craw so everyone could see he'd sinned and gone against God's commandment."

"That right?"

"Hell, I don't know, I'm just guessing. Sounds about right, wouldn't you say?"

He raises his head out of the newspaper and grins.

The razor catches. A drop of blood appears in the soapy lather.

I hear a car pull up outside and look through a part in the curtains. George already has his gun out.

"Relax," I say. "It's just those two girls we ordered."

"I shouldn't be screwing around," he says, putting away his gun. "I have a sweet woman waiting at home for me. It goes against God's commandments."

"So does stealing," I say. "It's a hell of a time to get religion on me, George. They're getting out of the taxi right now."

George looks glum.

"Fine," I say. "I'll take them both."

"Choc?"

"What?"

"Maybe it's too late for me anyhow what with all the robbing and so forth. I guess one more sin added to my account ain't going to make that much difference, huh?"

"You're the expert on such things."

"Sometimes I think about sex too hard, my leg goes to hurting where that fellow shot me. My hair look all right?" he says, glancing in the mirror over my shoulder, straightening his necktie.

Alfalfa Bill Murray

That damn Charley Floyd is robbing all the banks in my state. I tell the state police to list him as Public Enemy Number One in Oklahoma. I'm told catching Floyd would be like trying to catch a fart in the wind. I say I'm the goddamn governor and to go out and capture the son of a bitch, dead or alive.

"We ain't got the manpower to be everywhere at once," the head of the state police says. He's a big slope-shouldered son of a buck named Carter whose wife left him for another woman, or so it is rumored. The news, if it be true, must have taken all the starch out of him. He's got eyes like a water spaniel. Good man, but ruined, I think.

"Fine. Then I'll order out the National Guard. These bankers are all over me like flies on a shit heap to stop the robbing. Their insurance rates have doubled. I won't have some punk like Charley Floyd ruining my goddamn state!"

"You know anything about Charley Floyd?"

"Who the hell is Charley Floyd anyway but another punk trying to act like Al Capone? Shit fire, son, this is Oklahoma, this ain't Chicago. I won't have him messing in my state. You see that that boy's put on an ice block, you hear me!"

Before I can order the National Guard up to track down Pretty Boy Floyd, the bankers get the bright idea to pony up and offer a big joint reward, figuring the cops are like everybody else — poor — and it might inspire them to try a little harder to catch Floyd. The reward totals over six thousand dollars. Hell, I'm thinking about getting out my old pistol and going after the bastard myself.

Pretty Boy Floyd

The newspapers got me wearing steel hats and having bulletproof glass in my Studebaker and tires so thick the cops can't shoot holes in them. They say I live and sleep in my automobile and that I've got a machine gun mounted on the dash.

"Jesus, George, you ever read such crap?

George is trying to make water but all he's making are grunting sounds and shifting from foot to foot.

"I think I got the clap, Charley."

"Lucky you."

"It's not funny. I think it was that prostitute came in the cab last week gave it to me."

"You wanted her. You could have taken the other one. All I ended up with was the crabs."

"It's not funny, Charley."

"Then why you dancing?"

"Oh, hell," he moans. "Oh, hell."

Every time the cops close in on us, we escape. Sometimes we take hostages and make them stand on the running boards until we've cleared town then let them off where they can thumb a ride back. Once we did this and one of the tellers was a strawberry blonde young woman with freckles down her arms. George took a liking to her and while I'm driving the getaway car, he's flirting with her.

"You married, sugar?"

"Yes, and what's it to you?"

"That's too bad."

"Why is that too bad?"

"Because you look like the sort of gal who could stand some excitement."

"I'm about to pee my pants, mister, and fall off this damn car and you've got a great big gun in your lap pointed at me. That's about all the excitement I can stand."

George looks down at his lap at the Thompson.

"Oh you mean this?" he says. I can see the back of the young woman's dress is wet when we stop to let the hostages go.

As though things aren't bad enough, there are some petty criminals going around robbing banks and calling themselves the Pretty Boy Floyd gang. Hell, I don't mind hanging for things I do, but not things I don't do. I guess that's how the newspapers had George and me pulling every bank job in Oklahoma; we had all those imitators. What is it they say about imitation being the sincerest form of flattery? Maybe so, but I didn't care to have my name dragged through the mud by a bunch of redneck hayseeds. Still, what can I do about it if somebody wants to pull a job and call himself Pretty Boy Floyd? Leastways I never called myself that.

George and me pull a job or two then split up for a while, each going our separate ways. I go see Ruby and my kin while George goes sees his kin. We lay low. Even while I'm making love to my wife the papers got me robbing banks.

I must be a magician.

Charley comes and goes like time itself. He comes home rich, leaves broke.

"Why not save a little something?" I say.

He laughs.

"You mean put it into a bank somewhere?"

"I mean something for our future."

"I was thinking about buying Jackie a pony."

"And what, keep it in the apartment?"

"I was thinking we should move on."

"To where, Charley?"

"I don't know, Tulsa, maybe. You might like Tulsa; it's a lot bigger town than Ft. Smith. Lots more to do there. We could go out dancing on Saturday nights and not have to worry about it."

"Are we going to keep moving forever? Aren't we ever going to settle down and live like normal people?"

"Nothing's forever," he says.

It's the middle of the day and Jackie's playing with a neighbor child and there is frost on the glass. All the leaves have fallen from the trees and I look at Charley there in the wan afternoon light and he looks like some photograph taken by a sad photographer. He is the most handsome man I've ever met and sometimes when I look at him in these unexpected times, I crave him like crazy. I guess in that way I can understand how a dope fiend is about his dope because I feel like I'm addicted to Charley Floyd.

"Ruby —" he starts to say then turns and pulls me to him. I try not to act like I need him so bad but I can't keep myself from letting him pull me close. He brings his mouth down on mine and it tastes all warm and smoky. I wasn't in the mood a minute ago, but it only takes something like him kissing me to get me in the mood. I feel his hand trace down the front of me, down past my waist and it draws me into him like a magnet.

I try and talk to him because I don't ever want to let him know how strong his hold is over me.

"Look, kiddo," he whispers. "Now's not the time to talk about things, okay?"

"I should go get Jackie."

"He's fine, he's having fun with that kid next door. Let him have fun, Ruby. Let's me and you have some fun, okay?"

I stop trying to pull away from him. He tells me to ask him for it.

"Charley, you know I'm not like that, to be saying things like that." Charley can be dark as midnight when it comes to some things, but I wasn't ever raised that way, to talk like that.

"You're my wife, Ruby. What goes on between a man and his wife is sacred. I want to hear you say it. Say you want it. Say, 'I want it, Charley.' Let me hear it kiddo."

"I'm just not that way, Charley."

"Be that way just this once, okay? Let me hear you say it."

I try and say it, but it comes out so low he can't hear it.

"I can't hear you. Say it again."

"I want it, Charley."

"You want what, baby?"

"I want you, Charley."

"How do you want me?"

The light in the room seems to wrap round us.

"I want you inside me, Charley."

He lifts me off my feet and carries me to the bed.

"You make me happy, baby," he says, laying me on the bed. "I could never love anybody but you."

They are words I want to hear, want to believe.

We make love in the long silence of my thoughts. I try not to think of him with other women. I try not to think of everything that has happened to this point in our lives. I try only to think of the good and not the bad. After we're finished we lay there on the bed. Charley lights a Chesterfield and I can hear the tobacco burning.

"I'm sorry," he says.

"For what?"

"For making you say those things."

"God, Charley, if that was the worst part of it I wouldn't mind."

"I can't change, Ruby. It's too late."

"No it's not, honey. No it's not." I want to believe that it is not too late and I want him to believe that it isn't.

He sits up, his back a curve of hard muscle. He exhales a cloud of smoke up toward the ceiling. I watch it ascend, swirl, as though seeking escape, as though somehow desperate, and I feel a bit that way myself: like smoke seeking escape.

"I guess nobody understands what it's like to be me, but me," he says.

I guess maybe he's right. Part of me wonders if it was a mistake to leave Leroy. I had it nice with Leroy. Nice in a way I didn't have to worry, but not so nice in other departments. I don't know if I could ever find another man like Charley, or even one like Leroy if something were to happen to Charley. A girl only gets just so many chances in life and maybe I've had all I'm going to get. I am like the smoke Charley exhales.

I hear the night train off in the distance. Ruby is asleep next to me. I hear the train and it makes me want to follow it. There are times when it's good like this, when right after we make love and I'm lying there thinking how sweet life can treat you even when you don't deserve it, that I get the most restless. When things are going to hell, I feel calm, at peace, but when things are good, I'm all shot to hell in my heart somehow, wanting to move on, to leave the good thing I got and find something else.

The night train calls my name, long and low out over the rolling hills:

Charley Floyd, Charley Floyd
Where you bound but heaven's gates
Where you been but at hell's doorstep
Come on Charley Floyd, stop your
Running and get on board and let
Me carry you for a
while cross the
River and through the woods to a
Cold grave Charley Floyd, Charley Floyd
To a dark cold grave, Charley Floyd.

15

Pretty Boy Floyd

George is drunk on the seat beside me as we roll through the pitch-black Oklahoma night. Going to go see Ruby. I got word she saw a photograph of me and Beulah with our arms around each other and is steaming mad. It was Beulah's idea to get our picture taken. I'm such a sucker for a pleading woman. I got my window rolled down because it smells like a gin joint inside the car and the air outside is sweet across those dark hills I can't see.

"You better cut back on the booze," I say to Bird. "It's going to turn you blind."

"Not me, Choc. I can handle it."

We hit a bump in the road and his head lolls over to one side like he's got strings in his neck somebody cut.

"I don't want to get shot pulling a job and

you hung over so bad you can't watch my back."

"Don't worry about me," Bird says. "We ain't been killed yet. Hell, we ain't even been shot."

I light a cigarette and think of Ruby, how she's going to take it, seeing me with my arms around Beulah. I should have cut Beulah loose a long time ago. But now it's too late. Last time I went over to Bradley's to see her she tells me something that I don't know how to exactly take.

It was a hot afternoon up there in that spare bedroom and Bradley and Bessie had gone off to town for the day so it was just me and Beulah alone. I was standing at the window in my undershirt thinking how hot it was — too hot even to make love — when Beulah said, "I'm pregnant, Charley."

At first I thought she was joking, but I looked into her eyes and knew she was dead serious. She was sitting on the edge of the bed with tears running down her cheeks, sitting there in her slip.

"You sure?" I asked.

"Pretty sure."

"You could just be late, though?"

"I could, but I don't think so Charley, it's been almost six weeks."

"Things like that can happen though,

can't they?"

"Sure, I guess so. But a woman knows. She does, Charley. Come sit on the bed with me, please."

I wasn't so sure how I felt about the news. In a way I was sort of pleased she might be. I loved my son and it wouldn't be so bad to have another. But then I thought what it would be like having a son by each of them: Beulah and Ruby. The sky looked like a sheet of hot tin. Chickens scratched in the yard. Beulah's sniffling seemed to fill the room.

I went over and sat on the edge of the bed and put my arm around her.

"You angry with me, Charley?"

"No, why should I be?"

"I mean I guess if you didn't want it, we could do something about it."

I thought of my kid killed before he ever took his first breath, some guy running a coat hanger up inside Beulah and poking around until she bled bloody clots.

"Hell no," I said. "If you are, you are. That's it. I'll be his daddy just like I'm Jackie's daddy."

"Oh, God, Charley, I love you so much."

"Thing is, Beulah, I can't marry you. You understand that don't you?"

She didn't say anything for a long while

then said, "Sure, I understand you can't."

She took my hand and placed it on her tummy and said, "Feel." I rubbed around but it felt like it always did, round and firm. But something about doing that made me want her bad even though it was too hot for doing anything. Next thing I know we're kissing and I have her laid back on the bed and I can't resist her. And when I do it to her it's the best we ever did it. And afterwards even she said it was.

"Charley, that was so nice. It's like we were made for each other."

But right after we're finished, as I'm lying there, I'm thinking about Ruby again. Feeling guilty again. Wishing I was with Ruby. And when I am with Ruby, I'm thinking about Beulah. And when I'm robbing banks I'm thinking about what it would be like to live a straight life and when I'm trying to live straight, I'm thinking about robbing banks. I feel like I'm trying to live in two different worlds and can't find any peace in either of them.

We come to the road that turns off to the farm where Ruby is staying with Jackie — her father's place — and we turn up it only I kill the headlights as I do.

"We're liable to run into a cow or something," Bird says, slurring his words, as if he'd even know if we ran into a whole herd of cows. He still dances when he pisses even though the doctor gave him something for the clap. He says that's why he's drinking so much, to kill the pain he has when he pisses. He says it won't go away entirely because God wants to leave him a reminder about fornicating with whores. I tell him that's nuts. He says, "There's a lot of stuff goes on none of us know about — God's one great big mystery, Choc." I tell him he's still nuts.

I slow the car down to barely a crawl because I've learned to be cautious and not to trust nothing or nobody. I can see the outline of the house against the night sky: dark and lonely. Still I'm cautious. There's enough reward money on our heads to get a man to sit up all night with a rifle hoping to get lucky.

"You got bullets in your gun?" I ask Bird.

He fumbles around in his pocket and takes out his pistol. It looks big as a brick. He fools with it trying to check the chamber, slides back the slide and a shell kicks out and lands in his lap.

"Careful with that thing," I say. "You ever see the size of a hole one of those leaves in a fellow?"

"I know if you shoot a man in his pinky

finger with one of these, it will knock him off his feet," Bird says, happy as a child.

"That's what I'm worried about, you shooting me with that damn thing."

I think of how Beulah said she didn't feel anything when the police shot her in the head. I think if you got shot anywhere else but in the head, you'd feel it.

As we get closer to the house, there's a gate we got to pass through. I notice it's standing open. Something no farmer would do who has cows. I stop the car.

"Something's wrong, Bird."

"What?" He drops the gun on the floor, bends to pick it up. Somebody steps out of the shadows.

"Give it up Pretty Boy!"

I don't wait for whoever it is to identify himself. I shove the gearshift into reverse and hit the gas hard.

Gunshots. Bullets whang off the fenders, doors, trunk; one shatters the back window, another a headlight. Bird's hat gets shot off his head. The lane is muddy and the harder I give it the gas the more bogged down the wheels get spinning into the mud. I cut the wheel sharp.

"You going to fire that thing?" I yell at Bird, "or just let them shoot us like fish in a barrel?"

Bird sobers quick, starts tossing lead through the busted glass.

Bang! Bang! Bang! Bang!

Every time he shoots his pistol, flashes of light explode inside the car. I'm yelling at him but I can't hear what I'm saying. Slugs tear into the car but nothing hits me or Bird. Still, I get ready to bite one, hoping it won't hurt too badly.

"How the hell they know they ain't shooting innocent people?" Bird yells.

"Three o'clock in the morning, I guess they can figure out we ain't innocent people," I yell back.

If it weren't we were about to be slaughtered, it would almost be funny. The car is going maybe fifteen miles an hour back up the lane. I can hear the tires zizzing, flinging mud clots up underneath the frame as I give it everything I've got.

George says he sees the shadows running after us, the flames of their rifles and shotguns lighting up the dark.

He's yelling, "They couldn't hit a bull in the ass!" when something hot hits me in the ankle and my whole foot goes numb: my brake foot, not my gas foot.

I must have yelped because Bird turns to me and says, "What?"

"I think they shot my foot off."

He crawls over the seat and I crawl under him and he takes the wheel and I take the pistol and try not to think how damn much getting shot hurts. It feels like hot water is filling up my shoe.

I wonder is this it, is this the time they kill me?

Ruby Floyd Leonard

I should have known Charley would never change his ways. Somebody shows me his picture with a woman he's got his arms around.

"He was just acting like it was nothing at all," this friend, the wife of a guy me and Charley both knew and who I used to think was a true friend until she showed me that picture.

"They had it taken in Sallisaw. Me and Frank were there for the day and ran into them and Charley just said, 'Hey Iris, this here is Beulah Baird.' He had a handful of pictures taken in some studio they'd just come out of and gave me and Frank this one. I thought you'd like to know."

It was one of those things you wanted to know but didn't want to know and once I saw it, I couldn't deny my jealousy, my disappointment, my fire-hot anger.

"Oh, you know Charley's never going to

change," I say, but down deep, my heart is bitter and it is shattered.

I packed everything Jackie and me owned into two suitcases and I left all of Charley's clothes hanging in the closet. Let whoever moves in have them. I was mad enough to burn them but I didn't want to take the time, and we left Tulsa and moved to my daddy's place in Bixby.

It was where Charley came looking for me on the night they ambushed him and George and shot Charley in the ankle. I guess he loved me enough to risk his life, knowing that the police were probably watching the place. It left me all torn up. How are you supposed to love a man who cheats on you but will risk his life just to see you? My heart is bitter still and the worst kind of love is the kind you can't quit.

Bill Counts

A bunch of us looked at all that reward money the bankers placed on the head of Charley Floyd and said, "Hell if the regular law can't catch 'em, maybe we ought to." We knew that land as well as anybody, as well as Charley himself. Me and Erv Kelly decided to put an end to all this Pretty Boy business and put a little something extra into our pockets doing it. We'd both been law officers in the past, so it wasn't like we were green fish or anything. Shit, we could shoot. And Erv had taken down about a dozen different bank robbers when he was sheriff of McIntosh County.

"We'll shoot those boys like they was ducks," Erv said.

"Hell yes," I said. "Why not."

So we laid an ambush for Pretty Boy and old George Birdwell. And we sat outside that farm on long dark nights and drank a little shine out of mason jars and swapped a few lies and liked to have froze our asses off waiting for them boys to show up.

Then one night they come.

And I said to Erv, "That's sure as shit them."

"It sure as shit is. Ain't nobody drives up a lane in the dark with their headlights off at three in the morning but somebody that's got a reason to not want to be noticed."

Erv was packing a Thompson machine gun. We sort of made a joke of it before that night: "That's a lot of gun." "Yeah, it's enough gun for a couple of birds named George and Charley." "Pretty gun for a Pretty Boy." Stuff like that.

We held our breath until they got close. We'd had a lot of rain lately and the lane was muddy. It would be nice they was to bog down in it. They drove up to a gate I saw too late we'd left open. The plan was, soon as somebody stepped out of the car to open the gate, we'd hit 'em. Erv said something I'd never heard come out of his mouth before when he saw them stop and start to back up: "Fuck a damn duck!"

It was a dead giveaway, that gate. They stopped and started to back up and Erv went out there and yelled at them to stop, his hands full of that tommy gun; I guess he must have felt invincible or maybe he just had gotten tired of sitting out there in the dark night after night freezing his ass off. He yelled at them to give up.

He got shot six times (this I learned later) and fell squeezing the trigger of that Thompson tearing up the ground around his feet. Time I got to him he was dead, shot about every place a man can be. Hell, I emptied my rifle and pistol and even took up the Thompson and emptied it. The other boys that were with us that night, Crockett Long, A. B. Cooper, M. L. Lairmore, Jim Stormont and J. A. Smith, were firing too. It was like a goddamn turkey shoot.

But that automobile just kept on going with Charley Floyd and George Birdwell in it and I thought to myself standing over Erv, what a couple of lucky sons a bitches they were, and what an unlucky fellow old Erv was.

It eat me up to have to go tell his widow.

Pretty Boy Floyd

A week after the shootout, George says he needs cash and wants to rob a bank of his own since I'm laid up with a bullet in my ankle.

"Go ahead," I tell him. "It's a free country."

"You know I'd never run out on you, Choc."

"You been a good partner."

"Just I need the dough real bad."

"Go on. Just make sure you get a good man to watch your back like you watched mine."

"I will."

He stands at the door holding his Stetson in hands that are shaking from all the booze. He's gotten old fast since I first laid eyes on him.

"I'll come back round in a month or two and see how you're doing."

"Say howdy to your wife for me."

His eyes are reddened. He smells like a still. He hardly ever reads the Bible anymore. I feel sorry for him.

After George has gone I spend my time

writing letters to Ruby and to Beulah and to Bradley. I listen to the radio and smoke and watch the weather change. One day it is sunny and warm, the next cloudy and cold. Spring never was the best time of year because it's so unpredictable. Spring has a feminine quality to it because it is so quickly changeable in its moods. I think about a lot of crazy things laid up like I am.

I grow restless watching the changing weather.

I don't tell anybody in the letters I write back home where I'm hiding out. I read in the papers where one of the ambushers was killed that night at the farm. I don't know if I shot him or George did. I guess it doesn't matter. The papers say more than two thousand people came to the man's funeral. I wonder how many will come to mine.

I write Bradley that if they kill me, I want "Amazing Grace" sung at my funeral.

I write Mother that I'm fine, doing swell.

I write Ruby but don't expect to get any letters back.

I'm about to jump out of my skin.

I feel a sweetness descending upon me.

I see the face of Jesus one morning in the changing clouds.

Life is hard as a bullet.

16

Pretty Boy Floyd

I return to the Cookson Hills once I'm sure the place isn't being watched so closely. I spend the summer laid up with my bad ankle. By autumn I'm able to limp around some using a crutch. Bradley and me drive out to a lake where the leaves of the trees have turned red and gold and flutter like dying birds to the water. We drink beer and just sit there and I say, "It reminds me of when we were kids, don't it you?"

"I like the peacefulness," Bradley says.

"There was a time when I could hang out here all day long. But now I'm as restless as a cat in heat."

A fish splashes in the middle of the lake.

"What you going to do, Choc?"

"About what?"

"Ruby, Beulah, the cops, the rewards they got on you?"

"Hell if I know."

Bradley squats on his heels at the water's edge picking up stones and skipping them over the smooth water, one-two-three skips at a time. He's got quiet mysterious ways like Daddy Walter had and I never know everything he's thinking. I know if I were to let him, he'd become a hell of a bank robber. But there can only be one of us Floyds in the bank robbing business and I've already got the job.

"You know if you keep going they'll get you sooner or later."

"Yeah, well hell, we ain't none of us going to get out of this world alive."

He turns his head and looks back at me leaning against the front fender of his truck, the crutch under my arm. I'm like a wounded bird myself.

"I'd sure hate to get news they'd shot you dead," Bradley says.

"Dying might not be the worst thing that can happen to us," I say.

A pair of wood ducks glide down over the treetops and land at the far end of the lake. They swim together as though tied by an invisible thread. They remind me of the way Ruby and me were: how it feels like we're going through life tied together by an invisible thread neither of us can break.

"Mother's old heart would be broken you were to end up in a police morgue," Bradley says, skipping another stone. The ducks swim in a wide circle, preening each other's feathers. Then something startles them and they explode from the water, their wings beating furiously. But only one flies away. The other is caught in the jaws of a snapping turtle and can only beat the water furiously with its wings. The duck's desperation pulls the turtle half out of the water before the turtle's weight pulls it back down again.

"Goddamn," Bradley says. "You see that?"

I think about pulling my gun and shooting the turtle, because I know the desperation the duck must be feeling. But it's too far away to hit anything and all I can do is watch. There is a final flourish of agony then the duck is pulled below the surface.

"I hate a damn snapping turtle, don't you?" Bradley says.

My future is like that duck's I think: someday I'll be pulled down by the jaws of death.

"I guess I'll try not to let the cops shoot me," I say. "But if they do, then that's just the way it will be. Dead is dead. I can't see any way of turning back for me, Bradley."

"Ain't none of us would feel good about it you was to get shot," he says.

"Me included."

He grins.

"I guess not."

That night I dream I am dead, lying in a casket, mother and Bradley and E.W. and Bessie and Ruby and Beulah standing round me. Jackie crying for his daddy. I can't move, can't speak, can't tell them that being dead isn't anything like they think it is. In fact, it feels sort of pleasant. Then I am startled by something and see the snapping jaws of a big mossback eating away my flesh. I awake in a sweat and look out at the full moon that is as bright and round as a blind eye, my heart beating fast. I think about the duck that flew away and who is alone this night, like me, and wonder if ducks have hearts that ache.

A month later, George shows up at Bradley's and he's got a couple of guys with him I never seen before; one of them is a Negro with wavy hair slick with pomade. All three wear cheap gray suits under their long overcoats and felt hats. By now I don't need the crutch to get around. George introduces me to the guys with him. Johnny Glass is the Negro's name, and the other guy is C. C. Patterson who claims he's part Kiowa. He doesn't look like an Indian, not with those blue eyes. But half the white men running around in Oklahoma claim they got Indian blood in them.

"Let's drive out to that roadhouse we first met in and talk about something, Choc," Bird says.

I can tell right away this isn't a crew I want to be part of, but the thought of doing a little drinking with my old partner beats hell out of just sitting around.

We drive over to the same roadhouse in Aikens, only now it's being run by an ex-judge. The women who hang out in the place are all tramps.

Bird starts talking about robbing this bank in Boley. Boley's an all-colored town. Even Jesse James wouldn't rob the bank there.

"Don't you think you boys might be sticking out like sore thumbs?" I say. "I mean except for Johnny here."

Johnny Glass is a light-skinned Negro. His pomade hair ripples with light from the bare bulbs overhead.

"It's not like we're going to take up residence there," Bird says. "We're going to drive in, take down the bank and drive right back out again. Old Johnny here knows them people. Knows what to expect. Ain't that right, Johnny?"

"I know them people," is what Johnny says.

C. C. Patterson is tight-lipped. He keeps looking at this ugly tramp at the bar. She must weigh two hundred pounds. She's got coal-black hair and looks like Cherokee, if I know my Indians. Maybe that's why C.C. is looking at her, figuring they got something in common, both of them Indians, so to speak.

Bird is drinking so much I think his mind is going on him. He talks about how easy it would be to rob a nigger bank. He spills his drink because his hands shake, laughs even when nothing funny is said. I think the liquor has definitely rotted his brains.

"You still doing the shuffle when you piss, George?"

He laughs, says he isn't, then says, "You in with us, Choc?"

"Count me out," I say after we drink a few rounds.

"Easy money," Bird says.

"No, count me out."

The other two look relieved that I don't throw in with them. I guess they figure they've got enough guns to rob a "nigger bank." They drop me off at the house and the last time I ever see George Birdwell is when he drives away from Bradley's under light of a full moon leaning out the window of a '29 Hudson Hornet waving at me, a bottle of gin in his hand, his laughter trailing into the night.

Pink Brooks

I was cutting Raymond's hair when I see 'em. Two white boys and a colored boy pull up across the street at the bank. The colored boy stayed behind the wheel while those two white boys went inside the bank. I said to Raymond, "There's some trouble if I ever saw any."

Raymond's a big old boy with a big old head and he turned round and said, "Shit, Pink, I guess you sure enough right. Damn, that might be ol' Pretty Boy hisself. You think he come to rob our bank?"

"Sure ain't come to make no deposits," I say. "I'm thinking the same think you thinking, Raymond?"

"We damn sure better get us our guns."

And that's what we do.

We ain't the only ones that seen trouble that day. And we ain't the only ones got our guns that day. Money is precious and little and what we have, we aim to keep. And it don't matter if you white, Negro, red-assed Indian or Pretty Boy Floyd his goddamn self, you come into Boley to steal our money, you better be ready to go to shootin'.

We didn't have to wait long for something

to happen.

Pop, pop, pop! Gunshots all inside that bank, sounded like firecrackers going off.

Raymond say, "Shit, we in for it now!"

We don't get half out the door when we see 'em come running out. One of 'em is holding his neck. Looks like he's wearing a red scarf, only it's a scarf of blood. He staggers like he's drunk, then he go down before he reach the car. Me and Raymond open up on the other one with our guns. Knocked him off his feet, both of us hitting him 'bout the same time. Raymond say, "I got him." I say, "No, I got him."

The colored boy start they car up, tossing dirt with his tires tryin' to drive it away but he only got half a block, far as the drugstore on the corner. Half the men in Boley were in town that day buying shells because it was openin' of bird season. They shot that wild-ass nigger from both sides of the street, tore up that fancy car, shot it and him all to pieces. Wonder they didn't shoot they selves. The car ran up on the curb and knocked down a telephone pole, steam and blood coming out of it.

We learned later the one wearing the blood scarf was George Birdwell, Pretty Boy Floyd's partner. But it wasn't Pretty Boy with him that day.

"Birdwell," Raymond says when he hears the news. "Shit, we shot him like he *was* a damn bird, didn't we, Pink? And if old Pretty Boy hisself had come, we'd a shot him too."

I couldn't cut nobody's hair for two days, my hands was shaking so bad. And for two or three months, that's all anybody talked about: how it was we shot them bank robbers. The state police came and took the bodies off and we sure enough was glad to be rid of them. I guess nobody ever came to Boley to rob another bank it would be soon enough for me.

Pretty Boy Floyd

I read about George being killed. There was a picture of him and those other two guys — Johnny Glass and C. C. Patterson — old mug shots. The article told how they were shot and killed by the citizens of Boley. I guess Johnny Glass didn't know his own kind as well as George thought he did. The papers mention that George was a partner in crime of mine. They say I'm next. Hell, they could be right. Death keeps snatching my partners and sooner or later it will snatch me.

I tell Bradley the news.

"Damn, Choc. I'd say it's an omen. Hoover aims to get you."

"It wasn't Hoover who shot George and it wasn't Hoover who shot Billy Miller. Life guys like us lead is risky. That's all."

"Hell, even poor Beulah got shot. What makes you think you won't be next?"

"Because I got this," I say, and show him my lucky rabbit's foot.

"Let me ask you something," he says, looking at it.

"Sure."

"If it's so dang lucky, why ain't the rabbit still got it?"

I've got no answer.

Ruby Floyd Leonard

I get a letter from Charley, all apologetic about the photo with him and that woman. "I'm wounded, Ruby," he says. "Shot in the ankle. Guess how that happened? I was coming to see you and Jackie and the cops were waiting for us. I wouldn't even cared if they had killed me as long as I could have seen you and Jackie one last time."

Jesus, what am I supposed to say to that? My mother says I should go back with him.

"Every man is weak about some things," she tells me. I ask her about my father who, outside of Charley, is the strongest man I ever knew.

"He's weak about some things too, Ruby, don't think he isn't."

I watch Jackie playing so innocently, alone, without his daddy. It breaks my heart.

"Maybe I'm just not enough for him," I tell my mother. "Charley's got large appetites. Maybe one woman just can't keep him satisfied."

"Ruby, there ain't no woman completely enough for any man, just like there ain't no man completely enough for any woman. That don't mean he doesn't love you. Men are just the way they are. Charley surely loves you or he wouldn't have risked his life to come see you. Didn't he come and take you away from that man you married, and didn't you go with him? If that's not love on both your parts, I don't know what is."

"Did daddy ever cheat on you?"

She wipes her hands on a flour-stained apron, lights a cigarette and sits down across from me at the kitchen table.

"Not as far as I know of. But can you keep a secret?"

"Sure."

"I did on him, once."

Seeing her sitting there, plain and worn as a pair of overalls, I find it impossible to believe she could ever have done anything wrong in that way.

"You cheated on daddy?"

"I'm ashamed to admit it, but yes, I did. Just once. Five years after we were married. You were just real little."

Sun the color of butter spreads across the kitchen floor where Jackie is playing with a toy wood truck.

"It was with a preacher that came through here once with a big tent. I went to the revival because I heard this man could cure just about anything and your father and me weren't getting along so well. He was drinking a lot then and gambling and acting mean sometimes. Your daddy is a good man, but back then, he was being a fool because he loved liquor so much. I figured if this preacher could cure anything, I could go and pray he could cure your daddy of his thirst and bad ways. And maybe he could cure my empty heart in the doing."

My mother was not beautiful, and I never recalled her being so even in old photographs I'd seen of her when she was younger, when she and Daddy first got married. She was plain and tall and never smiled in any of the photographs.

I touched her sweet hand.

"The preacher had mesmerizing eyes and he let them fall on me and I guess I didn't mind. It was nothing like I'd imagined it to be, nothing like you might think. There was nothing romantic about it. We did it in the back of his church bus after everyone went home. At the time I thought it was something special, for some handsome man to pay attention to me. It made me feel alive inside again to know that someone as powerful as a preacher wanted me in that way. It seemed the greatest sin I could commit and I figured if I was going to sin, I was going to sin all the way. I was going to show your daddy I wasn't something to be walked all over. The feeling came over me hard and fast and it was over about as fast as it started and I cried for days afterward.

She got a faraway look in her eyes and I knew what she was feeling.

"I went home that night drunk on my thoughts. I remember the stars seemed so close I could reach up and touch them. But in a way, it made me feel dead when I awoke the next morning and realized the terrible thing I'd done. I realized that preacher probably took a woman in his bus about every town he stopped in. And I realized that what I done had hurt me as much as it would your daddy. I couldn't ever tell him what I'd done, and I never told anyone until just now. I'm glad I told you."

The smoke rose and clouded her features

and I couldn't imagine her doing what she'd just described. Not with any man, not even a bad preacher.

"Your daddy would have gone to pieces if he knew," she said, then stood and turned back toward the sink of dishes and began washing them and I began drying them and we did that in silence while Jackie played innocently on the floor lost in his imagination. I looked at him and thought: he's just another boy who will grow to be a man, filled with men's troubles that will spill over on whoever loves him. I pray he is not cursed with his father's sins. I wondered if that preacher Momma gave herself to ever thinks about her, ever feels sorry for what he did. I wanted to say to Momma, it's all right what you did, God understands better than any man could.

Pretty Boy Floyd

I send Ruby a letter and wait for an answer from her. I try and stay away from Beulah. Her belly's starting to get big. She still gets dizzy. Bradley says I sure got my hands full. I've got dead partners, too many women, a bullet hole in me, and the law on my tail. I guess you could say I've got my hands full.

Everything I read in the papers is how I'm Oklahoma's Enemy Number One. The governor says he'd just as soon see me dead as alive and that if his boys catch me, he'll make sure I get the chair. I don't know what I ever did to get so many people down on me. All I ever wanted was a decent life. I just went about it differently than most people. I just had the guts to do what it took to make my own way instead of standing in a soup line begging for scraps like a damn dog.

Tell me what's wrong with a man wanting to
be a man?
I think of Daddy Walter, giving credit in
Heaven
To all the sad angels and the rain
That comes too seldom is little but their
tears.

Time I got back to work, do what I do best.
First, I got to find me a new partner.
Someone to walk the line with Charley
Floyd.

17

Pretty Boy Floyd

I was getting my shoes shined at the barbershop when Richetti walked in. I hadn't seen him since we both worked the oil fields together. He was looking around like he wanted to steal something.

"Hey you," I said.

He looked at me with that innocent face that reminded me of my brother E.W.'s face.

"Charley Floyd?"

"One in the same."

He grinned so wide I could see all his teeth.

I give the shoe-shine man fifty cents and me and Rich go and have us a bottle of beer at a blind pig not far up the street from the barbershop.

"What you doing in Sallisaw?" I ask him.

He drinks his beer like a woman, sipping on it tenderly.

"Just looking for opportunities," he says.

"Last I heard of you they nabbed you for stealing typewriters."

"Oh, that was a long time ago, three, four years back."

"Seems like there's a lot better opportunities in this old world than stealing typewriters," I say, ribbing him a little. "Those damn things got to be heavy."

"You ain't wrong there, brother." He grins shyly. He has soft brown eyes you'd never suspect had a criminal's heart behind them.

"Guess who was in the state reformatory up there in Indiana with me," he says.

"How the hell would I know?"

"John Dillinger."

"He's making a name for himself all right."

"Real tough guy," Rich says. "Real ladies' man, according to him. I heard tell he's hung like a stallion."

"That's information I'm not interested in."

"Yeah, me either."

"What about you," I say. "You trying to walk the straight and narrow?"

"Me? I couldn't go straight if they paid me. No fun in it. You remember how hard it was working the oil fields."

"Yeah, I remember. That's why I'm not

working them anymore."

"Me either. Even stealing typewriters is easier."

We have a laugh, another round of beers.

"So what about you, Charley? You must be doing something I'd be interested in, everything I've been reading in the newspapers about you."

"I've got some new ideas on things," I say.

"I read where your partners have all ended up dead from lead poisoning."

"Yeah, but that was just bad luck on their part. Me, I'm lucky."

"You look like paint wouldn't stick to you."

I show him my lucky rabbit's foot. He rubs it, says maybe it will bring him luck too.

"You still doing jobs?" he says.

"Those were the old days," I say. "I've got other plans."

"No more banks?"

"Plenty more banks, just that I won't be the one robbing them. Figure it's time I became a boss. You still interested?"

"Hell, I'm all ears."

I tell him a little about my plans to become a gang boss, how I can hire guys to do for me what I used to do for myself. Tell him I'll do all the planning; let the other guys do all the robbing. Then I tell him I know a couple of real lookers in Kansas City and ask if he'd like to go there with me to meet them.

"I like girls."

"Who doesn't?"

"Nobody I know."

So we head back to Kansas City. Mostly because I don't know where else I can go and get a gang together, and to tell the truth, I'm sort of missing Beulah. I think of her big with my child in her belly and think maybe I ought to do the right thing by her. But then thinking about Ruby tears me all up. I wish there was a way we could all be family, Ruby, Beulah and me.

Beulah Ash

Charley and his new partner show up unexpectedly, no telegram, no phone call, nothing. Adam, the guy with Charley says his name is.

"Adam, like the first man God ever made," he says. "Adam Richetti." He's a nice-looking guy, sweet face; eyes that would make a girl believe anything.

"Rose around?" Charley says. "I'd like her to meet Rich."

Charley acts like he just came back from buying a pack of cigarettes instead of being gone for a couple of months.

I ring Rose up and tell her to come over. She says, why should she. I tell her Charley's in town and he's got a new beau for her. She says she'll be right over. I don't know how she does it, falls so hard for the guys Charley comes dragging in. Even though they're nice-looking guys, every one of them so far has ended up on a slab in the police morgue. This Rich probably will too.

We sit around and drink some hooch, Charley and me and Adam who says he was named after the first man. I'm glum and can't hide it.

Charley looks at me, says, "Something wrong?"

"Yeah, I lost the baby."

I was waiting for him to notice, but he didn't. He doesn't say anything for a long time. Adam sits on the couch with his hands between his knees like a little kid that's lost his way and is waiting for somebody to come and take him home.

"I'm real sorry to hear that, Beulah, when did this happen?"

"A few weeks ago."

"Hell, I'm sorry," he says again, then takes me in his arms and holds me tenderly. I think of what our son would have turned out like. Maybe it is just as well he didn't get born. Maybe it would be better if none of us had. I look at Charley and I don't see any future for any of us.

"Ah, it's okay, honey. Everything works out like it's meant to." I think he's truly disappointed we won't be having his son.

Rose takes her sweet time it seems getting there. We sit around and talk, me and Charley and this Adam. Turns out he's Italian. I just know Rose is going to fall all over herself for him. He's got little-boy brown eyes and a face a girl could kiss all night and she'll be crazy about him.

Pretty soon she shows up and right away takes a seat next to Adam on the sofa and they sit there like a couple of coo birds while Charley and me go into the bedroom.

"How you doing otherwise?" he asks, taking off his jacket and hanging it on the back of a chair. He's wearing a gun in a shoulder holster and has little sweat stains darkening his shirt under the arms.

"You mean like can I do it?"

"I missed you a lot, Beulah."

"I missed you a lot too, Charley. But I figured you had your wife to keep you company."

"No, no. I've not seen her in a long time, I swear. Here, look, I even got shot in the ankle and it laid me up for months. I've just been lying low is all."

He pulls his sock down to show me where he got shot.

"Broke some of the bones," he says. The wound is scabbed over. He takes hold of me and kisses me.

"I ain't had no action in a long time, I swear it," he says.

I know he's probably lying but I tell myself it doesn't matter if he is lying or not. I got a real thing for Charley Floyd. Still, I don't want to end up pregnant again.

"Charley, I'm not ready yet, you know what I mean."

He looks disappointed and sits on the side of the bed, his sock pulled down over his scabbed ankle.

"Boy, I was sure hoping we could do something, Beulah. It's not natural for a man to go too long without it. But if you can't, you can't. I understand."

I know if I don't do something for him, he'll just find another woman. Kansas City is full of women who'd do anything for a guy like Charley Floyd.

"Maybe there's something I can do for you, baby," I say and kneel down in front of him.

"Yeah?" His voice grows soft, almost a whisper as he threads his fingers through my hair. "I'd sure like it if you could do something to help me out here."

"Sure, there's always something a girl can do," I say.

He looks down into my eyes and I look up into his just before I lower my face to his lap.

Later we all go out, me and Rose and Charley and Adam. We have a nice shrimp and steak dinner and then find a dance hall. Charley says he can only dance slow now that he's been shot in the ankle, so we just dance slow. He presses up against me and whispers in my ear: "Thanks for earlier, honey. I was just about to go nuts."

"I love you, Charley. I'd do anything for you."

"I know you would. That's why I keep coming back, baby."

I look over and see Rose kissing Adam. It's like déja vu all over again.

Adam Richetti

I knew the minute I met Charley I'd made the right score. He's a solid guy, the kind you know you can trust once he takes to you. I once saw him whip a guy twice his size in the oil fields, over what I don't know. But Charley was fast with his fists and every time he hit this guy you could almost feel it.

It sounded like somebody socking a slab of beef. Charley mashed the guy's nose flat into a pulp of blood. I told myself right then and there, here's a guy you don't want to fistfight with.

So when I see him again in a Sallisaw barbershop getting his shoes shined I see how much he's changed. Sitting there in a natty charcoal suit, white silk shirt and tie, snap-brimmed fedora tilted back. Real cool customer, like butter wouldn't melt in his mouth. By now, Charley's as famous as John Dillinger and Al Capone.

"You want to throw in with me?" he says after we have a few beers and catch up on some things.

Hell yes, I tell him. We talk about that time I stole typewriters and went to the reformatory up in Indiana, same place Johnny Dillinger was. I'm surprised Charley would ask a guy like me to join up with him — a guy who served time for stealing typewriters. But he says, "I like you Rich, you're a solid guy and I need me a solid guy."

I read about how all his other partners went the way of an early grave, but that doesn't bother me none. You can choose to live a nice, safe long life and never do nothing, or you can take your chances and maybe live like a king. I never robbed a bank, but I'm damn ready by the time Charley's through talking to me.

We drive to Kansas City to meet his sweetheart, says she's got a sister that's as hot as a firecracker. "You're not queer are you?" Charley laughs. "Because you sure couldn't be queer with a girl like Rose."

"No, Charley, I ain't queer, whatever gave you an idea like that?"

"Some guys are, you know after they've been in the joint at an early age. Baby face like yours I can see where going to the joint early could ruin you on women."

"Oh hell, I guess I'm just going to have to prove you wrong."

"Not me," he says. "Rose is the one you'll have to prove yourself to."

We arrive at this place near downtown, this old shingled house and climb the stairs — rough-looking part of town.

That's where I meet Rose. Charley was right, I could practically feel the heat coming off her when she sat next to me. She smelled like a bunch of fresh flowers and before I knew it she was all over me. When Charley and Beulah headed for the only bedroom, Rose put her hand on my knee and said, "So, you just going to sit there, or what, Richey?"

I liked how she called me Richey and I

liked how her mouth tasted when I kissed her. The way she kissed, she acted starved for love. By the time me and Charley left the place, I'd made sure Rose was no longer starving for anything.

Charley says later to me, "So, you prove to Rose you weren't queer?"

"Yeah, I showed her real good how I wasn't." He laughs.

Ruby Floyd

I went to see a gypsy fortune-teller. She smelled like licorice. I wanted to know what was in store for me and Charley and little Jackie. Charley's been on the run again and I hear rumors he's back with that other woman in Kansas City and he's picked up a new partner. He was writing me love letters, but he hasn't written me anything lately and it's starting to feel the same old way and my heart is becoming bitter again.

"The thing that is troubling you now will soon be gone," the gypsy tells me. She's reading cards, her face pinched with concern as she does.

"What's that supposed to mean?" I say.

"There is a man who is the source of your troubles," she says.

"That's sure the truth."

"You are bound to this man until death."

"Oh, just terrific."

"But the end of your troubles is near."

I get a chill.

"Is something going to happen to him soon?"

She turns another card and looks at it. There's a drawing of a black skeleton on it. The skeleton's skull is grinning.

"His fate is written in the stars."

"Oh God, tell me what's going to happen?"

She turns another card.

"I see a place shrouded in mystery. I see a man running and other men chasing him. I see . . ." The fortune-teller starts breathing heavy, tells me that's all she can see — a man running with other men after him, that this place is surrounded by a cloud and that Charley runs into the cloud and disappears and never comes out again.

It makes no sense. I think the licorice I smell is something she's been drinking, for she leaves the room every few minutes then comes back and the smell is stronger.

"Just because you see a man running into a cloud," I say, "doesn't mean Charley's going to die."

"There is much we don't understand," she says. "That's all I can tell you about this man, except your troubles with him will soon be over."

It's all so creepy. The really creepy thing is, after I leave the gypsy's, I meet a man who looks a lot like Charley. I'm sitting in Walgreen's having a Coke thinking about what the fortune-teller said when this man comes in and sits next to me. I just caught a look at him out of the corner of my eye and I almost screamed. But then I see it's not Charley. The man introduces himself, says his name is Al and "Nice to meet you." And "What's a swell girl like you doing on such a hot day all alone?" And "Wouldn't you like to go for a walk?"

I look at the clock on the wall above the fountain. It's just a little after two in the afternoon. I feel so lonely. Next thing I know I'm in a hotel room with this Al who tells me later when he's getting dressed he's a traveling salesman and he'd like to see me again the next time he gets into town. I think about what my mother told me about her and the preacher and feel the same emptiness she felt. I don't say anything because I'm feeling more lonely than ever and when he comes over to the bed and kisses me it feels just like a knife going through my heart. I keep thinking about Charley running into a cloud and never coming out again as I lie there in that lonely strange room listening to the afternoon traffic. Nothing makes any sense anymore.

I end up crying my eyes out.

And when I finish and go into the bathroom to freshen up, I see the man has left ten dollars on the bathroom sink. And when I look up and see the face of the woman in the mirror, I start crying again.

For this is what I've allowed Charley Floyd to turn me into.

Pretty Boy Floyd

Beulah is silent and unmoving next to me on the bed and I can't sleep. I have a hard time sleeping anymore. I get up and smoke a cigarette and pace the floor and try to think of how I'm going to put together a gang, run the whole operation without taking too many risks. I'm starting to think long-term now, not just the next bank and the one after that — but as far as a year or two down the line. I want to get enough money together to buy a little ranch, maybe down in Mexico where the law can't touch me. I want to have Ruby and Jackie down there with me, maybe have some horses, live like a rich man. I hear the living down there is cheap and if I can put together maybe forty or fifty grand, we could live down there the rest of our lives, have servants so Ruby wouldn't have to do any housework or cook. We could just lie around in the sun and grow old together. The more I think about it, the more I'm sold on the idea. Beulah says something in her sleep and I turn and look at her and she's just another woman to me in this moment. The truth is, she's not Ruby and she'll never be Ruby and she'll never give me a son and I don't want her to. I got a son and his name is Jackie and I love him dearly.

I go and look out the window to see if any strange cars are hanging out or some guy is standing down in the shadows because it's become my habit to do such things. It's why I'm still alive and some of my pals aren't — because I keep a close vigil and don't ever let my guard down.

I lie down next to Beulah and try to sleep,
but I can't.
Instead I dream of things I want.
I dream of gorgeous things
Whilst waiting for the midnight of
My soul.

18

Pretty Boy Floyd

About the Kansas City Massacre — I just want to get the story straight. Me and Rich were staying in a nice hotel in Kansas City with Beulah and Rose when Verne Miller came knocking. Verne's a local guy connected to Johnny Lazia the big mob boss here in Kansas City.

"I need a couple of solid guys to help me out with something," Miller starts out saying as soon as he introduces himself.

"What makes you think we're solid guys?" I say.

Miller looks at Rose and Beulah, says, "You think we could have a private talk here?" I give the girls a couple of twenties and tell them to go shopping, which they're always glad to do.

"Let's not beat around the bush," Miller says. "Everybody knows you're a solid guy,

Floyd. And look this ain't no big deal what I'm asking for. Just a simple job."

Then he tells us what he needs us for is to steal a guy.

"We steal money not people," Rich tells him. I can tell the way Rich is acting he doesn't like Verne Miller much.

"You might for ten grand."

Rich whistles.

"Who's the guy, the President?"

"No, one of our guys," Miller says. "The cops got him and we want him back."

I know now why he's offering so much dough.

"I don't think we're the guys you're looking for here," I say. "We do jobs, like my partner says. This sounds like some serious business where a guy could get killed easily."

"You like to golf?" Miller asks me out of the blue.

"Why?"

"Because I like to golf. Maybe after we do this thing, we can go golfing."

Rich rolls his eyes.

"I don't shoot people just for the hell of it, Mr. Miller."

"Nobody's asking you to. We do this thing right nobody has to get shot, including us."

Ten thousand dollars is more than I ever

made doing a bank job and we're getting down to nickels and dimes because we haven't pulled a job in some long time. As usual, the girls are spending money like it was water. But hell, that's what money is for, to spend. Miller takes an envelope out of his pocket and drops it on the table.

"Half now, half when we finish the job."

"Count it, Rich," I say. He does, whistles again, says, "Five Gs."

"When and where?" I say to Miller.

He grins, says, "Yeah, I'll take you golfing after we finish the job. I bet you're about a five, six handicapper." I don't know what the hell he's talking about.

Verne Miller

Orders come down from Johnny Lazia we need to get one of our guys back from the police — Jelly Nash. In our business, you don't just let the cops take who they want. There is a price to pay for everything, now they got to pay it for taking Jelly. Me, I personally could give a shit less about Jelly Nash. He's a pompous little prick wears a toupee looks like a dead squirrel sitting on his head. I never trusted any guy who wears a rug. But Johnny tells me to get a couple of solid guys: "That Pretty Boy Floyd's back in town," he says. "Why not get him. The son of a bitch is an expert with a machine gun." Guys wearing hairpieces and guys with names like Pretty Boy. I wonder what the fuck crime is coming to these days with guys like that in it.

But I do what I'm told by the higher-ups and I go see Pretty Boy and offer him ten grand to help me get Jelly back. At first he says he only robs banks, but when I drop the dough in front of him he just says, "When and where?" He acts real cool about it, doesn't even count the dough himself — has his partner, this dago prick named Richetti do it.

Once we make the deal, I tell them when and where. That day comes the cops are bringing back Jelly, we set up outside Union Station. We set up so we can get the cops in a crossfire in case they don't want to too easily give Jelly over to us. We all got machine guns under our coats. Pretty Boy keeps telling me how he won't shoot anybody unless they try and shoot him first. I'm beginning to wonder if the guy's a sissy the way he keeps talking about not wanting to shoot anybody.

"Fine, fine," I say. "We don't have to shoot no fucking body."

We wait maybe twenty minutes then we see the cops coming out with Jelly in the middle of them — seven cops and Jelly. The street is full of people coming and going out of the station. Pretty Boy looks at me and I call over to him to wait until they start to get into the car, that we'll take them then. The dago Richetti acts nervous and I'm wondering if I've hired a couple of real pansies.

The cops are getting in the car, getting Jelly in the car, I make my move, step out from behind the lamppost I'm standing behind and shout, "Put 'em the fuck up!" I shout this two, three times. Pretty Boy and Richetti show themselves. We all got machine guns, and all the cops have got are pistols. You'd have to be crazy going up against machine guns with pistols. But whoever said cops have any brains to begin with. Next thing I know the cops are shooting at us. Hell, what choice we got but to shoot back?

So that's what we do, we shoot back.

Adam Richetti

I thought it was a crazy-assed idea from the start — trying to kidnap somebody from the cops. But Charley said ten grand is nothing to sneeze at.

"We ain't thugs," I say. "We're fucking bank robbers."

"You ain't nothing yet," Charley says. "You ain't been with me long enough to be anything." He's got the same look in his eyes as he did when he busted that guy's nose in the oil fields.

"Sure Charley, whatever you say. You're the boss."

"It's just we need the money right now, Rich," he says, trying not to be mad at me. He's got a quick fuse, but it burns out just as fast.

So I go along with it. But as soon as the cops start firing at us, I know Charley made a bad decision. We got no choice but to open up on them. Charley gets hit right off the bat. I don't think he got a shot off. The bullet knocks him off his feet. He gets back up, blood leaking from his shoulder, staining his nice suit coat. His machine gun is lying in the gutter.

The *burrrrr* of our tommy guns sends people scrambling for cover. The cops are popping off shots at us with their pistols. It's like a goddamn war: glass breaking everywhere, chunks of brick exploding up from the curb, the clang of bullets hitting parked cars. Two of the cops crumple to the sidewalk, one lying with his face in the gutter. I can hear the bullets whizzing past my head. I keep firing the Thompson, feeling it buck against me like it's some wild thing trying to get loose from my hands. I'm not sure I'm even hitting anything. Miller is firing his machine gun. He looks like he's enjoying it. I see the rear window of the cop's car explode — black Chevrolet sedan — see its body dimple with bullets. The tires go flat, whooshing air.

Charley is staggering around trying to get his machine gun out of the gutter. He's bleeding like a stuck pig, dazed as hell. The shooting seems to last forever, it's like a dream. But I can't stop shooting and Miller can't stop shooting and the cops can't stop shooting.

Then suddenly nobody's shooting back — all the cops are down on the ground or slumped over inside the car. Empty shell casings glitter in the street. There is the smell of hot grease and metal and gunpowder. Smoke curls out of the end of the barrel of my tommy gun like a gray snake. We're all just standing there, like we're frozen in time.

Miller says, "We got 'em."

"Got what!" Charley yells at him. "Tell me what the fuck did we get!"

We go over to the car and I pull open the door and Miller says, "Oh shit, that's Jelly."

I see a guy with a toupee dangling from

his shattered skull. Impossible to tell who it is, his face is half gone. He's lying over another guy who's dead. One guy in the backseat is making funny sounds in his throat, like water bubbling only it's him choking on his own blood.

We sure fucked this up, I'm thinking.

Pretty Boy Floyd

I'm getting tired of getting shot. It's something you don't get used to. If you can imagine what having a hot nail hammered into you would feel like, that's what getting shot is like, only worse.

When we're standing there looking at the bloody mess inside the car, at the cops lying on the ground, suddenly the ten grand doesn't seem like nearly enough. It wasn't supposed to be like this. I'm mad as hell, but I'm not sure who I'm mad at, Miller, or myself for letting him talk me into this thing. Rich says, "You're bleeding, Charley."

I don't even know where my machine gun is.

We drive away in a roar, Miller behind the wheel. He keeps saying, "Son of a bitch, son of a bitch," and driving fast, taking corners on two wheels. Off in the distance we hear sirens. The city slinks away behind us.

Later I get patched up by one of the doctors Johnny Lazia keeps on the payroll. His breath smells like tobacco and whiskey. Miller tells me later his specialty is bullet wounds and abortions he performs on the prostitutes Johnny runs.

"You're lucky, Mr. Floyd," the doctor says. "That bullet didn't hit anything vital, just took some meat out of you."

"Lucky, huh? You ever get shot?"

Verne Miller comes in right after I'm patched. He's drinking bootleg whiskey straight from the bottle and sweating like hell. He's got his coat off and is standing there in his shirtsleeves. His eyes are glazed but wild like an animal that's gotten trapped.

"We messed up, Floyd."

"No, you messed up. Give me the rest of my dough so I can blow this town."

"Sure, sure," he says. Then he paces the floor and drinks some more of the hooch and I can tell he's been hitting it hard because he's laughing between cussing. He's crazy as a loon.

"I'm a fucking dead man," he says. "We're all dead men, Floyd. You, me, Richetti."

"Not me and Rich."

"Sure, you too. Don't you see, we messed up, the heat will be down on us all. You think Johnny's going to let us live bringing that much heat on him? He'll cut off our heads and send 'em to the cops with an apology letter. This is the kind of heat even Johnny can't stand."

"Give me my dough, Verne, or you really will be a dead man, only it won't be Johnny who kills you." I still got my .45 and I show it to him.

"I'd have to get it from Johnny," he says. "That ain't possible now, we fucked everything up."

"You keep saying *we,* Verne." I want to kill him with my bare hands. I remember what Billy Miller said to me: never fool around with rats.

I go get Rich and we drive the hell out of Kansas City with just five grand blood money. The sky is flamingo pink over a city still asleep, and if you didn't know any different, you'd think Kansas City was the best place in the world to live with that nice pink sky hanging over everything. It all seems so peaceful, the city at dawn.

"Let me ask you something, Rich," I say as we drive toward the rising distant sun.

He's smoking a cigarette, the smoke curling up into this baby face, his arms resting atop the steering wheel, his chin jutted forward as he seeks an escape route. He doesn't look like a cop killer.

"What?" he says.

"How many of those cops did you shoot back there?"

"I don't know, Charley. I don't fucking know."

"They'll track us down for this, you know that, don't you?"

"Yeah. It was pretty goddamn awful."

We drive until nightfall, until the outer dark flows inside the car like black water and all I can see are Rich's features in the yellow glow of the dash lights, the red tip of his burning cigarette. I get this spooky feeling like we're two dead men riding around looking for a couple of innocent souls to steal. I wish I were home with Ruby and Jackie. I wish that I were a housepainter or even a baker — anything but what I am: a wanted man, probably a dead man.

Ruby Floyd

I read in the papers Charley is wanted for what they're calling the "Kansas City Massacre" — four cops shot dead, a couple of others wounded. The paper says the gunmen were trying to rescue a criminal who was also killed. Jesus, I can't believe Charley would do a thing like that. Charley has never shot anybody who wasn't shooting at him first. I burn the paper because I don't want Jackie to see his daddy's picture. Charley is out there somewhere right now running from the law, being chased like a rabbit by a bunch of guys with guns. The paper says they even got airplanes flying around looking for him.

I play the radio and try not to think of Charley alone in the world. I try and remember the times we danced, how he held me and told me how much he loved me. I try and remember the nights of our passion, the way his mouth tasted, the way his body felt. I try and think of that silly grin he sometimes got when I said something he thought was funny. I can't think of him the way he is now, running for his life. My love chases after him but can never quite catch him and hold him long enough to heal his troubles.

I've been made an offer to perform in a stage show: "Crime Does Not Pay." I'd play myself, the wife of Pretty Boy Floyd. The man who wants me to do it calls himself "the Professor" — of what I do not know. He's a slick talker, says we can take the show to the Chicago World's Fair where thousands would pay to hear a "living testimony" by the wife of one of the nation's most notorious outlaws. The living testimony of course would be all about why people shouldn't commit crime and how I personally can attest to that. The Professor wants Jackie to be in the show too.

I wouldn't do it but for our son. I've no money, no way of making much in these times. Charley sends some when he can, but nothing lately. The Professor is offering me twenty-five percent of the take, says we'll clean up in Chicago.

"We stand to make thousands, Ruby."

He has flattering eyes and a wet smile. I don't doubt that he has more on his mind than just making money when he looks at me.

It is only later after I signed a contract that I learned the Professor made a film about nudists he tried to sell but got arrested instead for "distribution of illegal and obscene material."

"I hope you don't expect me to take my clothes off and prance around naked," I tell him when I find out about his past.

"Why it was all just a big mistake, Ruby," he tells me. "It was a nature film about a way of life some people enjoy — sun worshipers! People just don't understand nothing about freedom and art! But that's a hell of an idea, you taking off your clothes, come to think about it." He laughs, but I don't see anything funny about it.

He wants me and Jackie to wear Indian costumes.

I hate Charley for what he's turned me into — a "living testimony against lawlessness." A goddamn exhibition like they have in the circus — like the Bearded Lady, or the Dog-face Boy!

Jesus, Charley, didn't our love mean more to you than that?

Pretty Boy Floyd

Later I hear Verne Miller got killed. Whoever killed him drove him up to Detroit and dumped him. The way I hear it, they'd worked the guy over pretty good, maybe tortured him before they murdered him. Why they drove him all the way to Detroit, I can't say, except that if Johnny Lazia was behind it, he probably didn't want even the stink of Verne's body within a thousand miles of him. I can't say he didn't have it coming, but from his own people? I don't know who I can trust anymore. That's the one good thing about family; at least you can trust your family.

Next thing I hear is Ruby's doing stage shows, her and Jackie. Some huckster has talked her into going around the country telling people how crime doesn't pay. It breaks my heart to think she would do something like that. I send her letters asking her not to do it but I don't get a reply. I call Bradley. He says he heard the same thing about her doing stage shows about me. Said he heard she was promised a lot of money to do it.

"Jesus, my own wife, Bradley. My own family."

"Hell, I know it," he says. His voice sounds weary. "Goddamn, Choc, did you do it, what they said?"

"Kansas City?"

"Yeah, Kansas City."

"I was there, but I didn't shoot anybody."

I hear the long silence of his doubt.

"You don't believe me do you Bradley?"

"Sure, I believe you. You're my brother. I'm supposed to believe you. I'm family."

"I didn't shoot anybody in K.C.," I tell him.

"The papers are quoting the FBI about how they're going to track you down, Choc, how they'll capture you dead or alive. That J. Edgar Hoover has sworn an oath against you."

I hear the tremble in his voice. It sounds like he's a long way off, like a train fading into the lonesome night. It feels like I'm a million miles away from him and all the rest of my kin. I close my eyes and see us all sitting around the table, Bradley and E.W. and all my sisters, Mother and Daddy Walter — a platter of fried chicken, biscuits, gravy, mashed potatoes, yams, peas, apple pie. Eating, laughing, later warm in our beds, the muffled sounds of voices coming from the other rooms, the warm black night like a blanket around us. I tell Bradley I got to go, and hang up quickly before I change my mind, or he changes it for me.

Not long after Miller is found bound by ropes, his body full of burn marks and ice pick wounds, somebody kills Johnny Lazia in front of his wife. Same people I'm guessing who killed Miller. Or maybe it was the cops who killed him out of revenge. Who knows? All I know is I not only have to worry about the cops getting me, but also the same people who killed Miller and Lazia coming after me.

"Rich, we need to get the hell out of Dodge and stay the hell out," I tell Adam.

"Then let's ride," he says.

And that's what we do: we ride the hell out of Dodge under a moon that looks like the grin of a dead man.

"Love Letters in the Sand" is playing on the radio.

One of Ruby's favorite songs.

I feel her dancing with me.
Somebody pulls down a shade.
Darkness everywhere.
Tell them Pretty Boy was here.

19

Pretty Boy Floyd

I find Ruby in the Pfister Hotel in Milwaukee. Nice place.

"What are you doing here?" I say.

"What are *you* doing here, Charley?"

"Is it true you're going around telling lies about me?"

"Oh, Jesus. You don't understand a thing do you?"

Jackie's asleep on the bed, wearing a little Indian suit — a beaded headband with a feather in it.

"You turning our boy into a freak?"

The street noise from down on Wisconsin Avenue skitters up the walls, enters through the open window: horns blaring, music, the *rat-a-tat-tat* of a jackhammer. The sky is as gray as my mood. My wife and kid turned into a pair of trained monkeys for the sake of making money I don't have to give them.

"You know how this hurts me, Ruby?"

"You ever stop to think of how what you're doing hurts me and your son?" she says.

"That's all I think about all the time. What else do I have to think about?"

"I'm sure you got plenty to think about, Charley. That whore girlfriend of yours, for one."

"Jesus, you know she doesn't mean anything to me."

"Like hell, Charley. Like hell."

Ruby lights a cigarette she takes from a silver case that's got her initials engraved on it. Not something you'd find in the five and dime. I wonder who bought it for her.

She stands by the window in her red dress that looks like neon on her and so good I can't take my eyes off her. If anything, she gets better-looking every time I see her. The dull light and cigarette smoke that surround her make it look like she's standing in a cloud. I get close to her, so close I can smell her and there's nothing like the way a woman smells to a man who wants her as bad as I want Ruby.

"I hate it we're like this," I say.

"You're not the only one." She doesn't look at me; instead, she looks out toward the lifeless Wisconsin sky.

"I need you now worse than anything," I tell her. I mean it, too.

"Charley, you can't just look me up whenever you get a little lonesome. I'm not just some piece of ass you can come get whenever you want it for god's sake. I'm not like that whore you keep on the side."

"Ah, Ruby, I wish you wouldn't talk like that."

"I didn't use to, Charley. I didn't use to."

Look at what she's become. I want to scrub the lipstick off her and scrub the hurt out of her heart and scrub away all the bad things I ever did to make her this way.

Adam Richetti is downstairs in the lobby waiting for me. They've got cops everywhere looking for us for what happened in Kansas City. He's wearing two pistols under his jacket just in case. The whole country is wild about taking the criminals off the streets. They captured Machine Gun Kelly in Memphis, and the Texas Rangers killed Bonnie and Clyde down in the Louisiana backwaters — no great loss there. They're going to kill us all before it's over with, me included. Hoover has got big rewards on all our heads: mine, Johnny Dillinger, Alvin Karpis, the Ma Barker gang. He says he's going to see us all in jail or dead, dead, dead.

I take five hundred dollars of the money

we got for Kansas City and I lay it on the bureau by the door, catching a glimpse of myself as I do in the mirror, Ruby reflected behind me still looking out at that empty sky.

"You take this and go back to Oklahoma," I say.

She looks around, sees the money I put on the dresser.

"I mean it," I say. "No wife of mine is going to be made a fool of. No son of mine, either. I'm Charles Arthur Floyd. I'm Pretty Boy Floyd."

"Goddamn you, Charley Floyd. Goddamn you."

She comes at me, her face a storm of anger, regret, pain. She's mad as hell — Indian mad, and I catch her up by the wrists, and before either of us knows it, we're kissing like it's the first time and the last time, like we can't get enough of each other and we're never going to get another chance. We spin and turn, embraced in anger and passion and I don't know what all. I'm hard and I'm pressing against her, my leg between hers. We find a wall and I pin her to it, my hands uplifting the skirt of her dress. The flesh of her thighs just above her nylons is soft and warm under my hands, like warm bread, and I feel the snaps of the garter belt holding her nylons up and unsnap them.

"Jesus, Ruby . . ."

"Goddamn you, Charley," she whispers. "Goddamn you."

I undo myself and push inside her and she is ready for me, more than ready and it's like it's always been between us. She clings to me all the while I'm moving in and out of her. She clings and cries in a soft, broken-hearted way, "Goddamn you, Charley." And before I know it I feel myself shattering inside her, feel her biting down on my neck to keep from screaming, or else to make me feel her pain.

I keep her pinned there, just holding her and letting her hold me and I can't tell if it is her tears or mine streaming down our faces.

Ruby Floyd

How can I tell Charley about the Professor, about the deal I made with him so I could earn enough money to keep Jackie and me alive without having to rely on handouts from family and strangers? How can I tell him and not go crazy and want to kill somebody?

Charley comes and goes like a ghost. One minute there, the next gone. No wonder the

FBI can't catch him. Even my own heart can't catch him.

He appears at my door at the hotel and the next thing I know we're doing it even though I'm mad as hell at him. Jackie asleep on the bed and I don't even know how or why we're doing it except I love him like no woman ever loved any man. Charley's got this power over me I can't explain — the power of love, or whatever you want to call it.

Later, we sit on the bed next to Jackie and Charley strokes his sweet innocent head and calls him a little angel as tears run down his cheeks.

"I hate it we have to be like this," Charley says.

"Then do something about it."

"What, Ruby? What can I do about it? What choices do I have? I give myself up, and they'll put me in prison the rest of my life, or give me the chair because of those cops who got shot. That what you want, to see them fry me?"

"Don't talk that way," I tell him.

"What would it do to him?" Charley says, looking down at Jackie. "What would it do to him to know his old man got electrocuted by the cops?"

"I'll write the governor," I say. "I'll write

him and beg him to give you mercy."

"Oh, fuck that," Charley says, suddenly angry. "Don't be such a dope, Ruby. I mean, Jesus, we're not dealing with kid stuff here. They got me murdering half the cops in the country and robbing all the banks."

"Charley, what are we going to do?"

He looks at me and his face softens into that handsome face I first knew way back in Aikens the first time we met at the dance. He's wearing a powder-blue suit and a silk shirt and silk tie, but he's the same farm kid I knew back then.

"I don't know, baby," he says. "I just really don't know."

And for the first time ever, I see that Charley is afraid. He kisses Jackie and says, "Buy him a nice suit with some of that money, huh. I don't want him running around dressed like a little Indian."

"I can't make you no promises, Charley. We got to live too, you know."

He starts to flush with anger again, then says, "Hell, I know you do, Ruby. After what all I've put you through. I know you got to do what you think is right for the two of you. Just do the best you can, huh?"

He kisses me softly, then slips away. My love cannot hold him. The love of his child cannot hold him. Nothing can hold him now except maybe the arms of angels.

Adam Richetti

Me and Charley drive all night out of Milwaukee. Charley doesn't say too much. Instead he bites on a bottle of whiskey pretty steady. I want to ask him how it went with Ruby, but I can smell perfume on him and pretty much guess how it went. It's been a long time since I had a woman and smelling that perfume made me want to find one. I asked him if we might stop long enough while we're in Chicago and get a couple of girls but he doesn't say anything. It starts to rain.

"We are going to Chicago, right?" I say, after a long time of driving in the wet darkness.

"Yeah," he says. "We're going to meet Johnny Dillinger."

"Well, now that sounds like a solid plan."

He passes me the bottle and I take a bite then pass it back.

"I think we can do some good joining up with Johnny," I say.

But Charley doesn't say anything. He's usually pretty jovial, but not tonight and not lately.

"Women," I say. "They'll drive you nuts.

Can't live with them, can't live without them."

"Ain't that the truth."

We see the lights of Chicago off in the distance twinkling like a thousand diamonds dangling from a black velvet curtain.

"Look," I say. "I'm all for joining up with Johnny Dillinger, but I got to score me some pussy, Choc. I mean I'm walking around like I got one foot nailed to the floor. That's what that stuff will do to you, you go too long without it."

He looks at me with about as close to a grin as I've seen lately.

"Damn it, Rich, you think there's anything worse God ever made than a woman for driving a guy nuts?"

"I'd sure as shit like to see it if there was."

"Me too."

Off to my left I can see the city's lights floating in the black waters of Lake Michigan. I can smell the water through the open wing vent and it smells like good fortune to me. I think we're going to do us some good joining up with Johnny Dillinger. He's been developing quite a reputation since I last ran into him up at the reformatory. The way I see it, Pretty Boy Floyd, me and John D will be quite a force to be reckoned with. But right now all I can think about is what

I ain't had in awhile and it's driving me crazy.

Pretty Boy Floyd

I'd put a call in to Dillinger before we left Milwaukee, told him I was on my way to Chicago. He said, sure, come on Pretty Boy. Did you know they killed about all of us, that fucking FBI did?

I told him I'd been reading the newspapers same as him.

We're a dying breed, he said. Then he laughed and I could hear the phlegm crackle in the back of his throat and music somewhere off in the background and a woman's laughter.

I told him we'd be arriving the following night and he told us where to meet him — at a diner named Joe's Hash House in Cicero.

"You think you can find it?" he said.

"Yeah, I can find anything," I said, "and a good thing too, because Richetti couldn't find his nuts with both hands."

Dillinger laughs like hell, says, "Okay then."

"They say he's got one the size of a salami," Rich says as we get near enough to Chicago to see the city lights.

"What the hell you talking about?" I say,

because I'm only half listening to the conversation since we left Milwaukee. Some of it is Rich saying something about how he wants to get laid when we get to Chicago.

"Johnny," he says. "I heard tell when we were up in Michigan City together he had one big as a salami."

"Seems like you mentioned it before," I say. "You got a thing about how big Dillinger's dick is?"

"No, I ain't queer or nothing," he says. "It's just that everybody was talking about it up there in the reformatory."

"Sounds like you're queer for the guy."

"Hell no! Only thing I'm queer for is quim."

"Oh hell, just find us Cicero on that map, will you."

Boozers and sex addicts.
I feel I'm part of a
traveling circus.
& crazy clowns everywhere
my eyes full of stardust.

20

Pretty Boy Floyd

We meet Dillinger at the diner. He's with a hot little number calls herself Irma. Rich is about to pop his eyeballs staring at her. Dillinger acts as though he doesn't care that Rich is practically eating Irma up with his eyes. John Dillinger is a real cool customer.

"You see where the FBI's got that little prick Baby Face Nelson as Public Enemy Number One?" Dillinger says, tapping a newspaper with Baby Face Nelson's photograph on the front page.

The guy seems a little bit snobbish when it comes to certain things like his reputation as a bad man. He wears red socks, I notice, when we walk up to the booth he and Irma are sitting in. Irma's hair is dyed platinum and she has it bobbed and her skin is as smooth and pale as milk. She's leaning on Dillinger like he's a life raft and she's sinking in an ocean of regret. He hardly pays her any attention. She pouts, laughs, smokes her cigarettes and drinks a chocolate malted. Her lips are a little red bow with a dab of malted froth which Rich and me watch her lick off.

"Who cares who the G-Men list as number one?" I say. "Better him than us, right? Let him take the heat."

"I guess you got a point, Pretty Boy," Dillinger says.

"I don't much care to be called that."

He takes his cigarette from the ashtray where it's been smoldering and takes a draw from it and exhales through his nose French style. His hair is slicked back and his eyes try and look right through me. He is wearing a dark blue suit like a banker would wear and a silk tie held by a gold clasp. He's a good dresser except those red socks just don't go with anything. But who's going to tell him they don't?

"Sure, whatever you want, Floyd," he says. "I'll call you fucking Santa Claus that's what you want me to call you."

"I'm Adam," Rich says to Irma and holds his hand out for her to take it.

"Nice to meet cha," Irma says and offers Rich her hand, which has a ring on every finger. It's a fine hand, slender with long fingers and red-painted nails — the same color red as her mouth. I can almost hear Rich thinking where he'd like Irma to put that nice hand of hers. She giggles when he takes it and says, nice to meet you too.

"I'm ready to do some business, you?" Dillinger says. He's got this low, rough voice sounds something like a tire crunching over gravel.

"That's what we're here for," I say. "To do some business."

"You I heard of," he says, talking about me but looking at Rich. "But you, I don't know."

"I was up at reform school in Michigan City with you a long time ago," Rich says.

"No shit."

"Yeah."

"What were you in for?"

Rich snorts. He's too embarrassed to say.

"Stealing typewriters," I say. "Boy wonder here got nabbed stealing typewriters."

John grins and the grin borders on being almost evil.

"Let me ask you something," he says to Rich.

"Sure."

"How you figure to make any dough stealing typewriters?"

"What'd I know? I was just a kid."

"I bet you probably got a hernia carrying 'em." Dillinger snorts.

Irma giggles. We order cheeseburgers and French fries and some cherry Cokes.

John Dillinger

Irma and me meet Pretty Boy Floyd and his partner, a guy named Richetti. Innocent-faced little cocksucker, that's for sure. He's got eyes and a boner for Irma right off the bat, tongue hanging down like a goddamn meat tie. I don't care, because everybody knows once Johnny Dillinger has boned a girl, she's his for life. Let the little dago prick slobber all he wants.

Pretty Boy says he wants to hook up and pull a few bank jobs. Hell, I ain't opposed, except I know through the grapevine that all Pretty Boy's partners have gone down from police bullets. Either Pretty Boy is real lucky, or his partners are real unlucky. I see he limps a little. I ask him about it, he tells me he got shot in the ankle trying to go see his wife. I ask him was it worth it, getting shot in the ankle. He says he doesn't know because he never got to see her, had to shoot it out with a bunch of farmers with guns. I tell him the worst thing you can do is get into it with a bunch of hayseeds packing heat. He says yeah he knows.

While me and Irma were sitting there waiting for them to show, I read in the Chicago *Tribune* where the Feds got that little prick bastard Baby Face Nelson listed as Public Enemy Number One. The punk has no style. All these guys getting attention because they got Baby faces, or Pretty faces, or innocent faces like this Richetti guy. What's this world coming to? Maybe the Feds figure guys with pretty little baby faces will be easier to bring down than me. Hoover. What's he know?

I'll give Pretty Boy one thing: the guy knows how to dress. Richetti, on the other hand, dresses like what he is: a wop just off the banana boats. He reminds me of every dago I ever met, greasy little bastards with hard-ons.

"Rich here is looking to get laid," Pretty Boy says, after we've had a little something to eat and discussed a bank in South Bend I think might be an easy job.

"I'll bet he is," I say.

"What's that supposed to mean?" this Rich guy says.

"Whatever you want it to mean." I don't try and hide the fact I don't like the fucker.

"Hey," Pretty Boy says, trying to be the peacemaker. "We're all here just to have a good time, make a little money, right?"

"Sure, sure. I know a club where the booze is good and the women are easy," I say, to try and show I'm a guy who can make the peace when I need to make it. What the hell, ain't probably none of us are going to live very long — might as well live fast and have some fun for as long as we can.

"Just money and pussy," I say, "There ain't nothing better in life."

Pretty Boy and Richetti follow me and Irma into Chicago, him driving his canary yellow Ford roadster. Son of a bitch has got style I'll give him that.

Adam Richetti

First time I lay eyes on Johnny Dillinger's woman I'm gone. I ain't had no quim since the last time me and Charley took Beulah and Rose out in Kansas City before the shootout. Something about a gunfight makes me horny as hell; me and Choc have been on the run ever since, no time to get paid, no time to get laid. All I'm getting these days is a visit from Rosy Palm and her five sisters. So when I first lay eyes on Irma I'm ready to do something rash if I have to because I can tell she's got eyes for me too.

And when she shakes my hand, she scratches a fingernail across my palm, which means only one thing. But I have to watch myself here because I hear that not only has Dillinger got one the size of a bratwurst, but a hair-trigger temper to match. That, and we're here to do some business with the guy and if I fuck it up, either he or Charley might shoot me. But someway, somehow, I just know I got to have Irma.

We all go out to a speakeasy and the music is loud and the booze good and there are plenty of girls to be had if a guy wants. Charley takes up with a redhead right away who is sitting with a couple of other girls. I guess I could move on one of the other girls at the table, but I don't want to. It's funny how a guy can get something in his mind that's as crazy as trying to take another guy's girl from him. It's like some sort of an addiction. And after awhile you ain't sure if it's the girl you want as much as it is just to see if you can get her. In this case, it's not only crazy it's stupid. But then I never claimed to be no genius.

Dillinger starts drinking hard and throwing his money around, to impress Irma I suppose, maybe to impress Charley too. He flirts with the cigarette girl who comes around and sells him a pack of smokes. He acts like Irma doesn't mean a thing to him. Which is fine by me, because underneath the table she's scratching my palm again and I'm going nuts with desire.

Finally Dillinger says he has to take a leak and leaves the two of us alone. Big mistake. Charley is dancing with the redhead and I can tell he sure as hell isn't going to be lonely tonight.

"What you want to do about this?" I say to Irma.

"You mean this?" she says, scratching my palm again.

"Yeah, that."

"I don't know, what cha got in mind, Richy?"

"I got in mind to take you out into the parking lot," I say.

"Oh you do, huh?"

"Don't tease me, Irma, I'm about to bust my pants."

"Oh, is that what that is?" she says, her hand tracing upward on my thigh until she reaches my hard. "I thought maybe you were packing a pistol in there."

"Jesus," I say. "Let's get out of here."

"Oh, we can't Richy, Johnny will be back any second. He'd kill us both, he thought we was up to no good."

I must have had a look on my face that made her pity me, for the next thing I know she's got me out of my pants and is stroking me right there under the table and talking baby talk to me at the same time, saying things like, "Oh sweety, you like what mamma's doing to you?"

I can't even talk.

From way across the room I see Dillinger coming out of the lavatory.

"Hurry up," I whisper to Irma, "Johnny's on his way back to the table."

She got a grip on my pistol like you wouldn't believe and I can tell this ain't the first time she's ever done something like this. She's a real pro.

"That's some gun you got Richy," she's saying.

I'm squirming in my seat because it's feeling like heaven what she's doing to me and I know if Dillinger comes over to the table there's no way he's not going to notice what's going on. I'm asking myself am I ready to take a bullet in the head for this.

"Hurry up!"

"I'm hurrying, baby. Sweet mamma's hurrying to make her man's gun go off."

Her breath is warm and syrupy sweet and she's tossing me like I'm a martini she's making for party guests.

Dillinger is getting closer.

Christ, I know he's going to catch on even before he gets to the table, he'd have to be blind not to see what's going on.

But I'm so close by now I know there's no stopping what's about to happen. I'm at that place — caught between panic and pleasure. I got to decide: do I let Irma get me off and take one between the eyes, or do I have her stop?

Dillinger's about ten, fifteen feet away now. I see him reaching inside his coat. I figure he's reaching for his gun. The whole table could be knocking up and down for all I know. My legs are shaking so bad I know I couldn't get up and run if I had to. The music is loud, fast, like jungle music. People are dancing like crazy, there's smoke everywhere, laughter, loud voices. I feel myself erupting.

Some guy taps Dillinger on the shoulder and he turns and speaks to the guy just as Irma is pulling my trigger, cooing in my ear. . . . "Oh Richy, what a nasty little boy you are."

I'm dizzy, ready to take a bullet I have to. Irma keeps squeezing my trigger until I'm out of lead.

I clasp my hand over Irma's, say, "That did it." She says, "Don't I know it" and excuses herself saying she has to go to the powder room. I try and look cool just as Dillinger finishes talking to the guy and comes over and sits down across from me. He lifts his drink and says as he's watching Irma disappear through the crowd, "I bet you'd like to get in her pants, wouldn't you?"

I don't say anything.

"Well, forget about it, *goombah.* Because once a girl has had big John in her, she ain't interested in nobody else."

He says this real smug, but not as smug as I'm feeling just then.

I purposely spill a drink in my lap, grab a napkin and make the excuse I got to clean myself up. Dillinger looks at me like I'm a mutt. Maybe I am. My legs are like rubber, but I'm feeling higher than I've been since we shot all those cops back in Kansas City.

Thing like this, I ain't never going to forget, long as I live.

Pretty Boy Floyd

It's later back in our hotel room that Rich tells me what happened at the speakeasy.

"You nuts, or what?" I say. "Dillinger would have caught you, he'd have put a bullet between your eyes. So would I was it my girl."

"Tell you the truth," he says, "I was ready to die if it came to that. . . . You can't even imagine how damn good it felt." He is lying on the bed in his undershirt and trousers and his shoes on. A .45 in a shoulder holster dangles under his left arm.

"For a lousy piece of tail," I say. "You risked getting shot and messing up our deal over something you could have done for yourself."

"Yeah, but believe me, it wouldn't have been nearly as good I was to have done it for myself. I've been doing it for myself for days now," he says. "And you know what the best part was?"

I'm looking out the window like I always do these days, looking for cops or the Feds. Ever since Kansas City I know the heat is on worse than it's ever been. J. Edgar Hoover would like nothing better than to see his boys put me on a block of ice.

"The best part was," Rich says, without me asking, "was getting her to do it right there in the joint with everybody sitting around. I got John Dillinger's girl to do me right there in front of everybody, including him."

Rich has been drinking a lot lately, a lot more than I'd like him to. Half his words come out slurred. Why is it I always got to hook up with guys who drink too much? Maybe that's what got them killed — the booze made them sloppy.

"That kind of thinking will get you killed," I tell him. "Get me killed too if I'm with you."

He leans over and turns off the bedside light and the room goes dark except for the neon glow of a theater marquee across the street. I feel like I'm in another world. Two seconds later Rich is snoring, working off his drunk in his own world. Me, I'm alone again. Even when I'm with somebody, I'm alone. Earlier I had taken the redhead at the club I'd been dancing with out to my car and we ended up in the backseat, our pants down around our ankles, but the whole time I was feeling alone. Even when she was calling my name, I was feeling alone.

The sweet times have become a bitter taste in my mouth.

I am a river that no longer flows free.

The star fallen from the sky.

The yesterday, of all yesterdays.

The man without a shadow.

I am condemned.

21

Pretty Boy Floyd

We rob the bank in South Bend. It turns into another shootout, Homer Van Meter, one of John Dillinger's guys takes one in the leg. In turn somebody shoots the guy who shot him — I don't know who, I just know it wasn't me. We get away with almost four grand — split four ways, it's a grand apiece. We eat pie in a café in Elkhart and discuss our future as a gang. Van Meter isn't shot as bad as we thought.

Dillinger says, "Shit, I think I'll go back to flying solo."

He looks at me, at Van Meter, back to me.

"Suit yourself," I say.

"Sure John, whatever you say," Van Meter says. "This ain't exactly working out like I hoped it would."

We eat our pie and drink our coffee in silence for a while, then Dillinger says, "It's just that a grand won't last me a week the way I spend dough. Irma likes to shop like you wouldn't believe. Last week she came home with all new satin underwear. Red. Costs me almost fifty bucks just for stuff she puts on so I can take it right back off again. Dames, what you going to do?"

"Why didn't you make her take the underwear back?" Rich says.

"Take it back! What are you, nuts? Don't you know anything about women?"

The thought of Irma is still twisting around inside of Rich like a worm in a hot skillet; he still talks about her every damn night and I know he's trying to needle Dillinger.

"Women like Irma," Dillinger says, "you don't say no to, especially when it comes to them wanting to make themselves sexy for you." Dillinger is smoking a Lucky Strike, has his fedora pushed back. He's as tough as a cop.

"Let me tell you something there, dago," he says to Richetti. "Two things I'm an expert on are women and banks."

I'm waiting for the other shoe to drop from Rich's mouth — like him telling Dillinger how he got Irma to give him a number under the table in that speakeasy. I give Rich the eye to warn him he better not even dare open his trap about that business. Two things will get you killed quicker than anything with guys like Dillinger: stealing their money, and stealing their women.

"You got to do what you got to do, John," I tell him. "Just like me and Rich have to do what we got to do."

"Sure, I understand that," he says. "We're all pros here, right? I mean I just can't get used to working with a crew. I've always liked going solo, guess I always will till the day the feds gun me down."

Van Meter excuses himself saying he has to go to the bathroom, he thinks maybe his leg is bleeding again. He's got a vial of cocaine pills he's been taking since he got shot and his eyes are dreamy.

Dillinger orders another slice of cherry pie, eats it and smokes and drinks his coffee in between bites. After we leave the café and go our separate ways, Rich says, "That cherry pie was the same color as Irma's red mouth."

"It's a good thing he didn't find out about you two," I say, "or I'd be looking for another partner."

"You want a drink of this?" Rich says, extending a pint bottle of bourbon that's half gone.

"Lay off the juice, okay?"

"Wadda you my mother?"

"Maybe we should call the girls, because something has to bring a little pleasure back into our miserable lives."

"Say, that ain't a bad idea."

I shrug, maybe I should pack up, head back to Oklahoma and find Ruby and make peace with her.

"Yeah, let's call the girls," Rich says. "I can't go the rest of my life on that hand-job Irma gave me, now can I?" He grins and winks; he's hard not to like in spite of his weakness for booze and dames.

That evening we drive back to Toledo and call Beulah and Rose and tell them to take the next train and meet us there. They squeal like schoolgirls. Afterwards, Rich and I find a brothel down on Summit Street near Cherry Avenue where they've got nothing but Chinese girls working. It's a warm night and you can smell the stink of dead fish from the Maumee River drifting up toward the city.

"I never had a Chinese, you?" Rich says.

"No, that's why we're going."

"Jesus, I hear they got them slanty pussies, you think that's true?"

"I hope not," I say. "I'm trying hard to go straight."

Rich laughs like hell. He's a good audience for my jokes.

That night I sleep in a tiny hard bed with a girl named Mai. She's pretty and small and has skin like a porcelain China doll and there's something about her that makes me want to be gentle with her. She says to me at one point early on, "You want to love me rough, it okay."

"No, I don't want to love you rough," I tell her. "I want to love you easy."

Her English is pretty good and afterward when we're lying in bed in the dark and I'm smoking a cigarette, she begins to tell me about her family in Canton province.

"The only Canton I know is about a hundred miles from here," I tell her.

"No, no, not that place," she says all serious, like I don't know the real difference.

She tells me her mother and father are old and that she has several brothers and sisters — all of whom are still in China, but one sister she calls Lu. Says this Lu came to America with her and they worked in the brothels for a time together in San Francisco, Denver and Detroit before here. She says her sister met a rich man in Detroit and they got married, but then there was this accident and her sister ended up dead but that she didn't know exactly what happened or why and never could find out anything more about it. She says this in a quavering little voice like she was about to cry, but didn't.

"I'll bet your sister was pretty, just like you," I say.

She snuggles against me like a child. I put my arm around her and feel like hell because she seems too nice and innocent to do this kind of work — sleeping with guys like me for money. But money makes whores out of everybody. It's not something I feel good about, the things I've done for money. But like little Mai, I'm probably going to keep on doing those things until I can't anymore.

Beulah Baird

"Guess what?" I say to Rose, the evening when Charley calls from Toledo.

"It's them, right? It's Charley and Rich."

"They want us to catch the train to Toledo and meet them there."

"Oh gawd, we gonna?"

Sometimes I wish Rose would do some of her own thinking. I guess the good Lord gave her the looks and me the brains. Sometimes I wish it were the other way around.

"We could stay put and keep seeing Marvin and Eddy," I say. Marvin and Eddy are two local hoods whose gift, you might say, is strong-arming people. Marvin's the one I've been putting in time with and Rose has been hooked up with Eddy.

"Jeez, I'm about tired of those goons," Rose says.

"So I should tell them yes?"

"Yes!" She squeals like a kid. I take my hand off the receiver and tell Charley we'll catch the next train, can he wire us some dough for the tickets.

"Sure," he says. "I'll go down to Western Union and wire it now."

I still get dizzy sometimes when I move too fast. I guess getting shot in the head you got to expect that. So I try not to move too fast, but Rose and me are packed and down at the Western Union within the hour. After, we catch a cab over to the train station — the same station they say Charley and Rich and Verne Miller shot all those cops. It's raining and the streets outside the station are wet and the streetlights are reflected in the wet streets and it all seems so goddamn lonely like because it's late at night and there's just me and Rose and those empty wet streets and the sound of trains.

We are sitting on the hard wood benches, the tickets for Toledo in our purses when a couple of sailors come up and sit across from us and start a conversation.

"Where you girls headed this late hour?" one of them says. He's young, pink-faced, like a farmboy. Good-looking kid.

"We're going to Toledo to meet our boyfriends," Rose pipes up.

"Oh yeah?" the sailor says. "What's the matter, Kansas City got no real men you got to go all the way to Toledo?"

"Real funny," Rose says. "But our guys are special."

"What's so special about guys in Toledo?" the other sailor says. He's older and has a moustache and looks like he's been around a lot.

I nudge Rose with my elbow so she doesn't say too much.

"Nothing," I say instead. "We're just the kind of girls who are faithful to the men we love."

"Oh," the older sailor says. "Where have I heard that before?" He nudges his buddy. "Ain't all dames the same, though."

"Ah, I don't know," says the younger sailor. "These look like some pretty swell girls." Then he looks at me and says, "How about we take you girls for a drink while you're waiting for your train. There's a nice little club just down the street."

"We better stay here," I say.

Then Rose pops up and says: "Excuse us a moment while we go powder our noses" and jerks me by the arm toward the ladies' room.

"What's with you?" I say, once we get into the lavatory. It smells like industrial soap, and that isn't all.

"Why not go with them for a drink?" she says. "Our train don't leave until six in the morning."

"Because," I say.

"It's just a drink," she says. "I mean who's to know?"

"Rose, we going to be tramps all our lives? Go with just any man who asks us?"

"Probably," she says. "As long as we got the looks that guys are still interested in. Someday we might not have our looks, then what? You ever think of that?"

She's got a point, though I don't know quite what. We end up going with the two sailors whose names turn out to be Jerry and Stu and we have a pretty good time but get a little loaded and end up with them at a fleabag hotel a block from the train station. We barely make it back in time to catch the morning flyer.

"Jeez, Rose, we really are trampy," I say as we watch the wet Missouri countryside drift away. Rain runs over the window like tears.

"It's just the way it is, Beulah," she says. "We're just a couple of girls trying to get by with the gifts God gave us. What's the difference between us and some gals who get married to the wrong guys? I mean in a way, all women are tramps, but at least we're happy. We ain't stuck with some guy all he wants to do is sit around and listen to the radio."

I think of Charley, of dead cops, of wet streets and the tattoo the older sailor had on his chest — a large blue anchor out of which grew gray curly hairs. The weight of his anchor feeling like it was pressing onto me and dragging me down to the bottom of some deep, deep ocean. I knew the day would come when men would no longer want to buy us a drink or call us long distance and tell us to meet them somewhere or give us dough for dresses and perfume. Still, it didn't make me feel any better knowing what we were, what we'd always been.

Ruby Floyd Leonard

I got two letters today: one from my ex saying that he had filed for divorce and one from Charley saying how much he missed me and Jackie. I didn't know which one to read first, so I just picked the one on top.

Dear Ruby,

I have seen a lawyer and filed for divorce from you. I kept thinking you'd change your mind and come back to me, that you'd see that Charley Floyd doesn't love you the way I do. But it is evident now that you aren't coming back and never will. I guess some men are just fools and I was one of them. Just like you're a fool for Charley Floyd. Well, all I can say is, no man ever loved you more than me, Charley Floyd included.

Your former husband,
Leroy

My darling Ruby,

You probably heard about my latest troubles — that whole business in Kansas City. What they're saying about me isn't true — I never done it — shot any cops. You know me. I'm a lover, not a killer. How's Jackie? Give him a big hug and kiss for me. Me and Rich are on the lam still because the cops are never going to believe I'm innocent and if they catch us we're both dead men, I can tell you that with all certainty. I plan on coming back to Sallisaw soon, to see you and Jackie and Bradley and E.W. and Mother. I miss you all so terribly and this ain't no kind of life for any man. I wish to God I'd never started down the road I did. But it's too late to have regrets now. I am going to try and find a way to get out of the country, Spain or France maybe. Rich says Italy is nice — that's where his people come from. Maybe we'll go there, but I mean to come and get you and Jackie and take you with me. I could start over in a new country, maybe start a little business, be a regular Joe. What do you think? Send me your reply general delivery Buffalo, New York. That's where I'll be soon.

All my love, Charley.

P.S.

I sure do miss all the good things a man misses with his wife and hope you feel the same. It breaks my heart to think you might find yourself another man. I don't think I could stand the news were I to hear of it.

Both letters make me feel a little torn up inside. Why can't love be easy? Why can't we just find somebody and love them forever and let them love us forever? The Professor comes out of the bathroom wearing a bathrobe and smelling of bay rum. He has skinny pale legs and large ears and halitosis.

If Charley ever found out it would break his heart, just as my own is broken whenever I think about what our love did to us.

I shudder when he touches me, brings his sour mouth near mine.

Pretty Boy Floyd

I have a dream that I'm talking to Jesse James. We're in his house in St. Joe, sitting around having coffee and I see a crooked picture on the wall. I know what's going to happen and I want to tell him, "Jess, don't straighten that picture, because if you do, Bob Ford's going to shoot you through the head." But I can't get the words out.

He seems like a nice man, very soft-spoken, and says, "I hear you robbed more banks than me and Frank and the Youngers put together."

How does he know?

He has a wife and two lovely children; they all have blue eyes, just like Jesse.

"She's my cousin, you know," he says when his wife brings us fresh-baked cookies, kisses him on the forehead and drifts away. "Lots of folks said it was wrong for me to marry my cousin. But I never did abide by what other folks thought." He leans forward and takes a cookie and dips it in a glass of fresh goat's milk. "And you shouldn't either, Charley."

I feel I'm in the presence of glory. Jess has grown a beard and wears a red cravat and carpet slippers. He has a stack of newspapers by his chairs; some are several months old, for I can see their dates.

"It's a good thing," he says, munching the cookie, drops of milk dew in his beard.

"What's a good thing?" I say.

"Oh, you know, Charley. This," he says. But I don't know what he means.

One of his children floats into the room, hovers there in the air between us and floats out again. I hear strange moaning from another room, then a woman crying and realize that the floating child is my own son, Jackie, and not Jesse's boy.

I look and the picture on the wall is straight. I feel relieved, for now he won't have to stand on a chair to fix it and have Bob Ford fire a pistol into his skull. Jesse's wife returns only it is not his wife, but Ruby, and she comes and kisses him on the mouth and his hands run over the swell of her hips and she moans with pleasure and I can hardly stand what I'm seeing.

He looks past her, one blue eye fixed on me as if to say, See, I can have any woman I want including Ruby.

I am fevered with hatred and when he

says, “Oh, look, that picture needs straightening,” and pulls free from Ruby’s embrace, I stand and wait for him to step up on the chair and when he does, his back offered up to me like a sacrifice, I pull my .45 and kill him. The explosion wakens me. Only it’s not a gunshot but a clap of thunder outside the window — a morning storm that has swept down on the city with a fury washing the streets and my dreams clean.

The radio crackles with static. Rich is staring out the window and says, “Look at them trees blow. Why hell it might be a tornado.”

My mouth tastes like an ashtray and my heart is a kicking against my ribs trying to free itself from my chest.

“I hope that storm don’t delay the girls arriving,” Rich says, turning away from the window. “I got me a large problem that needs taking care of.”

I can see from the open loose way he wears his bathrobe he has an erection.

I turn my eyes away, ashamed, for him, for me, for the whole world.

22

Pretty Boy Floyd

The sun is an orange ball of flame sinking into the dark waters of Lake Erie. Wind with the kiss of snow behind it sweeps down out of Canada where they make some of the finest whiskey I ever drank. Me and Rich try our hand at fishing — he doesn't know shit about fishing, even how to bait a hook. The girls sit huddled in their coats drinking peach schnapps asking when can we go back to the apartment we've rented.

The way I see it, we're just a couple of regular guys out with our gals fishing and acting normal, except there is nothing normal about it. I used to love to go fishing with Daddy Walter and E.W. and Bradley — just the four of us. We'd catch catfish — big brown ones had blue whiskers and slippery as eels. We'd catch a mess of them and take them back to the house and Daddy

Walter would have me and Bradley drive nails through their heads to a board so E.W. could take a pair of pliers and skin them. Mother would roll the meat in flour seasoned with salt and black pepper and fry them in hot grease. My mouth still waters when I think about it.

I catch two sheepshead and a carp. The sheepshead are fragile creatures and die easily once caught. I try and explain this to Rich.

"Some creatures are like these fish," I tell him. "They can't stand getting caught — they can't stand it so much, they just stop living because they'd rather be dead than caught. I'm like that too." He is nipping on some Canadian whiskey and his face is knotted in confusion about why we're even out here on a pier with fish poles in our hands, the weather cold enough to snow. The carp I pull in is heavy as a water-filled boot.

"That's one big ugly son of a bitch," Rich says, when I reel in the carp. "What we going to do with it?"

"Eat it. But before you can eat it you got to cut out the mud vein." I run a finger along the back to show him where the mud vein is.

"I ain't eating nothing that's got mud in

it," Rich says bitterly.

The girls make faces — "*Eew, eew,* we're not going to eat that slimy thing."

"Then you're just going to starve," I say. It's a mean joke, but I'm feeling a little mean.

The carp has a little oval mouth and its head looks way too small for its body. It has sad little white eyes and scales that shine like dimes under the autumn sky. It slips out of my hand when I take the hook out and flops around on Rich's shoes. Rich pulls out his .45 and threatens to shoot it, until I finally toss it back into the lake and watch it swim away.

We drink the liquor to stay warm and smoke cigarettes as the girls shiver inside their coats while the wind tugs apart their new hairdos. They bitch and moan and Rich keeps threatening to shoot the next fish I catch and it all gets to be so goddamn ridiculous I want to laugh. Hell, it's the most fun I've had in a year.

The only time we feel free to go out in public anymore is after the sun goes down. All day I pace around in the apartment while Rich reads *True Detective* and cuts out stories about us and pastes them in an album. He draws circles around the eyes of John Dillinger and blacks out some of his teeth whenever he finds a photo of him. Most of the stories about us are such lies they're hilarious. The girls read magazines about movie stars and paint their nails and try to get us to do something with them — which ends up being mostly you know what. The girls go out alone sometimes and get their hair done and window-shop but buy little because our funds are drying up. Rich and I haven't pulled a job in months.

We talk on and off about robbing a bank over in Canada.

"Those Mounties always get their man," Rich says.

"How do you know?"

"That's what everybody says."

"Who's everybody?"

"Everybody," he says.

"I want to know who everybody is. You're always saying everybody says this and everybody says that. So who the hell is everybody?"

We argue over the least little thing just to have something to do. It's all this being cooped up that's got us all on edge. Even the sex gets boring after awhile. Rich says to me one night when we go out to get some cigarettes and whiskey — "It's starting to feel like I'm banging my sister, doing it with Rose."

"You banged your sister?"

"No, I ain't never banged my sister," he says. "I'm just saying it's getting to be old hat, is all. I'm about ready for something new, ain't you?"

I have to admit I am too; it's like eating steak every night. No matter how much you might love steak you don't want to eat it every night.

"Maybe we should trade off," I say.

This gets Rich's attention.

"You think they would go for it?"

"Rose might, but Beulah never would."

It takes a second for the joke to sink in.

"Shit," he says. "You're probably right."

I miss Ruby. The more I'm with Beulah, the more I miss Ruby.

"Let's take a trip," I say.

"Where?"

"Aikens. Maybe rob a couple of banks along the way."

"What about the girls?"

"It might do them some good to have a little break from us. We're probably getting to be like eating steak every night to them."

"Steak?"

"What makes you think they're not just as tired of us as we are of them?"

"Steak, huh? Tube steak maybe." He grins.

"Yeah, right."

We tell the girls when we get back we'll be gone for a while. We tell them we're going to go do a few jobs. They want to come with us.

"You remember the last time you were with me when we tried to pull a job," I say.

Beulah touches her head, says, "Do I ever."

We tell them we'll probably be gone a couple of weeks. They don't protest all that much, especially when we give them a hundred bucks.

Next day we drive west, the sun rising out of the dark lake like it's keeping an eye on us. By the time we get to St. Louis, the sun is sinking into the rolling hills, the last rays of light flaring across the land and we have to put the visors down.

I'm always glad to be west of the Mississippi, close to home.

Bradley Floyd

Charley calls long distance, collect, says he and Adam are heading our way and for me to keep an eye out for the law and to meet him outside of Aikens on such and such a day at such and such a time at such and such a place. It's good to hear the voice of my brother even though he sounds weary. I can only imagine the strain he's been under.

I read all the time where he's killed this person or robbed some bank or taken hostages. I read where he supposedly killed all those policemen in Kansas City in a botched attempt to free some crime boss. I read where J. Edgar Hoover has issued a death warrant for him. But it can't be Choc. It can't be the older brother I played baseball with and went fishing with and who tried to keep everybody feeling happy by pulling pranks and joking. It can't be that Choc Floyd.

"How's mother and E.W. and the girls?" he says.

"Everybody is fine. Ruth got married and Flossie had a baby girl."

"Gee, that's good news, ain't it," he says. "I can't wait to see you all."

"How are you doing?"

"Me? Good as gold, kid. Never better."

But I know that he's just putting on an act. Charley never wants anybody to worry about him. All the letters he writes home talk about what it's going to be like someday when we are all together again. And sometimes it's not what he says in his letters, it's what he doesn't say that troubles me.

"Guess what?" he says.

"What?"

"I had the damnedest dream the other

night. I dreamt I was talking to Jesse James."

"That is pretty strange."

"Yeah. It got me to thinking was it possible that maybe I'm him . . . you know, maybe his spirit came back from the dead and I'm him reincarnated."

"Jesus, I don't know much about stuff like that," I say. "That something you learned in the big city, that stuff about reincarnation?"

"Yeah, you really need to read more, kid. I've been doing a lot of reading lately. Trying to figure out what it all means, this life and the next one."

"You think there's a next life after this one, Choc?"

"I'm beginning to believe there has to be. Least I'm sure as hell hoping there is."

There was something fatal in his voice, like a man standing on the railroad tracks with his foot trapped under the rail watching the train coming toward him.

"Maybe we can talk about it when you get here," I say.

"Yeah, I'll see you in a couple of days, kid."

There is a click and he is gone and I realize that we can all be gone quick as a click, quick as a gunshot, quick as a breath.

Adam Richetti

Charley is always on me about my drinking. I ask him what it has to do with him what I do. He says he doesn't want to get shot down dead because I'm a boozehound. I tell him we're probably both going to get shot dead whether I drink or not. He says, "Yeah, but probably a lot sooner than later you keep it up."

My life has come down to this: pussy and drinking, and neither one are getting the job done lately. We ain't robbed nothing since South Bend and all we do is hang out in the apartment and sometimes go out and fish at night. Fish! Jesus H. Christ. We're like a bunch of damn retards.

I like to draw, but I know I'm not any good at it and never could make a stinking dime doing it. I wonder sometimes why God makes people like me: people who don't have no gifts for anything but raising hell and doing wrong. Why does he make some people like me and Charley and others like Charles Lindbergh and President Taft — guys who do great things? I don't get it. It's a crazy world and we're all crazy for living in it. And maybe guys like Charley and me know that and we just do whatever the hell we want to do because we know no matter what we do, it doesn't count for anything. We're never going to be the President of the United States or some hero. Our fate was sealed the moment we stuck our heads out of our mommas' cunts and looked around.

Drinking and being with women makes me feel good. Ain't I got as much right to feel good as Lindbergh and Taft and guys like that?

We drive out of Buffalo and head for Oklahoma. There is a pair of machine guns under a blanket in the backseat. We're what the FBI calls "armed and dangerous" and we plan on staying that way.

We stop in Pittsburgh to have a late lunch and the air is gray with smoke from the steel mills. They got three rivers running right through downtown and they all look dirty and cold, like if you were to jump in them you'd die instantly. The whole town has a stink to it.

"What do you think?" Charley says, eating a roast beef sandwich.

"About what?"

"About maybe robbing a bank here?"

"Hell, why not. It looks like the kind of place that deserves getting some of its banks robbed."

The waitress has a lazy eye but I ask her if she'd like to go out back with me because right now I could go for just about anything different than what I been getting lately.

"Do I look that desperate?" she says, when I ask her.

"No, but I sure as hell am."

"If I had a nickel for every guy who came in here like you," she says, "I'd be rich."

Charley is in the phone booth back of the place calling his brother in Oklahoma. I can see him through glass with chicken wire in it, a little light on above his head. I wonder if a guy could screw a girl in a telephone booth, what that'd be like.

"I got some good Canadian whiskey out in the car," I tell the waitress.

"Is that supposed to turn me on or something?" she says.

"Might loosen you up a little."

"You see this?" She shows me the third finger of her left hand that's got a little silver wedding band on it.

"Yeah, so what?"

"My old man is the cook here. You want me to go get him and see if he'll give his permission for me to go out back with you?"

"Forget about it. I don't want no trouble."

It's starting to rain, which only makes Pittsburgh look more like a place you want to be from and not in.

I take out some cash to pay for our meal,

the waitress looks at it.

"You a salesman or something?" she says.

"No," I say. "I'm a bank robber. Make good money at it too."

"What about your friend back there, he a bank robber too?"

"Yeah, we're notorious. We live the high life."

She looks skeptical, the lazy eye of hers trying to judge whether I'm telling the truth or pulling her leg, which I'd like to pull but for real.

I put a five-spot on the counter, tell her to keep the change.

"Jeez thanks," she says. "Maybe I heard of you two — my husband reads detective magazines all the time."

"Listen," I say. "If I tell you who we are, I'd have to take you along as a hostage."

"Maybe that wouldn't be such a bad thing."

For a moment I almost think she really would want to come along. Then I think what Charley would say if I brought this dame with us. He'd probably throw us both out.

"You were to have come in yesterday, I'd probably have let you take me hostage," she says.

"Why yesterday?"

"I just found out this morning I'm pregnant, going to have a kid." She says this like someone who's been given a life sentence in the state pen. She jerks her head toward the kitchen. "Al's always wanted me to have a kid. Me, I'd just as soon travel all over the country, maybe even rob a bank or two than have a kid. I was always kinda of wild until I met Al."

"You want to know something?"

"What?"

"You're a lot better off right here, having the kid, trust me."

She fills my cup with more coffee, only this time she has a lot sweeter look on her face than before.

"Hey, that stuff I said, about going out back and having a drink with me. I apologize. I'm not as bad as I come across," I say.

"I know you ain't. And I know you guys don't rob banks. You're probably traveling salesmen, probably sell Bibles or encyclopedias, right?"

"Yeah, you're right," I say.

Funny how a little decent conversation can make you feel decent about yourself and about life in general. I tell her it's too bad she's married because she's the kind of gal my mother would have approved of me bringing home to meet the family.

"Thanks, that's a nice thing for you to say."

She smiles and I want to kiss her, but don't. I see her looking out the big picture window at the cars going by. I know that feeling she's got.

Pretty Boy Floyd

We rob a bank just outside Pittsburgh and for the first time I don't feel right about it. There was a guy wearing his work clothes and you could tell he just got off at one of the mills and was cashing his check. I told the clerk to go ahead and cash the guy's check and give him the money and me and Rich took the rest. It made me think that maybe we were stealing the food right out of people's mouths by robbing banks. Rich said I shouldn't worry about it, that we weren't stealing nothing from poor people, we were stealing from the rich guys.

"How you know for sure we're not hurting the little guy?" I say.

"Hell, you ever seen a little guy that owns a bank, buster?"

Still, I feel funny about it for the first time, seeing how that fellow was dressed in those grimy work clothes, the soot creased in his skin from years of slaving away in the mills, his dirty hands taking the cash for the check, the look of relief when I didn't take the few lousy bucks they paid him to break his back all week long. I think of how I'd feel if it were Daddy Walter or one of my people getting robbed of what little they had.

We drive down through the Ozarks and I'm still thinking about it and wondering why this time it got to me, and not all those times before. It's not supposed to get to me, things like that; that sort of thinking will get me killed fast.

I look at Rich who is driving and I see a dead man. I wonder if he looks at me sometimes and sees a dead man too. We're just two dead guys driving toward another sunset.

And another sunset after that
&
until we reach the last sunset.

23

Pretty Boy Floyd

Bradley is waiting for us outside Aikens, just like I'd asked him to do. He's standing in the hot dust next to a weed-choked ditch. Got a straw hat knocked back on his head and chewing a stem of grass. He looks like Daddy Walter. He grins when he sees our flivver pull up and me lean out.

"Whoa boy, you ain't changed a lick," he says when I step out of the car. "Look it you, dressed like a damn banker, that fancy suit, those two-tone shoes. Where's your gold watch?"

I guess maybe I do look like a swell for this neck of the woods. But I like the way a good suit makes me feel like I am somebody and not just some thug robbing banks for a living. Not just some crop-picker, either.

We stand around and chew the fat and once or twice a car or a truck drives past and we turn our backs pretending like we don't want to get a face full of dust, but really so nobody can see our faces. This land is full of my people and friends, but the Feds have got all sorts of rewards out for me and you never know who your true friends are; even Jesse James got shot by his cousin for a few bucks and the glory.

I ask after the family and Bradley says they are all doing fine, says mother is fixing a big Sunday dinner. I don't even realize it is Sunday. The land is still under the heat of an Indian summer day, quiet like a dozing dog, and the red dust coats my shoes. The land has a feel to it like I've never left. The only thing that's changed is me.

We drive the back roads out to mother's place and she throws her arms around my neck with tears running down her cheeks.

"This is Adam Richetti," I say, introducing Adam. "He's Italian."

Mother greets him like he's one of her own.

"Hope you like to eat," she says. "You look like as though you could stand some meat on you."

Rich acts shy, gives her that innocent face of his and says, "Yes ma'am, I like to eat about as much as anything. Us Italians are big eaters."

Some of my sisters are there, Ruth and Rossie May with her new husband and baby, and so is E.W. He's shot up like a weed since I saw him last.

In spite of everybody being there, the place is lacking without Daddy Walter in it. While the food is being prepared, we boys drive out to Daddy Walter's grave. All that's left of Daddy Walter are memories and the small white stone mother paid to have placed at the head of his grave, wind skitters through the grass grown over it. We stand and smoke cigarettes and Bradley passes around a mason jar of shine.

"Drinking's legal now," I say. "No need to still sip corn."

"I know it," Bradley says. "But I prefer it over that taxed whiskey."

The shine is clear as drinking water and hits you like a mule kick.

"This some of yours or did you buy it off somebody?"

"Bought it off somebody," he says. He doesn't say who; old habits are hard to break.

"Remember when Daddy Walter ran a little shine?"

"I was with him lots of times," Bradley says. "We'd race like hell down all these back roads, sometimes with our lights off so the law wouldn't catch us."

"That's why they call it moonshine?" Rich says. "Cause you hauled it at night?"

"Yes sir," Bradley says. "We once hit a dang cow standing in the middle of the dang road. Couldn't see him cause there wasn't any moon that night. Liked to have throwed us through the windshield. Wrecked the front fender of Daddy Walter's Chevrolet, tore his bumper all to hell and busted the headlights off. We both got bumps on our heads."

"Wrecked the cow too, I'll bet," Rich says, grinning over the lip of the Mason jar.

"Wrecked him hell, killed him. We ate cow for three months."

A raven lands in a lightning-struck tree and caws down at us like he's trying to tell us something, warn us, maybe. For a second I feel like I'm standing in that nether-world where Daddy Walter is — the sky has an odd color to it like unpolished brass and I feel like I'm shrinking.

"I sure would like to shoot that machine gun," E.W. says.

"You weren't supposed to notice it," I say.

"Hell, Choc, it's right there under them blankets under the backseat."

"Ah, go ahead and let him," Rich says.

"I'd just as soon you not get to liking

shooting machine guns," I say to E.W., but the look of disappointment on his face causes me to relent.

"Go ahead and get it," I say.

He comes back carrying it like some sort of precious animal, stroking its barrel.

We polish off the shine and I tell Bradley to run the jar out on the prairie, which he does and perches it on the trunk of a dead blackjack tree. I show E.W. how to take the safety off.

"Lean into," I tell him. "She'll jump back on you if you don't lean into it."

He fires a burst that chews up ground ten yards in front of the Mason jar. "Hell, son," Bradley says. "You ain't never going to be a good bank robber shooting like that, let me have a try."

Bradley straddles his feet apart and leans into the Thompson and cuts loose a burst and the jar shatters, the pieces flung into the air like diamonds. He looks pleased with himself.

I take the gun from him and wrap it back in the blanket and tell E.W. to put it back under the seat.

"It's one thing shooting jars," I say. "It's another shooting a man that's shooting back at you."

"Hell, I know it."

"No, I doubt you do."

"Let's go eat some chicken," he says.

I get a bad feeling because when I look, the raven is still perched in the tree; not even machine gun fire scared him. It's a bad sign, I think.

Joe Prince

How I met Pretty Boy Floyd was over Cora shaking her ass. Every weekend night she'd go down to the Dew Drop Inn to shake her ass and I'd go in there to watch her shake it. I never been much good with keeping a woman, but Cora's one I'd like to try and keep. She's my third wife and the best-looking woman in Sequoyah County. My friend Bobby Horton ribs me on how I got her in the first place.

"What'd you do, put a pistol to her head when you was sheriff to make her marry you, Prince?"

Hell I sort of feel like maybe I'm going to have to put a pistol to her head before it's all said and done; either her head or mine, or maybe both. Ever since I met her, my life is going to hell in pieces, Cora just being one of those pieces.

Saturday night I go down to that shitty little honky-tonk and watch Cora shake her ass for anybody willing to watch. She's drunk half the time now that prohibition is over and drinking is legal again. Not that prohibition ever slowed her up much — she'd just find somebody had a bottle or a jar and go off with them like she went off with me one night. Neither of us planned on falling in love. I did, but I'm not certain Cora did even though she said she did.

She said that night, "Prince, you got the biggest pecker on any man I ever knew, and between you and it and this shine, I'm about deep in love." Well, I was too.

So it's Saturday night and I come home from a long haul of taking a load of cantaloupes over to Ft. Smith, because that's what I do now that I ain't sheriff anymore — drive truck over the road — and there she is shaking her ass with some swell.

The swell is wearing a suit and two-tone shoes and he and Cora are pressed up against each other like they're Siamese twins. The music is slow and low-down, the kind of music makes you fall in love, or out of it, and the air is full of blue smoke and laughter and glasses clinking against each other. I'm drinking from one of those glasses and watching my wife dancing with some guy looks like stink wouldn't stick to him and feeling like I need to bust his head because of the way Cora's all up against him.

Bobby comes over and says hidey. But I'm in no mood to talk.

Cora is practically letting the guy put it to her right out on the dance floor; I feel like there's a stove in my head.

"What cha gone do?" Bobby says seeing me watching them.

"I'm gone bust somebody's head," I tell him.

"Hers or his?"

"Both maybe."

"You want, I'll jump all over that sumbitch like he was a red-headed nigger."

"Nah, you stay out of this, she's my wife."

"I think you could bust his head with no trouble," Bobby says. Bobby is drunk and I know how brave a man can get and want to bust somebody's head when he's liquored up. Hell I put enough of 'em in jail to know.

Next I know I'm between Cora and the swell.

"This is my wife," I tell the swell.

"She's a damn good dancer," he says. "You're a lucky man."

"I don't need you to tell me that. Down here in Sequoyah County, we don't let other men mess with our wives. Maybe that's the way they do it wherever the hell you come from."

I've seen this face before, but where I can't say.

"I know what they do down here in Sequoyah County," the swell says.

"Jesus Christ, Joe, don't make a scene, huh?" Cora says. "Me and him were just dancing."

"You stay the hell out of this, woman." I guess I'm more mad at her than him, but you can't just hit a woman in the mouth every time you feel like it. I'm not that kind of guy, and besides, I know it wouldn't do any good with Cora — she'd just leave me flat out.

"What the hell you expect me to do," she says. "Stay home all alone while you're gone all the time?"

"I'm trying to pay the rent, goddamn it." I sound lame and weak and I don't want to in front of this guy, or Cora.

"How about I buy you both a drink with my apologies," the swell says.

"Hell no, I can buy my own drinks."

"I just dropped in for a little fun, mister. I'm not looking for trouble."

"Well, it's a little too late for that," I say, because you can't just back down from some guy you caught mauling your wife.

Then too, everybody knows I was once the sheriff of Sequoyah County and how would it look I was just to let her shake her ass without doing something about it.

I tell the guy he's any sort of man he'll come with me outside so we can settle things. Cora tags along behind us. The night air feels cool and good against my hot stove of a head. Gravel crunches under our shoes. I'm trying to think of a way I can settle this without violence, because for all the shit I been through in my life, I hate violence.

"Let me explain something," the swell begins by saying. "I'm not after your wife, I just like to do a little dancing. I used to come here all the time to dance. I even used to go down the road to the dances in Aikens. Hell, I've danced all over this state. I'm just a dancing fool. I don't mean any disrespect to you or your wife."

"That's what you call what I seen you two in there doing, dancing?"

"Oh, go to hell, Joe Prince," Cora says.

The swell reaches in his pocket and I reach for a sap I keep inside my coat and he says, "Whoa up, I'm just getting me a cigarette" and pulls out a pack and offers me one.

"You're a real cool customer for somebody who dances with other men's wives," I say.

"No sir, I'm just having me a smoke is all," he says.

Then somebody steps out of the shadows and I think it's Bobby but when I see who it is steps under the pole light, I see it ain't Bobby.

"Hey," the man says. He's got his hand in his coat pocket and whatever he's got in there is the shape of a pistol. I've seen enough to know.

"We're just out to have a good time," the guy says. "No point in anybody getting in a scrap, is there?"

"You threatening me?"

"No," he says.

The swell says, "You know who that is?"

"I don't give a shit who that is, if he's threatening me, we got us a problem."

"No, he's not threatening you. And I'm not threatening you, and surely Cora isn't threatening you either." He says this as calmly as anything I ever heard.

The guy with the hand in his coat pocket says, "You ever hear of Baby Face Nelson?"

"That who you are?" I say.

"No. I just wondered if you ever heard of him."

"What is this, some sort of joke?"

The guy laughs, then the swell laughs. And pretty soon Cora is laughing.

"Say," the swell says. "I'm really sorry about what happened. Let's just call it a night, okay?"

"Come'n, Joe," Cora says. "Let's go back inside and have a drink. Hell, honey, you know I don't love nobody but you, and there ain't no man could steal me away from you and that big thing of yours."

So that's what we do, go back inside and everything is all right again until I catch her the next time, only the next time, she ups and runs off with the son of a bitch she was shaking her ass for. Good riddance I say. It's later that same year I learn the swell Cora was shaking her ass for was Pretty Boy Floyd. How do I know? I saw the photo they took of him in the newspaper after they shot him. I can't say I was real tore up over it. But I realized how close I came that night to getting killed.

Pretty Boy Floyd

I *lay* out in the yard staring at the stars. Crickets chirp in the night and frogs belly up from down in the ditches and I can smell the dry red dust and imagine I'm turning into dust again — like they say we do in the Bible.

I think about all the people that have died since time began, buried in the same earth

I'm lying on, how there's probably a million times more people under the ground than on top of it. Only right now I'm the one on top, but soon I'll be joining all those millions of other silent souls. It doesn't seem fair somehow to get a taste of life only to know it's going to be over so soon.

Jesse James looked up at the same sky I'm looking up at now, saw the same stars in the same places and maybe had the same thoughts. Everybody who ever lived throughout all mankind has looked up at those same stars. It feels strange to think they have and I have.

I see a shooting star.

Horses laugh somewhere in the night.

It's over, it's over.

Darkness, take me away.

24

Pretty Boy Floyd

I remember even though it was Indian summer that it was so hot the land buzzed with heat when I got the news about John Dillinger. I was in a hotel room in Muskogee wishing it would rain. Rich knocked on my door, a newspaper in his hand and said, "You see this?"

A pretty little girl lay half asleep across the bed, her slip like a pink silk skin, barely covered her hips and back. I had met her at a roadhouse the night before while Rich was busy drinking himself crazy and tossing dice with three men in coveralls.

I rubbed sleep from my eyes and fumbled for my Chesterfields while Rich took up a chair near the window. The room had a hotplate but there was nothing to cook! The light was so bright coming through the window you couldn't look at it and I remember hearing the land buzzing like the thrum of a million grasshoppers — like a chorus of death.

I stood there in my shorts and undershirt and waited for Rich to tell me what it was in the newspaper he was reading that had him worked up. He hadn't combed his hair and it stood wild on his head and his shirt was stained. He looked like a hobo.

"They shot Dillinger in Chicago last night," he said.

Outside of me, John Dillinger was the last of the real good bank robbers in my book.

"Dead?"

"As hell," Rich said.

"Jesus."

"They're going to kill us all, ain't they, Charley? That fucking Hoover is going to kill us all."

The inside of my mouth tasted like a back alley, but I lit the cigarette wondering if maybe Rich was right — they were going to kill us all. If they killed Dillinger — one of the most cautious men I ever knew — they would get me sooner or later.

"Some skirt working for the G-Men did a number on him," Rich said, reading the news article. "Says she was wearing a red dress and that was the signal to the cops it was him with her . . . says they came out of some movie theater and they shot him running away."

Like a dog, I'm thinking when Rich reads me this. They shot John Dillinger down just like a dog.

The girl on the bed stirs, turns over, opens her eyes — they are violet — and looks at me, then at Rich before closing them again. Her mouth is small and pretty and I remember what it was like kissing it, how she made little noises when we made love, like a little kitten mewing over warm milk, how she moved under me sweet and sexy. It was things like that I'd miss most if the cops got me: the sweet sexiness of women, a woman like Ruby. I'd miss driving the back roads in a new roadster, wearing nice clothes, spending all that easy money. I'd miss reading about myself in the newspaper and I'd miss the respect people gave me. I'd miss my family, too: Bradley and E.W. and Mother and my sisters. But what I'd really miss and what really hurt to think about was my boy Jackie, how he'd grow up without a daddy, how I'd grow cold in my grave without him.

"Son of a bitch," Rich says angrily. "I never thought they'd get Dillinger."

"I thought you never cared for the guy," I say, the cigarette tasting dry and hot in my mouth.

"I didn't, much. I mean I guess what's so unnerving is the fact they got him so easily. Shot him to pieces, him running away."

"I know lots of guys they got just like that," I say, thinking about Billy Miller and George Birdwell. Good men who weren't afraid of anything, who didn't run away, and they still got them, still shot them down like dogs.

"Yeah, but Christ, Dillinger!" Rich whistles because he still can't believe it. "The way he escaped all those jails. Had to be a skirt that done him in. Only a skirt would get a guy like him to drop his guard. Says here the lady in red was named Ana Sage. Least it wasn't Irma that brought him down. I knew Irma was too good for the guy, she'd never done him that way."

"Dillinger's no different than anybody else. He's no different than me or you," I tell Rich, but something in me is feeling dark like a closet you can't see into.

Rich looks at the girl on the bed.

"Quim," he says. "It makes guys like us crazy."

"Still, what kind of life would it be if there weren't any dames in it?"

"Not worth a damn, that's for sure."

"I think we better head back east," I say. "We've been hanging around here too long."

"Yeah, I got the willies."

"Me too."

John Dillinger

It was a nice evening to go to the picture show. Polly says we should go to the theater to see a movie. She suggests the Marlboro. But Ana pushes we go to the Biograph where they've got "iced air" and we can all cool down and spend the evening. Ana Sage is Polly's friend and is practically living with us.

I'm a sucker when it comes to dames. Ana says, "Good, good," in the hunky accent she has when we agree to go to the Biograph. Foreign dames never did much for me and I'm only going along with it because Polly wants to.

We walk down the streets of Chicago and even after the sun goes down you can feel the heat coming up from the pavement right through your shoes. We take our time because in that heat there's no reason to hurry. Ana tells Polly that Clark Gable is playing at the Biograph.

"*Manhattan Melodrama,*" she says.

She says it's about gangsters — a crime story, so that makes it okay with me. Mr. Gable and I have the same sort of moustache and maybe that's why the dames are crazy about me. I ain't one to complain.

Street lights come on and I can see lights wink on in the windows in some of the buildings where people live up over the stores. There are times like this I think it would be nice to have a regular life, one where I'd be coming home from work after a long day and the wife would have my dinner ready. Afterward I'd go in and prop my dogs up and read the newspaper and listen to the radio. But then when I think about it some more, I realize it wouldn't be for me — I'd get bored as hell with a life like that. Me, I got to have lots of action.

We get to the theater and I buy three tickets and we go in and find our seats, Polly on one side, Ana on the other, me in the middle. Polly's wearing some nice perfume and I like the way she smells there in the dark as we wait for the show to start. Ana seems nervous, fidgets and I say, "What's with you, you got ants in your pants?"

She laughs, says, "No, no, I'm very okay," real serious like those foreign dames can be.

We sit there in the dark and the newsreel comes on and right there on screen is a story about me, old mug shots of me when I was in the joint and J. Edgar Hoover looking in the camera and telling everyone how guys like me aren't going to be around much longer. It was goddamn spooky, them showing Hoover then showing a mug shot of me that time they had me in Michigan City and I made that gun out of soap and escaped.

But at least it's dark and nobody knows I'm sitting there watching myself except for Polly and Ana. Polly leans close to my ear and whispers: "That's you, Johnny."

She squeezes my leg when she says it, like a promise for what's going to happen after the show when we get back to the apartment. It's not such a bad life, being John Dillinger — it has its rewards.

Ana is still fidgeting and I tell her to stop it.

I guess as smart as a guy can be, he never knows what's going to happen to him next or I would have known why she was fidgeting.

We watch Gable and it's a pretty good show and when it's over we all get up to leave. I'm thinking about how hot it's going to be back at the boardinghouse once we get there but how that's not going to stop me from making love to Polly because I've been thinking about it the whole time since she squeezed my leg.

We step outside the theater and pause there for a moment and Polly is saying to me, "Let's go get something to eat, Johnny. . . ." when I see a guy standing in the shadows of a doorway. A match flares up and shows his face as he lights a cigar and something cold snakes through my blood, because a guy like me just knows danger when it's around.

I start to run. I mean I really fucking start to run. Then something snaps through my flesh, my blood, my bone . . . and then something else and something else and I'm running, but I'm falling too.

I hear Polly screaming and I wonder what she's screaming about and the last face I see is Ana's leaning over me there in the shadows, her red, red dress like neon in the night.

Dames, I'm thinking as the white light surrounds me.

Pretty Boy Floyd

We drive familiar highways, like lemmings to the sea, Rich says. Where the hell he comes up with some of the stuff he comes up with I don't know. The ribbon of pavement turns into tracts of dirt, then back to pavement again. I've traveled this land it seems a thousand times and it never gets different and it never stays the same.

"We should rob every fucking bank from

here to Buffalo," Rich says.

"Don't be stupid."

"Why the hell not, I mean if we're going to go out, let's go out in a blaze of glory."

"Not like Dillinger, huh?"

"No, hell no not running from the cops."

"We wouldn't get as far as St. Louis were we to try robbing every bank."

"You gone soft, Charley? All that stuff Hoover is saying how he's going to bring us to bay, how he's going to have his boys shoot our asses off, that making you go soft?"

"I want to see my son again. I miss my kid and I miss my wife and I miss what I once had."

"Well, not me," he says. "I don't miss nothing except what I ain't got yet."

He's drinking heavily and I think he must know the same thing I do — we've got no future.

"Give me a hit off that bottle," I say.

He looks surprised.

"Ain't you the one always preaching about my drinking?"

"Yeah, but I'm not now. What the hell difference is it going to make in the long run." He hands over the bottle and I take a nip, then give it back and he takes a nip, and back and forth like that until the bottle is empty — a dead soldier, as they say — and Rich tosses it out the window and I hear it shatter on the pavement.

We drive into the long night and sleep in the car along some river I don't know the name of. The sound of running water in the darkness makes everything seem right in a world of wrong. I hear Rich talking in his sleep, cursing, threatening ghosts that's haunting him, kicking against the door with his foot. Tired as I am, I can't sleep much. I lie there and listen to that nameless river until I hear a whippoorwill singing my name: *Pretty Boy, Pretty Boy, Pretty Boy.*

I write Ruby a letter in my mind:

> My dearest darling, how I miss you and little Jackie and how I wish you were both here with me tonight. I'm in a beautiful place and the moon is standing over the trees. There is a river here I don't know the name of but will name it after you — the Ruby River — and after Jackie, the Beautiful Boy River. How is my brave little man? Does he ever ask about me? What do you tell him? I hope you keep me in good light with him for I never meant to do anything that would hurt either of you. You know that, don't you? My God how did things go so wrong for all of us? Please

write me and tell me it will be all right, that things will be all right again and that we will soon be a family again. I want that more than anything, for us to be a family again. All I think about is you and Jackie, my little man. How I would love to be holding you both right now.

I hear a noise off in the dark and my letter ends as I put my finger on the trigger of the machine gun. I listen. Nothing. I listen. Nothing. I let out my breath and stare out into the darkness for shadows and shapes but nothing moves and I've lost the letter in my head but think that if I concentrate hard enough, it will somehow reach Ruby.

Angels stand at my foot and head
Their arms outstretched, their
Faces white as stone and in the far
Night someone is singing in a
Baritone voice — Daddy Walter
— "Come nearer Jesus"
Pretty Boy, Pretty Boy, Pretty Boy,
The whippoorwill trills.

25

Pretty Boy Floyd

The news on the radio is I'm Public Enemy Number One now that they have killed John Dillinger. Rich says, "Take a look at you, Charley, you're the most wanted guy in America."

Like that is supposed to mean something to me. The only thing it means is I've been moved up on the death list of the G-Men.

We have been back in Buffalo three weeks and I'm about to go crazy with pacing, watching Rich get drunk, drawing pictures and arguing with Rose. Listening to the girls complain about how we can't ever go out in the daylight, how there's no money to spend works on my nerves like fingernails across a chalkboard. Rose especially gets on my nerves because she complains the most. Beulah too, though, can really drive me nuts at times. I feel like climbing the walls. I think of the days when fishing in the sun made me happy. I think of pie dances and the girls I held so close I could smell their fresh-washed hair. I think of what it was like to sweat in the harvest fields — hard but honest work that left me tired but ready for a night of fun. I think of Daddy Walter taking me for a ride in his truck when I was just a boy, how he told me he had to go see a man about a horse when I asked him where it was we were going, but the truth of it was, he sold a little illegal whiskey and I didn't mind at all because it was all so mysterious and a grown-up thing to do. I think about lonesome roads.

I have dreams in which I'm running. There are woods all around and the land is hilly and there are men chasing me and I have a hard time running because my feet are like cement and no matter how hard I try I can't get away. All the men have guns — machine guns and shotguns and pistols and rifles and I've got nothing to defend myself with. Over every ridge there are more men. Behind every tree stands a man with a gun aimed at me. They are mean-eyed men who know no mercy.

Daddy Walter sits at the foot of my bed some nights and I think I'm dreaming him too, but I can't be sure. I awake with sweat soaking through my undershirt and the room is quiet except for the soft little snores coming from Rich and Beulah and Rose.

"Charley," Daddy Walter says, his face drawn into a purse of sad flesh. "My dear sweet boy. Oh God what sins have I committed that have fallen onto you? What did I do so wrong as to have my boy chased down by the law?"

I feel the weight of his sadness in my being until I am utterly sad too.

"I sure do miss you and everyone else, Daddy."

He shakes his head, his eyes dripping misery. He is dressed in clean overalls and a white shirt buttoned at the throat and has his hair combed into place. He looks just like Bradley, only older with silver hair. He looks just like I saw him in his casket.

"I've done some real wrong things in my life Daddy Walter."

"I know you have son. We all have."

"I killed a couple of men, but I didn't mean to kill anybody."

"I know you didn't. Just like that damn fool who killed me. I know he didn't mean to do it. We just got to arguing over some shingles and our anger got the best of us and he killed me. That's how it probably was with you — you got into a fix and killed those men but you never meant to."

"No, I never did."

The room smells strange — that's how I know Daddy Walter is really there, because in dreams you don't smell anything.

The strange smell is like wet clothes, like how wet clothes smell when they are washed in rainwater and left to dry in the sun.

"You got my bad seed in you son," Daddy Walter says, his voice a tremble. "You got the bad seed in you that was in me — the original seed that was in Adam and given to Cain and caused him to slew his brother Abel. You got the bad seed that is in all men. Only with you, it worked its way to the surface and caused you to do things I didn't do and things most men wouldn't do. You ain't to blame, Charley. You ain't to blame. But you are going to have to pay just the same as if you were to blame. Do you understand what I'm saying?"

Then Beulah stirs or Rich coughs or a car backfires out on the street and Daddy Walter fades away. And every time he returns we have this same conversation.

I dream sometimes about my old partners — George Birdwell and Billy Miller. They got holes in their heads and no eyes and walk around like the ghouls you see in the picture show with Lon Chaney as the dead monster.

Sometimes the dreams choke off my air and sometimes I get hard and have to wake Beulah up and shove it between her legs — it is the only way I can get any relief. She never complains and I kiss her mouth while I'm doing it to her and taste the unpleasantness and afterwards lie next to her and smoke a cigarette and stare and stare into nothingness and realize I am a man with nowhere to turn. The world is full of people waiting to kill me. My own damn misfortune. I am too miserable to cry.

Bradley Floyd

I saw Daddy Walter standing out in the yard in the moonlight, his hands shoved down inside his coveralls. He was just standing there and I came out on the porch in my bare feet and called his name. He turned and looked my way and motioned for me to come stand in the moonlight with him and I did and he said, "I saw Choc just a few minutes ago. I'm afraid his time is near up."

"But you've been dead a year," I say.

"I know it, but the dead are privy to things the living are not, so listen to me close, boy."

He told me that Choc was about to be murdered and I asked him how and where and when.

But Daddy Walter simply shook his head and said, "It was foretold since the beginning of time. His story and mine and your'n have all been foretold — written in the book of life. Look it them stars — that's where I live and that's where Charley will be living soon, and you and your children and their children."

I looked up and the stars seemed close enough I could pluck them with my fingers like they were boles of cotton. Daddy Walter touched the brim of his hat and a thousand stars fell to earth and fire lit the sky and the world spun beneath my feet.

Daddy Walter had a hole in his head where the neighbor man shot him over shingles and I could see the stars and the moon through the hole. Seeing these things caused me to shiver so hard I wanted to scream.

I went inside and wept for an hour, the cold bare floor against the soles of my feet, and cursed the sin that had been heaped on our family.

Ruby Floyd

The Professor says he wants me to dance with him in a jar of water.

"What?" I say, for I don't understand such talk.

His eyes are crazy.

"It's the dope," he says, "makes me talk this way."

His hands are clammy upon my breasts, his breath the scent of a rotted flower.

I hear the drumbeats of my ancestors who were left dying on a wintery plain shot full of holes by soldiers. Their dead faces are frozen in crooked grins as though they enjoyed somehow the murderous rapture of their killers. Their spirits cascade through time like a waterfall that washes my heart clean of everything but sin given to me unwillingly.

My son — Charley's and mine — sleeps peacefully with innocent dreams sugarcoating his head.

"Dance with me in a jar of water," the Professor insists.

I have the money Charley gave me pinned inside my dress. I will take the next train home because all this talk of "crime not paying" is a meadowlark with broken wings, a faux lesson sold like taffy to the curious willing to pay a dime to hear it. But my Charley isn't any more evil than the Professor or the preacher who would sell you Jesus on a stick if he could. I think of my mother, the preacher who sold her more than just a little Jesus. And what Charley Floyd is, is twice better than what most men are and

I'd rather be Charley Floyd's wife than the dance partner of a dope fiend.

"Go to hell," I tell the Professor.

He sits on the bed and laughs and laughs.

"You're just another tart Ruby Floyd who would sell her ass for the price of admission. Why you've made as much money off old Pretty Boy as I have. He's our cash cow. We're a two-headed monster living in the same dream. *Har, har, har.*"

The mark I leave on his cheek is pink and the shape of my hand.

That same night the train carries Jackie and me back to Oklahoma.

I vow to wait for Charley even if it takes forever.

Melvin Purvis

Mr. Hoover sends down orders that he has an empty grave needs filling in the cemetery of the doomed. Says the headstone reads: Pretty Boy Floyd, and all I got to do is fill it. Says, make sure you fill it soon, Purvis. I want old Johnny Dillinger to have company in hell.

So the FBI lists Pretty Boy Public Enemy Number One. Good, good. Kill the salty dogs, take out the trash, all that. It's my job and I aim to see it done. I killed a lot better than that punk Charley Floyd. I write his name on a bullet and put it in my vest pocket then go eat myself a good meal because you never know what the next day will bring.

Ol' Melvin's on you now Pretty Boy. Beware, beware.

Pretty Boy Floyd

I can't stand these walls anymore. I tell the girls and Rich to get ready to roll.

"Where we going?" he says.

"I don't know, but wherever it is there will be no more hiding."

I give the girls five hundred dollars and tell them to go buy us a car — "Ford V–8 is what I want. Make sure you don't get anything but a Ford V–8."

Rose says in a smart aleck way: "Any particular color Charley?"

Soon as they leave I say to Rich, "We get on down the road a ways, I'll buy them bus tickets back to Kansas City."

"Good idea," he says. "I'm ready for some new quim anyhow, ain't you?"

"I've been thinking about your idea."

"What idea is that?"

"About robbing every bank in America."

"Go out in a blaze of glory?"

"Yeah, something like that. Why not."

"Hell yes. I mean let's live until we die."

"That's what I've been thinking. The law is never going to give up until they shoot us down. Even if we were to turn ourselves in they'd shoot us just for the headlines."

"We don't stand a snowball's chance in hell, do we," Rich says.

"No."

The girls come back with a white V–8 roadster.

"White?" I say.

"Sure," Rose says. "White represents purity."

"Pure as the driven snow," Rich says sarcastically. "Like you two. Ain't none of us been pure as the driven snow since we were babies."

"I resent that," Rose says.

"Resent anything you want," Rich says.

"Jesus, you don't have to talk to me that way."

"Shut up and get in the car."

We drive off into the dusky night gliding along the shores of Lake Erie where the city lights wink in the dark mean waters so eerily it makes the hair on the back of my neck raise up.

But I've come to accept my fate. I just want to see Ruby and my son again, one last time before they kill me . . . those men in my dreams.

I bid each moment a final good-bye.
I know this will be my last trip.
Tell them Pretty Boy is coming home.

26

Pretty Boy Floyd

Fog. All we see is fog. It is like we've driven into a cloud. Rich says he can smell the Ohio River. I say, where? Out there somewhere, he says. The girls are asleep in the backseat. They look like exhausted angels, like the burdens of life have simply struck them into fitful repose. Rose sleeps with her head in Beulah's lap. Rich says, look it them two. I wonder if they ever did anything nasty with each other. My mind is a million miles away.

I lose the road, find it again in the fog. I can hardly see the front end of the car.

"Slow down, Charley. We might be headed right for the river. It could be we will just drive off into the river and drown. Jesus I don't want to have to go out that way — drowning."

Somewhere the sun is shining, but not

here, not now. Somewhere the sky is blue and perfect like the eye of my wife, but not here, not in this place.

I am trying to light a cigarette when I hit the telephone pole. One minute it's not there, the next I bang right into it jarring the girls awake. Rose has drool on her lip, her hair is disheveled and her lipstick smeared.

"Holy moly!" she yelps sitting up. "What'd we hit?"

"Fog," Rich says. "First we hit fog then we hit that damn telephone pole. Of all the stinking rotten luck."

"My head hurts," Beulah says. I turn to look at her and she has that dizzy look in her eyes like she gets ever since the cop shot her.

I climb out and check the front end and the radiator is hissing steam and piddling water. I can't help but slap my hand down hard on the fender I'm so damn mad at myself. We sure are having a bad time of it.

"Where we at?" I ask Rich. Rich is an Ohio guy, has some people living around here somewhere.

He looks around at the fog.

"Paris, France?"

"Don't be a wise guy."

"Ohio is all I know."

"Yeah, where at in Ohio? You're supposed to know this country. You're the one who's got family down here."

He looks dumb-faced and I want to hit him and I don't know why except that I want to hit somebody for the dumb luck we're having.

I look at my watch; it's almost ten in the morning.

"I saw a sign just a ways back that said 'Wellsville, One Mile,' " Beulah says.

"I thought you were asleep, how could you see anything?"

"I was just resting my eyes, Charley, that's all."

"Hey, if we're near Wellsville, I know where we're at," Rich says.

Maybe our luck is about to change. I have to believe that it is.

"Listen," I tell the girls. "You two are going to have to hoof it into town and find a garage. Me and Rich can't show our faces. Get somebody to come get the car and when you get it fixed drive back here and pick us up."

Rose rubs her cheek as though she's had it with the lot of us. Rich and I watch them disappear into the fog, their heels clicking on the paved road.

"Let's get those blankets and our guns

and get off this road," I say.

We climb a fence and the grass is wet and slick as we climb the hill beyond it. Somewhere in the fog we can hear cows lowing. It is like we're in a strange dream.

"You could eat this stuff with a spoon it's so thick," Rich says about the fog.

"We may have to we don't get that car fixed up in town."

"Maybe there's a bus station we can drop the girls off soon. I can't hardly stand Rose running her mouth no more." Rich is half hung over and grumpy.

We spread the blanket somewhere on the hill and sit there in the fog unable to see three feet in any direction.

"You think with those cows we're hearing there might be a bull around?" Rich asks.

"Better make sure that machine gun is cocked and ready in case there is."

He laughs. The whole situation is ridiculous, I know. But somehow I don't see anything funny about it.

Edwin Harp

I got up early, like I always do and had my coffee and bread and thought about all my youngsters asleep in the other rooms and thought what a blessing children can be except when times are hard and there's never enough to eat and the whole country is up against it. I had me a pear orchard and figured I best get up there early to pick me a peck of pears if'n we was going to have anything to eat that morning or that day. Pears may not seem like they would be good enough to sustain a family of ten, but you'd be surprised at what you'll eat to keep the hunger from gnawing out your belly. And besides, I've et a lot worse than pears for breakfast.

I rousted my oldest boy Brat and told him to get on up and put on his coveralls and come with me. We each grabbed us a peck basket and headed on up to the orchard. Hell if I'd known what was waiting up there for us, I'd headed into town and begged for a handout.

Fog lay all over everything, which ain't unusual that time of year. The cold night air comes in over the river and you got yourself a mess of fog. But we were used to it and Brat can practically walk asleep anyhow and knows the way as good as I do, so we went up there to where the orchard was. Time we got up there, the sun had burned some of the stew off and we could see two fellows sitting on a blanket.

"Why them's tramps, daddy," Brat said. "I bet they hopped off the train and is aiming to walk into town so the train bulls don't get 'em and bash in their heads."

Brat surprised me seeming to know a lot more about tramps and trains and train bulls than I would have ever give him credit for. We get lots of hobos coming through these days begging for handouts and maybe Brat's gotten to know a few. You know how boys can be when they get a certain age.

But soon as we got close enough to them men, I could see they weren't no tramps of any kind. They was both dressed in suits and wore neckties and one had black-and-white shoes. Seemed damn strange to me, men like them sitting up on a hill in the fog. I put the bug in Brat's ear about not asking any questions, said we should just keep walking like nothing at all. But by then, one of the fellows said, "Hey, who are you two?"

"Why my name's Harp," I say. "And this is my boy, Brat."

"Brat?" the other fellow says. "You a brat?"

"No mister, I ain't," Brat says.

The man sort of chuckled.

"Where you going?" the first man asked. I learned later it was Pretty Boy Floyd. I went down to Sturgis Funeral Parlor there in East Liverpool and had a look at him after they shot him and he looked about the same only a bit more peaked by then.

"Why we're just going to pick us some pears from my orchard yonder," I say.

"Pears? They any good, your pears?"

"Fair," I say. "It's been kindly a dry year this year."

"That so?"

"Yes sir. But them pears is still okay — a little hard maybe."

I nudged Brat to move on and we went and kept going and never did stop to pick any pears. We went on through the orchard and down the other side to Wilson's little store and called Chief of Police John Fultz down in Wellsville and told him about these two strangers.

"What you think those men are doing just sitting up there in your pear orchard?" John says.

"Hell if I knew that I'd not need to be wasting my time calling you, now would I?"

After I hung up Brat said, "Now what, daddy?"

"We go home and wait for the police to come."

"But we ain't picked any pears."

"We'll pick us some pears later."

That's all I had to say and I'm glad I didn't go back up there for what happened later.

Police Chief John Fultz

I got a call from Ed Harp about two men sitting up by his orchard on a blanket. He said they were dressed like a couple of city types, suits, ties, said one had on black-and-white shoes. Said they looked shady. Somebody had robbed the bank in Tiltonsville, I figured it was the same guys sitting in Harp's orchard. I called Homer Potts and Bill Erwin and told them to get over to my office and bring their shotguns and when they did I deputized them.

"What's the story?" Homer said as we got into my car and drove up toward Harp's orchard.

"Maybe nothing," I said. "But maybe we just might have us a pair of bank robbers sitting up there on a blanket."

"Why'd bank robbers be sitting on a blanket in Harp's orchard?" Bill says.

"Hell, if I knew why bandits did anything they did I'd be head of the FBI," I say.

We parked the car in Harp's lane and started out from there, the way Ed said him and his boy went.

"Now don't go shooting just anybody," I told the boys.

"I ain't shot nobody since the war," Homer said.

"I ain't never shot nobody," Bill said.

"Any luck you won't have to today, neither."

The fog was still pretty thick, though some of it was burned off from the sun. Next thing I knew a fellow was pointing a gun at me.

Pretty Boy Floyd

I heard them grunting before I saw them and said to Rich, "Somebody's coming up the hill."

"Those two pear pickers?"

"I don't know, but if it is them, I'm damn sure going to find out why they're so interested in us."

I had a bad feeling because nothing was going right since we left Buffalo — it seemed like everything was going against us, including the weather. Then I saw three men come out of the fog, one of them had a pistol in his belt and the other two carried shotguns so I threw down on them and told them they better stop right where they were. They seemed surprised. They always seemed surprised.

"Why we're just on our way down to the rail yards," the man with the pistol says when I asked him what the hell they wanted.

"You gonna shoot trains or something?"

"No, fellow, we ain't aiming to shoot no

trains. But there's rabbits around and we sure as hell will shoot a rabbit we see one because times are tough and a rabbit ain't a bad thing to eat you cook it right."

You don't have to talk to a man more than a minute to know he's lying.

Before I knew it Rich popped off a shot at them and they scattered like quail but not before the man I was talking with jerked his pistol and started shooting back. The other two flat dropped their shotguns as they ran down the hill. I don't know how many times we shot at each other but nobody hit anything and that was another sign things were going bad for us.

We all ran in different directions — it was every man for himself, like it usually comes down to in a gunfight. I headed up through the orchard while Rich headed off down the hill into the fog. I didn't look back. I kept running, because that's all I could do was run and hope it was enough.

Ruby Floyd

I was in the yard hanging fresh washed-clothes when the sky darkened suddenly from a single small cloud passing in front of the sun. I looked up and thought that one little cloud in that whole big sky has caused the world to go dark. And in those few moments, the air turned cool and goose bumps welted up along the length of my arms, for it seemed fully unnatural that such a thing could happen.

I went inside and called Bradley, I don't know why.

He said, "What is it, Ruby?"

"I don't know, but I think something bad has happened to Charley."

"What'd make you think a thing like that?"

"A woman just knows certain things that can't be explained."

"Lord, I hope you're wrong."

"I hope I am too, but I know that I'm not. Something bad has happened to Charley."

Bradley was silent for a long time. I was too. Then he said, "Maybe we should pray for him."

"I never found a prayer yet that would fix anything, have you?"

"About all we got is prayer," he said. "Pray to Jesus that he'll save Charley."

I hung up and went outside and the sun was bright again. But the strange part was, that one little cloud was nowhere to be seen. It was like the sun burned it up for daring to cross its path.

Adam Richetti

The worst thing about that day was abandoning my friend. I never thought I'd be the kind to run at the first sign of trouble. But when that fellow started shooting at me all I could think about was how all Charley's other partners had gone down to a bullet. I wasn't ready to die. I don't know if a person ever is. I should have killed the guy, he was that close to me, but every shot missed and that told me my luck wasn't any good that day and if I didn't run I'd be a dead man. So I ran.

I got to a house and tried getting inside but the door was locked and I about busted my fists trying to bang that door down then I heard someone say, "I can shoot you where you stand, or you can give yourself up . . . it don't make a piss of difference to me."

And when I turned around it was that same fellow I should have killed — I don't think I could have killed him that day with a stick of dynamite. I thought of poor Charley up there in that fog running round in those hills, maybe being hunted like a rabbit. They'd have every copper in Ohio after him, if he wasn't already dead. I just had a bad feeling that this time he wasn't going to get away.

I saw the dull sun bleeding through the fog and thought the fog was about the only friend Charley had left now if a friend he had at all.

Pretty Boy Floyd

I come through the trees of the pear orchard and almost smack into those two boys who had throw away their shotguns earlier. Only by now, they had picked them up again and I cut loose with the Thompson about the same instant they cut loose with those shotguns. I heard one of them scream, then I turned and ran until I hit some rocks that I threw myself behind and waited. I waited a few minutes then saw something moving around in the lifting fog and treated it to a lead sandwich before the tommy gun jammed. I heard whatever it was fall over with a thud then waited until the last gauze of fog burned away. I see I shot a cow.

There wasn't anybody having much luck that day including that damn poor cow, but as long as I was still breathing, I had a chance and a chance is all a fellow like me can hope for.

I feel the world withdrawing whatever
sympathy it may have had for me
Like an old lover who's lost all her passion

and desire and has walked
Out the door on me, has caught a cab
never more to be seen or heard from.
The world, I think, has just written me a
Dear John letter.

27

Pretty Boy Floyd

That pear-picker was right: those pears were hard as stone, but they were all I could find to eat while I kept to wood and orchard and hillside. Once I fell and slipped in a dirty creek and got my knees wet, and I tore a sleeve on a fence of barbed wire and I must have looked like hell when I came down at last onto a road across which I saw some men bent under the hood of a truck. I figured I'd ask them politely for a ride to Youngstown, a place where I knew some people who could help me out. If these fellows refused, I'd offer to pay them, and if they still refused, well hell, I still had my .45 and not many men will refuse you with one of those in your hand.

By this time the fog had burned off and the sky was that perfect blue sort of sky you get that time of year, crisp and clean and not a hint of winter in it. I wondered if the cops had got Rich or the girls. Jesus I felt bad for the girls even though I was about sick of their company.

"How do," I say to the men under the truck's hood.

They are wearing faded overalls and you could tell looking at them there wasn't probably fifty cents between them.

They look around without coming out from under the hood; one is holding a distributor cap in his greasy hand. Two have on stained caps.

They sort of grunt and I say, "I'd pay one of you gents for a ride to Youngstown."

They stare at me for a long spell, then one says, "You broke down somewheres?"

"Yes, way back yonder, five, six miles."

"Well, we could go get your automobile and tow it into Wellsville," the fellow says. "I got a tractor we could tow it with."

"No sir, she's got a busted axle and I don't have time to sit around two, three days waiting for a new one to be sent. I got me an emergency in Youngstown."

They blink. One leans off to the side and spits.

"My wife," I say, hating to tell a lie on one of my own because you do, it could come true. "She's sick as hell."

"Boy that's a piece of tough news," the one holding the distributor caps says. "I'd sure enough give you a lift but this dang truck probably is needing some parts as well and I don't know if Earl can get them sent down today, or maybe even by tomorrow."

"I'd pay twenty dollars," I say.

The one who spat shuffles his feet and says, "I got me an old car and I'll take you to galdang China for twenty dollars."

"All I need is just to get to Youngstown," I say.

"I live just up the road a piece."

I follow him while the other two duck their heads back under the truck.

I look at the sun slipping up through the trees on the highest hill and see cattle eating away at the damp grass and it feels like the day is going to turn out right after all — that maybe my luck is changing. My spirits lift, like the fog.

Melvin Purvis

Word comes by telephone some local law down in Ohio have captured Adam Richetti and they have Pretty Boy Floyd boxed in some burg called Wellsville. I ask if the identification of Richetti is confirmed. It is. I order a plane to take me down there. Pretty Boy doesn't know yet just how long an arm the FBI has got but he's about to find out.

By the time I get down to Ohio every local farmer in the area is armed to the teeth and half the cops in the state have been called in. It looks like a turkey fuck and I can see a bloodbath: farmers shooting cops, cops shooting farmers, everybody shooting everybody if somebody doesn't take charge of the situation and organize things. All the talk is about Pretty Boy Floyd and reward money. They are as excited as a bunch of churchwomen at a bake sale. "We'll show bandits what they get they come around these parts!" That sort of talk. Someone says a bank nearby was robbed. Everybody has got hot blood.

I talk to a police chief named Fultz.

"It was the goddamndest thing ever happened to me," this Fultz says. I show him a photograph of Pretty Boy. He nods. " 'At's him. Jesus we were so close to each other we could have shook hands."

"Might have been better that you slapped some cuffs on him, you were that close."

"Hell, I woulda, but that little Italian started shooting and then Pretty Boy started shooting and then I started shooting."

"The way I hear there were three of you to just two of them," I say.

"Yeah, but my boys were just a couple of local men I deputized. You wouldn't expect them to stand up to a gunfight with Pretty Boy Floyd."

"Then why'd you deputize them?"

He looked at me like I was something he stepped in, but I didn't give a shit about that.

I wanted to take custody of Richetti but Fultz refused. I guess his feelings were hurt that I impugned his story.

"Look Chief, we have to work together on this thing, don't you see," I say to him to smooth his feathers. "We don't, you'll have more dead men scattered around these hill than cow pies. Look at these boys, armed with everything that will shoot a bullet, their dicks hard for a fight. You don't want a slaughter, now do you?"

He relented somewhat, but still wouldn't let me take custody of Richetti. He did allow me to interrogate him though. I acted grateful but down deep saw the chief as a hayseed.

Richetti was leaning on the bars when I went back to where they had him locked up. He looked like a captured monkey, face full of surprise that he had been caught at all. I guess he thought as long as he was with Pretty Boy Floyd, wasn't nothing could touch him.

I told him who I was. He went pale.

"You're the one that killed John Dillinger," he said.

"Yes sir and I aim to kill your friend I get the chance."

He shook his head.

"You'll never get Choc."

"Choc, huh? That's what you call him?"

"Nobody's got him yet and you won't either Mr. Purvis. You wouldn't happen to have a cigarette would you?"

I offered him a cigar and he looked sort of comical smoking it. A photographer from the local paper came in and took our picture.

"I'll get him, Mr. Richetti, don't you worry about that. Consider yourself lucky you're not out there with him in those hills or I'd be getting you too. You don't want to see your friend shot dead, why not just tell me where he's headed."

"He's not as bad as they say he is. Charley's a standup guy. Best I ever knew."

"He's Public Enemy Number One, Mr. Richetti, and that's all I need to know about him. He didn't get to be number one because he's a sweetheart."

"They've told a lot of lies about him, about me too. We never hurt nobody."

"How's that cigar?"
"Good."
"Enjoy it while you can."

Pretty Boy Floyd

The man I follow up the road says his name is Wesley and that he used to be a carpenter but that everything's so bad he can't hardly get any work because nobody can afford to have him build them anything.

I offer him a cigarette and ask, "How far up this road you say your place was?"

"About half mile more," he says. "Jesus was a carpenter."

"So I heard."

"You read the good book?"

"I have. My daddy was often in it."

"It's a precious thing to do, read the good book."

"I never heard of it hurting anybody."

"No sir, and it won't neither."

We finally arrive and there's an old black sedan parked in the lane of a shotgun shack needs painting. The left back end of the sedan is hanging low like it has a busted spring and there is bird shit splattered all over the roof and hood and fenders.

"Looks like you haven't run it in a while," I say.

"No sir, I don't run her much because of

what gasoline costs these days — twenty cents a gallon. I mostly walk when I can."

Surprisingly the engine fires right up when he turns the key. The seats are dusty, but by this time I'd be happy to ride in a honey wagon if I had to just to get to Youngstown and as far away from this place as I can.

We start off down the road and he says, "I don't suppose you have another one of them Chesterfields."

I light it for him and check through the back window to make sure there aren't any cops on our tails. Ahead is just a narrow ribbon of dusty road that looks like a road of freedom to me. I take a deep breath and hold onto it like a prayer. Maybe I'll get to see my wife and son after all.

We drive about three miles when the sedan sputters and dies.

"What's wrong?"

"I done run dry of gas," he says.

I feel like I just swallowed a stone and curse that my bad luck isn't going to let up on me.

"I could walk into Wellsville and get a can if I had a dollar," the fellow says.

I give the poor brute a dollar for his time, but I sure am not going to wait for him to walk to town and learn who I am and come back with the law.

After he heads up the road I take off the opposite direction.

"Daddy Walter," I say. "If you're listening to me, tell me what to do."

I hear a bird chirping — a redwing blackbird standing on the head of a cattail.

"That ain't you is it Daddy Walter?"

The bird chirps again, jerks its head my direction then flies off abandoning me. I think that old bird knew what was going to happen and didn't want to have to see it. I guess right about then, I got myself ready for whatever it was that was going to come for me. I guess I knew I was near the end — maybe like Jesse James must have known he was near the end that day in the parlor when he offered his back to Bob Ford. Maybe he knew it was the easy way out — letting someone kill him. Maybe he just got tired of running and hiding and couldn't bring himself to take his own life so he let someone else take it for him. I suspect that if that was true, it was because he was a man of honor, for it would take a certain honor to offer yourself as a sacrifice.

I feel weary but I can't be like Jesse was. I can't just let them kill me because it is the easy way out. I say aloud, "Ruby" over and over again. "Ruby and Jackie" hoping maybe their love will save me.

Melvin Purvis

We drove over to another little town — East Liverpool — to coordinate our efforts after we got a phone call from a local farmer about some man having stopped at his house and asking to be fed. The farmer said the man was a stranger, dressed in a suit but looked dirty and like he'd slept in the rain. It had rained that night before after we'd spent the entire day looking for Floyd. So it seemed like legitimate information.

Floyd was proving harder to track than a fox.

But something else occurred that night besides rain: I dreamed I killed him. I woke up feeling full of piss and vinegar and ready for a fight. Pretty Boy Floyd's running days would soon be over.

Pretty Boy Floyd

I see a farm and go up to it, desperate now, more desperate than I have ever been because I can feel a darkness growing in me and I'm scared a little because I've never felt anything like it before.

I'm surprised there aren't any dogs around to sound an alarm with their barking. I knock on the door, one hand in my pocket wrapped around the pistol. Whatever it takes to save my neck I'm prepared to do. I see an old car parked by a corncrib.

A woman who reminds me of my own sister opens the door and says, "Yes?"

"I'm afraid I'm in a fix," I say. "I am ashamed to admit it, but I got a little drunk last evening and run my car off the road into a ditch. I don't know where I am, but I'm so hungry I could eat the ears off a donkey. I'd gladly pay for a bite to eat — just anything at all, a little cooked meat if you have it."

She looks at me and she looks out beyond me. She is suspicious, but then with a good heart tells me I can wash up over in the rain barrel around the side of the house and then come on in the house.

The water is sharp cold but feels good when I splash it over my face. It tastes like tin roof when I drink some of it. I don't care. I clean up as good as I can, use my wet fingers to comb down my hair. I tuck in my shirt then go into the house and sit at the kitchen table. The smell of frying meat almost makes me faint. It has been a day and a half since Rich and me got into the gunfight. I don't think I could have eaten another pear if someone paid me.

"I don't suppose you'd have a newspaper?" I ask, anxious to see what they were saying about the gunfight.

"Yes, I get one every day delivered," the woman says, and brings me the paper. And there it was, front page, all about me, how the law was looking for me, how they'd captured Rich and taken Beulah and Rose into custody. The only saving grace is there wasn't a mug shot of me in the paper yet.

I eat the fried pork chops, greens cooked in bacon grease, biscuits, turnips mashed with butter on them, coffee, and a slice of apple pie. It is about the best meal I ever ate and I put ten dollars on the table next to my plate even though the woman protests saying it's only the Christian thing to do, to feed a hungry man.

"I always pay my way," I say. I know she could use the money. I ask her which way I need to go to go to Youngstown.

"It's about thirty miles from here," she says.

"Yes'm, but I have got to get there in a hurry, my wife's real sick and needs me."

"Oh dear."

"I saw an old sedan out along your crib."

"It belongs to my brother Arthur."

"He around nearby?"

"He was sharpening an ax out back."

"Maybe I'll go out there and ask him if he'd give me a ride into Youngstown."

"Well, good luck to you, mister." The

woman says this in such a kindly way I want to kiss her on the cheek.

"Yes'm."

I go out back and climb in the automobile and find that the key is in the ignition. I'm not above stealing a car.

"How do, mister."

I look up and there stands what must be Arthur, for he has a sharpened ax in his hand.

"Your sister said you might be willing to carry me over to Youngstown," I say.

"What'd make her say a thing like that?"

"Maybe because I asked her if you would."

He shakes his head doubtfully.

"I don't think I could."

"I'd pay you ten dollars."

"You look kindly run down to have ten dollars cash money on you."

I show him the money, put it in his hand.

"I reckon I could take you far as the bus line in Columbiana."

"That's good enough."

Hope rises.

Arthur Conkle

I told this man who'd come up to our farm offering to pay me ten dollars for a ride to Columbiana to wait while I went inside and got my hat. I made sure I took hold of the keys because I could see this fellow wasn't the sort you'd trust your car keys or nothing else to.

"Ellen, who is that man outside?" I asked my sister.

"I don't know but he seemed nice enough," she said. "He gave me ten dollars for a meal."

"That fellow must have a pocketful of ten dollar bills because he gave me one to haul him to Columbiana."

"Are you going to do it?"

"I guess I don't have much choice."

"Why not?"

"I think he's dangerous and I wouldn't want him to know that I think that. If I refuse to take him, he'll know that."

Ellen told me to be careful. I said, "You're preaching to the choir" and went outside and got in behind the steering wheel and drove out onto the road. If I'd known what was going to happen in the next five minutes I'd have hid under my bed.

Pretty Boy Floyd

We get as far as the road when I see the cars coming toward us from both ways.

"You called the police on me didn't you?" I say, reaching for my pistol.

"Hell, I ain't even got a phone!" the man shouts.

I stick my pistol in his face and say, "I hate a liar worse than anything. I ought to shoot you."

"Go ahead you son of a bitch!" he says.

But hell, what good would it do to shoot him? I'll need every bullet I have. I leap from the car and begin to run. I am so damn tired of running. And yet I can't stop. Something won't let me. I run until my chest burns until I see Ruby behind watery eyes standing far out in that farmer's field.

I run toward her.
Her arms are held out.
"Ruby," I call. "Ruby."
She becomes an angel and flies away.
A dark cloud passes in front of the sun
winking out my life, I think.

28

Pretty Boy Floyd

I run back toward the house, toward the outbuildings. I hear the scream of brakes and car doors slamming and men shouting. I run with their turmoil at my back, my shadow out in front of me like I'm chasing it. I wonder is this death: a man chasing after his own shadow? I have darkness inside of me and now darkness outside of me, like my soul is trying to escape before the terrible death comes to gather me up.

"Stop! Put up your hands, Floyd! Stop or we'll shoot!"

I slip, my knee strikes a rock, I am back up, running hard, running in a crazy zigzag way. I'm not going to make it easy for the bastards.

"Stop, goddamn it!"

I jump behind a corncrib and take a look back at the men who want to take my life.

I'm all out of breath. I see men with rifles and shotguns — a thousand black eyes staring back at me. I could kill a few of them, but I couldn't kill them all. And if I can't kill them all, why kill any of them? I'm not a killer. I'm just a bank robber, just a fellow who has tried to make a good life for himself.

"Floyd, come on out!"

Shit, I say to that. I'm not going to make it easy for them to kill me.

I look out toward the field where I saw Ruby standing. She's not there anymore. There's just grass and all this open space between me and salvation. It looks like a mile across, but is probably just a few hundred yards.

Melvin Purvis

I light a cigar and tell one of my agents to take up a position on the ground with the machine gun.

"He shows his face from behind the corn crib you know what to do," I tell him. "I don't want to go back to Hoover empty handed."

"Yes sir."

It was Agent Bailey, I believe.

For a short time there was just this great silence, the sort that country has to it. I looked around and saw all these fellows with shotguns and rifles and pistols and they were all just as quiet as if they'd been in church. I don't even think a meadowlark sang in those few moments. The sun broke over the tops of the hills and sent forks of brilliant light splaying down over their slopes. It was just like a bucolic painting you might see hanging in a church somewhere. I thought of Jesus and I thought of God and I thought this wasn't a place even they'd want to be, its beauty and quiet aside, for there was a pallor of death everywhere. Even the air smelled like dead flowers.

It was the calm before the storm, I thought. It always gets that way. Like the night we killed John Dillinger. It was quiet that night too. It had rained some and the streets were empty of traffic and there was just the glow of the theater's marquee awash in the wet streets, a lovely liquid red like fresh blood flowing. The other agents and I stood in doorways waiting for the show to be over and there was this absolute peaceful stillness descended over the city. I could hear the burn of my cigar.

The calm before the storm. Goddamn, it was arousing.

Ruby Floyd

Something awakened me.

I had been dreaming that Charley had come home and he was there with me and we were making love. He was just like he was the first time I met him. The really beautiful thing was, he wasn't in any trouble, the cops weren't after him. We were just two normal people in love and happy together and Charley was saying how happy he was as he kissed me and touched me in that way only Charley could do.

"I love you Ruby. I'll be good to you always. We'll have us a nice little life together. We'll buy us a little house and raise our own food and I'll hunt and fish and we'll have babies and grow old together just like our folks did."

"Oh Charley, will we really?"

"Sure we will. Why I've never been happier, have you?"

Then something awakened me from the dream and I felt terrible and dark inside. I went to the window and looked out. The sun was just breaking over the horizon and it was the color of a wound. A soft wind stirred the trees. I stared at the horizon hoping I'd see Charley coming up the road, but all I saw was the bloody sun rising up from the earth like it did every day and like it would do every day for all time — even after Charley and me and all of us were gone. Like it would do for Jackie and his children and their children. Like it would do eternally, and the thought of such things made me deeply sad.

I thought for a time it was just my imagination that something terrible had happened to Charley. Then I felt a sharp pain in my ribs and another in my chest and another that pierced my neck.

"Oh God, oh god!" I knew they were killing Charley.

I fell to the floor weeping and prayed my tears would find his face and give him some small comfort — like a warm rain.

Pretty Boy Floyd

Between the corncrib and the woods was only the field. All I had to do was make it across that open stretch of ground and to the woods bordering the far side and I'd have half a chance. I ran that field a dozen times in my mind as I peeked through the slats of the corncrib at the army of men waiting to kill me. I'd been in a lot of close scrapes and had lived to tell about them. That time in Bowling Green, for instance, when the cops and me and Billy Miller weren't more than twenty feet apart and I lived to tell about it. Lots of times I should have been killed but I wasn't. I asked myself why this time was any different and couldn't come up with an answer. But that awful darkness stayed in me, and it never had before.

I remembered all the banks I'd robbed and I remembered the women I'd loved and the roads I'd driven down. I remembered my whole life and it didn't seem but a blink of an eye. I asked myself, how long you expect to live anyway, Charley Floyd? I was tired of running, of being hunted.

That damn field looked longer every time I looked at it.

Through the slats of the corncrib I could also see one man calmly smoking a cigar while all the others knelt or lay on the ground or stood with their feet apart pointing their guns in my direction. But that one fellow just stood there calmly smoking his cigar. I figured he was running the show and it was him that I was most afraid of.

The woods beyond the field seemed to grow farther and farther away. I could give myself up, or try to, but I had a feeling that if I tried, that fellow smoking the cigar would make sure the only way I went anywhere was in a pine box. I was down to apples and ashes.

I took a deep breath before I took for that field. I knew it would be like trying to swim across the ocean. Fear, hope, dread. It all feels the same you think hard on it long enough.

I took a deep breath and went.

Ellen Conkle

Arthur and me were standing at the window looking out. He'd rushed in saying how there was going to be a killing.

"I was right about that fellow," Arthur said. "I think that is Pretty Boy Floyd. Jesus Christ, Ellen, every policeman and farmer with a gun in the country is down on our road!"

I remembered how nice Mr. Floyd seemed to me, the way he chewed his food with his mouth closed, like a real gentleman. I remembered in one spare moment while I was fixing him breakfast and watching him sort of out of the corner of my eye what a handsome man he was, even though his clothes were dirty and torn. Funny what a woman thinks sometimes when she looks at a handsome man and she's got none of her own. Funny what your mind will do if you let it get away from you.

We saw all those men out by the road with their guns aimed at the corncrib. I felt sad that they would kill Mr. Floyd and told Arthur he must do something to not let them kill him on our property.

"It's too late for any of that. They aim to kill him and I guess by God if that is Pretty Boy Floyd, they will." Arthur seemed feverish. "I should go get my gun and join them."

"No! I don't care who that man is, nobody deserves being shot down like some poor animal."

"He is a rabid dog. He's killed all sorts of men and robbed banks and probably raped women too! Jesus Christ Ellen what in hell's wrong with you?"

I pulled away from the window and went into the parlor and took up our old family Bible and held it to me and prayed that there wouldn't be any killing that day. I didn't want to have to see that handsome man killed. I prayed God he would not let it happen.

Then I heard the crack, crack, crack of gunfire and I knew that it was too late for prayer or anything else.

Pretty Boy Floyd

For some crazy reason the old gospel song "Amazing Grace" starts playing in my head. I remember singing it on hot afternoons in the dry Baptist church in Aikens when I was a boy. My mother and Daddy Walter sang it too and so did Bradley and E.W. and all my sisters. Our voices raised as one to where it didn't sound bad the way we sang it — Daddy Walter's basso underneath, supporting all our voices, his hand on my shoulder.

I run across the field toward the woods, that song playing in my head over and over and it feels as though my feet aren't even touching the ground. I run with ease and I no longer hear the shouts of the angry men behind me, nor the whine of their bullets, nor naught but the voices of that spiritual as though angels were gathering round me, shielding me, carrying me to freedom.

I call out to Ruby and to my boy Jackie, for I think I see them once more there at the edge of the woods. But my voice is lost in the chorus — *I once was lost but now am found . . .* And I am uplifted and the fear is shed from me like old skin. My shadow is nowhere to be seen, eaten by the sun.

And I know that neither man nor bullets nor death can touch me.

I know at last I have wings.

I am a young eagle flying.

Melvin Purvis

He darted out from behind the corncrib just as I suspected he would do and ran toward the field. I said to agent Bailey and the rest of them — "There he is, don't let him reach those woods."

There was a rippling of gunfire all down the line. The first shot hit him and spun him around. I could see the bullet had broken his right arm for it hung limply at his side. I don't know how so many of those bullets missed him, but they did, chewing up the field around him. He righted himself and started again for the distant woods. He made about another twenty yards when another bullet knocked him down. He rose slowly, bravely and began running again, only this time he was staggering like a drunk, trying to drag the weight of himself along. I think he knew there was no way in hell he was going to make those woods even before the bullets started striking him.

There was a slight incline in the land and he made it to that before he fell again, bullets tearing up everything around him. He lay there for several seconds and I told the boys to stop shooting. Agent Bailey's machine gun had jammed.

Then for a moment, not more, there was this awesome silence that overtook us and seemed to quench whatever violence lay in the bellies of those men. We held our breaths waiting to see what Pretty Boy would do next.

A long crow, its wings black and sharp against the sky, flew overhead and cawed breaking the stillness with the surprise of a glass shattering.

Like a phoenix, Pretty Boy rose to his knees and looked back toward us. Even at that distance I could see he'd been hit several times; there were ribbons of blood flowing from him. He knelt there in the dirt, his pistol still in his hand and I could see he was trying to get to his feet, but hadn't the strength.

"Should we finish him, Mr. Purvis?" one of the farmers said.

"No. He's already finished."

Maybe it was just my imagining it, but for a pure moment it seemed like the sun shone directly onto him causing him to glow in its light and I could not help but think that something completely unnatural had happened in that moment.

Then he fell again, rolled over on his back his arms outstretched as though offering himself to the heavens and did not move.

"Let's go gather him up," I told the others, and we ran toward where he lay.

He wasn't yet dead when we reached him.

I asked him if he was Charles Floyd.

He looked at me and said something strange: "You say I am."

I'm not a religious man but I've read the Bible enough to know that's exactly what Jesus said when asked by Pontius Pilate if he was the King of the Jews.

"Don't mess with me Charley. I know damn well you're Pretty Boy."

He offered me a half smile then said, "I guess you'll have to find out for yourself, you're the smart guy."

I told Agent Bailey to go find a pay phone and call Hoover and tell him we had Pretty Boy Floyd.

I looked down into the youthful face of our prey. The sun blinded his eyes and I told some of the men to carry him over to the shade of a nearby pear tree.

I asked him about his past crimes. I asked him was he in on the Kansas City Massacre. I asked him about different banks he had robbed. All he would say was, "I wish I could see my wife and son. That is all I want."

His wounds were grievous. I knew he was dying.

Pretty Boy Floyd

Daddy Walter kneels next to me, says, "Well, this is it, Charley. I've come to take you home boy."

I ask if Ruby will be there.

"In a little while she will be, and so will Jackie and all the rest of the Floyds."

I feel a sudden surge of joy knowing I will be with them again.

"You lived your life as well as you knew how to live it, son. Nobody is going to hold that against you. You won't have no more worries, it's all over, the bad part."

"I never meant to hurt anybody."

"No, I know you didn't."

"These men here shot me, Daddy Walter."

Daddy Walter looks at them each and every one — they don't seem to notice him. I remember they said Mary came and saw that the stone had been rolled aside and went in the cave and found two angels sitting at the head and foot of the place where the body of Jesus had been lying. Why I remember this, I don't know, except I still believe I can escape my situation. For didn't they find the tomb empty?

"Yes, I know they shot you, Charley," Daddy Walter says about the men sitting round smoking cigarettes — some of them even laughing. One has a box camera and is taking pictures, says, "Smile for us Pretty Boy."

"They did what they thought was right," Daddy Walter says. "That's all a man can do, what he thinks is right."

"I don't hold it against them that they shot me."

"Forgiveness is a virtue."

"I know it is, Daddy."

"You about ready?"

"No."

"We're out of time, Charley. We best be going."

And the angels said to Mary: "Why are you crying?"

"Why are you crying, Daddy Walter?"

He lifted me up as though I was nothing at all and I saw the blue sky and the darkness in me felt gone and I felt like nothing but air.

Daddy Walter and me fly toward the sun and I feel my soul aflame, the darkness gone, the light in me.

I am free of all my troubles.

29

Mamie Floyd

They sent my boy home in a baggage car — like old luggage found. I sent Bradley and E.W. down to bring him on home, for I could not face seeing Charley coming home that way.

It rained that morning but when I heard the train whistle blow far off, the sky was clearing and the sun broke through the clouds, and the air became as fresh as I'd ever known it to be.

I waited on the porch until I saw the black ambulance coming up the road, Bradley's old sedan behind it. I sent for the girls — Charley's dear sisters — and they came as well and we were all there to greet him.

"You're home now son, and home you'll stay," I told him when the men carried his coffin on up the steps and into the house. We set him up in the living room.

Ruby called and said she'd heard the news and I could hear Jackie crying in the background.

"You coming?" I asked.

"I can't."

"I understand."

"I wish I could but I can't."

"I know you loved him as much as any of us."

"I loved him something terrible," she said. I believed her. I knew Ruby and her people and they weren't the lying kind.

"Mother Floyd," she said. "I just want to say how sorry I am he's gone."

"You take care of yourself, Ruby. You and the boy come around when you can — you know you're always welcome here."

"Will you do something for me?"

"Course I will, child."

"Kiss him good-bye for me."

I promised her I would and I did.

Bradley and E.W. sat up with me that night and the girls slept in their beds while moonlight struck down in the yard. Bradley and E.W. took it hard, but took it like men and I said, "I'm about tore up." They said they were too and we cried.

They started coming in the morning — folks from all over the state wanting to see my child — Pretty Boy Floyd. They drove their automobiles through my garden and parked all over my yard and in the fields and everywhere they could without regard or respect. Some were friends and neighbors of ours, but a lot of folks we never knew showed up too. They took pictures of the house and some tried to steal whatever wasn't tied down for souvenirs and I told Bradley and E.W. to go out and run the worst of them off and they tried but finally came back in and said, "They's just too many to run off." Of course there was no point in calling the law for help.

Charley was a hero to some of those people and to some he was just a curiosity. Reporters came and tried to talk to me and I told them to get the hell gone or I'd be the next Floyd to take up a gun.

I hated I couldn't bury my son quietly. But then Bradley said, "Charley might not have minded, Ma. He always did crave a lot of attention."

My son's lips were cold when I kissed them. Cold like stone and not lips at all. He wasn't just thirty-one years old and too young to die the way he did. I guess I just lost my wits when they closed the coffin lid for I don't remember much beyond that moment. Later when there was just the family gathered round the table together, I asked was it over.

"They all gone? Those strangers?"

"Yes, Ma, they're gone — been gone for hours now."

"I guess they saw the circus for free."

Bradley said, "You had a spell."

"I saw Daddy Walter," I said.

"When?"

"When I was having the spell."

They didn't believe me, I could tell. But I know what I seen.

Nobody said anything for a long time.

"He come to take Charley with him," I said, "Daddy Walter did. Come to take him over to the other side."

Bradley started to say something then changed his mind.

"They said they'd wait for the rest of us."

"Who said?"

"Other side of what?"

"The river we all have to cross someday."

"Yes'm."

That's about all I care to tell about it.

Bradley Floyd

I tried not to think about Charley too much. There, when it first happened, all I could do was think about him. I wondered how he must have felt in those last minutes after they shot him then carried him to the shade of a tree and he knew he was dying. I tried to think what I'd think was it me done like that. I don't know what the hell I'd be thinking, but if I know Charley, I imagine he was mad they did him that way. And I imagine he was brokenhearted he never got to see his wife and son again. I know he loved them, and I know he'd hate to have them hear about the way he died — running from the law. I don't think he was running from the law so much as he was running toward a dream.

Charley had a lot of pride.

I picked up the newspaper the other day and saw where they killed Baby Face Nelson. He's about the last of the real bad outlaws. I know him and Charley didn't care much for each other. I guess they're somewhere in the same place now.

Ruby Floyd

The doctor says I'm dying. I got cancer. My life seems like a broken trail littered with nothing but bad luck and tears. Jackie comes to see me. He's all grown up now and as handsome as his daddy.

"How long the doctor say I got?" I ask him.

He looks away.

"It doesn't matter. It's not mattered since

they shot your daddy."

He holds my hand and gets me glasses of water.

My body has betrayed me just like the men in my life betrayed me.

"You were the only really good thing to happen in my life," I tell him.

Sometimes we talk about Charley. He asks me to tell him everything. I can't. Some of it I don't remember and some of it I don't want him to know. I only tell him the best parts. How his daddy was a good dancer and how he could make me feel special when he wanted to and how he dressed like a swell and drove fancy cars.

"It must have been hard for you," my sweet son says.

"Come kiss your Mamma."

I close my eyes when I feel his tender kiss grace my cheek. And when I open them again, it is Charley kissing my cheek.

"I've come for you, Ruby."

"Yes, Charley. I'm ready to go. Let me just put a few things together."

"You won't need anything."

I take a deep breath.

"Will it hurt much?"

He shakes his head and smiles sweetly.

"It will just be us again," Charley says. I feel his strength enter my body and take away the pain.

"Just us? Forever?"

"Forever, I promise. Say good-bye to Jackie."

"Good-bye my sweet son."

"Good-bye, Mamma."

Charley is waiting by a sunlit door, his hand outstretched and I go to him and take it and . . .

Beulah Baird

Everybody is gone now but me.

Rose died from a disease she caught from a man and too much alcohol and maybe of a broken heart, too.

Adam Richetti was put in the gas chamber and they say he went hard.

E.W. became the sheriff down in Oklahoma and died of old age.

I guess Bradley is gone, too. I heard he is.

Mother Floyd lived to be almost a hundred and outlived her boys.

Ruby died of cancer.

Melvin Purvis killed himself.

Maybe Jackie is yet alive. I hope so. He was the apple of Charley's eye.

The rest I've lost track of — Charley's sisters and such.

I've turned my life over to God now.

I know what it was to live a wild life, to be

the girlfriend of Pretty Boy Floyd.

How many women can say that?

We had us a good ride.

Jesus, Charley, didn't we have us a good ride.

ABOUT THE AUTHOR

Bill Brooks is the author of ten previous novels, including the critically acclaimed *The Stone Garden: The Epic Life of Billy the Kid.* He's a journalist and teaches creative writing. He lives with his wife in the Blue Ridge Mountains of North Carolina.

The employees of Thorndike Press hope you have enjoyed this Large Print book. All our Thorndike, Wheeler, and Kennebec Large Print titles are designed for easy reading, and all our books are made to last. Other Thorndike Press Large Print books are available at your library, through selected bookstores, or directly from us.

For information about titles, please call:
(800) 223-1244

or visit our Web site at:
http://gale.cengage.com/thorndike

To share your comments, please write:
Publisher
Thorndike Press
10 Water St., Suite 310
Waterville, ME 04901